SMILING

IRISH

The Summerhaven Trio

KATY REGNERY

Here's to the lass who smiles
when life runs along like a song.
And here's to the girl who can smile
when everything goes dead wrong.

—Traditional Irish toast

For Henry and Callie,
who enthusiastically listen
to the G-rated version of every book
their mother writes.

I love you both
to the moon and back
times a million.

Here's to Ireland!
How we loved you.

xoxo

CHAPTER ONE

Bang. Bang. Bang.

Tierney Haven opened her eyes slowly, rolling to her side to look at the digital clock on her bedside table, but it was as dark as the rest of her room. Reaching over, she tapped the clock with her fingers, but nothing happened.

Lightning split the sky in jagged white streaks, brightening her room as thunder cracked and rumbled outside.

Power must have gone out.

"Anyone home? Wake up!"

Bang. Bang. Bang.

It took her a moment to realize the banging that woke her wasn't thunder; it was coming from downstairs. Someone was knocking on her front door, yelling for her to wake up.

"Ian?" she mumbled, rubbing her bleary eyes and sitting up in bed as a fist slammed into the downstairs door again.

"Open up!" yelled the voice, growly with impatience and unmistakably male.

"*Damnú,*" she sighed in her mother's native Irish, swinging her legs over the side of the bed as more lightning lit her room with a brief phosphorescent strike. She plucked her glasses from the bedside table and put them on. The last time someone had pounded on Tierney Haven's door at two o'clock in the morning, it was her brother Ian on a bender. He'd shown up out of the blue, after several months of living on the streets of Boston, and scared her to death.

"Why, Ian?" she muttered as a dark heaviness filled her heart. "You were doing so well!"

Bang. Bang. Bang.

She slipped her feet into waiting slippers and padded from the side of her bed to her bedroom door, making her way down the dark upstairs hallway to the stairs.

"I'm coming, Ian, you *diabhal*!" she said, reaching for the railing.

Four and a half months of sobriety down the drain, she thought, blinking back tears with every step she took. Four and a half months of Tierney and their brother, Rory, shepherding Ian to AA meetings and supporting his recovery. Four and a half months of hoping—every day— that Ian was closer to lifelong recovery. Four and a half months that made a person believe that four and a half months could turn into forever.

She swiped at her useless tears and lifted her chin as she reached the tiny landing, turned, then continued downward. Crying wouldn't help Ian. She needed to be strong now.

He'd likely rage around her cottage for a while, drinking whatever he had with him, before breaking down in tears and finally passing out. At that point, Tierney would need to pour any remaining alcohol down the sink and hide his keys and phone. The vomiting would begin when he woke up and last for a day or two. She'd eventually need to call Rory to come and help. But not yet. She could handle things until morning, and then maybe Rory could come over for a few hours before his camp day began.

Maybe she could get one of the docent interns to lead tours of the museum today. She hoped so, because Rory would have to get back to Summerhaven by breakfast, which meant Tierney would be back on "Ian duty" until tonight when Rory could come back and relieve her for a few hours.

"What a fucking mess," she muttered, stepping into her tiny living room, the hulking body of her drunk brother silhouetted by another slash of lightning in the stained-glass window on her front door. "*Cic maith sa tóin atá de dlíth air.*"

You need a good kick up the arse.

"*Damnú air! Oscail an doras!*" he yelled back. *Damn it! Open the door!*

Oh, great. His bloody Irish was top-notch tonight…which meant he was *beyond* shit-faced, because his Irish was always best when he was on a bender. She took a deep breath, then unlocked and unbolted the door, turning the knob and pulling open the heavy Spanish-style antique door so that Ian could fall inside.

With no outdoor light overhead, she could barely see the man in front of her, but when another bolt of lightning rent the sky, the first thing she noticed was that he had no hair. He had a buzz cut. And the second thing she noticed was that his unbuttoned shirt flapped open in the wind to reveal a chest covered in tattoos, including one that ran from shoulder to shoulder and read, "Destroyer."

Ian has long hair, her horrified psyche whispered, *and no tattoos.*

"Need a phone. Lemme in."

A hand landed on her upper chest, pushing her back with such force that she was knocked off her feet and flew backward about five feet before landing on her ass. The

3

stranger stepped into her living room and kicked the door shut behind him, turning briefly to bolt the door before facing her.

Multiple strikes of lightning through her windows lit up the man standing against the door. Tall and thickly muscled, he had no hair, a torso covered in ink, the butt of a gun peeking out from the waistband of his soaked jeans, and bare, dirty feet.

"Where are you?" he demanded, whipping his head right, then left.

Pitch darkness settled upon the room again, the wind howling outside and the rain beating on the terra-cotta roof of the old caretaker's cottage.

Tierney, still sitting on the floor where she'd fallen, frozen with fear, remained silent.

"Where…*the fuck*…are you?" he yelled breathlessly into the black room.

Did he realize that she'd fallen when he pushed her? She drew her legs to her chest, making herself as small as possible.

"I know…you're here!" he bellowed, his voice breathless and his speech stilted. "You opened…the fucking door!"

Scooting back as quietly as she could, Tierney's back touched her bookcase, and she slid slightly to the left, into the corner created by the bookcase and stairs. Meanwhile, she heard the stranger, who must have pulled his gun from his waistband, cock the hammer back.

"*Aiteann.*"

He growled the word, his voice low and furious. Tierney sucked in a breath, shivering. *Aiteann* was the most

4

vulgar of all Irish curse words, and although she'd heard it once or twice before during summer trips to Ireland with her family, it had never been directed at her.

Thunder blasted outside again, and Tierney wrapped her arms around her legs and bent her head, curling into a ball and staying as still as possible. Maybe he wouldn't see her when the next bolt of lightning followed, lighting up the room.

As she huddled in the corner, waiting for the inevitable flash of light, a million terrible scenarios flooded her mind. Murder. Rape. Assault. Kidnapping. But what made her heart clench with desperation was the thought of never seeing her brothers again, of never hearing her father's voice or smelling her mother's perfume, Inis, ever again. Had she been a good enough sister? A faithful and loving daughter? Did they all know how much she loved them?

The lightning cracked, tearing open the sky and illuminating her cottage.

"There you are!"

A hand landed on her head, the fingers tangling in her hair and yanking hard. She cried out in pain, her knees scraping on the brick floor as he dragged her into the middle of the room, shoving her against the side of the couch before releasing her.

"Don't you dare…scream."

Scream? What was the point? She lived alone on thousands of acres of state land with no neighbors for miles. Even if she did scream, no one would hear. Her heart thundered in her ears, and her eyes burned with tears, but she bit the insides of her cheeks, refusing to cry, refusing to give him the satisfaction of a single sob.

Though it was dark as coal all around her, she could tell that he was squatting down in front of her. She could hear him breathing, shallow and loud, the whistle of a wheeze as he exhaled.

"Where's...the phone?" he demanded.

Her breath caught in her throat, making it impossible to answer.

"Where...is it?" he yelled at close range.

Speak, Tierney, speak!

"It's...I mean, um..."

"Where is the...the *fucking* phone?" he growled, his warm spittle landing on her cheeks.

She only had one phone, and it was charging upstairs on her bureau. She'd never had the little cottage wired for a landline.

"I don't have a...I mean—" She stopped speaking when she felt cold, hard metal slide against her temple.

"Stop...stalling! Give me...the goddamned phone!" he said, the words faster and angrier as they flew from his lips.

"*Éist liom!*" she begged in Irish, the muzzle of the gun still flush with her face. *Listen to me!*

Whether she saw a shadow of movement or just felt it, she wasn't certain, but there was a thread of surprise in his voice when he answered her in Irish:

"*Labhair.*" *Speak.*

"My—my phone is u-upstairs. On m-my bureau."

He lowered the gun. "Stand up. We'll go...get it."

Gulping softly, Tierney braced her hand on the couch and stood up. He reached out in the darkness, grazing her breast through her nightgown before sliding his hand to her arm. Gripping it tightly, he said, "Lead the...way."

SMILING IRISh

After living in the same place for five years, Tierney could walk about her cottage blindfolded, so it was easy for her to find the stairs and start climbing. But was it a mistake to lead him to her bedroom? Should she be fighting him off down here? What could she do? *What can I do?* Could she push him down the stairs? Sure, but maybe his gun would go off. *No, don't push him. Fight later, when you don't have a gun at your back.*

As they rounded the landing, she suddenly remembered an article she'd read about kidnapping victims. It advised if you were ever in a hostage situation, you should try to humanize yourself to your captor. It made them more likely to spare your life.

"You're…" She paused, trying to calm her erratic breathing and figure out a way to connect with him. "You're Irish."

"Shut up," he grunted, and for the first time, Tierney heard something else in his voice. It wasn't a feeling or an emotion. It was…*pain.* Raw pain. Real pain. Physical pain. He was in pain. That's probably why his speech was so breathless and stilted.

"*An bhfuil tú ceart go leor?*" she asked, trying to keep her voice gentle. *Are you okay?*

"I told you…to shut…the fuck up. K-Keep walking," he panted, shoving her forward as they reached the top of the stairs.

In the close space, she lurched forward and hit her forehead on the closed bathroom door in front of her. She gasped with pain. "Ow!"

"F-Fuck," he growled. "I didn't—sorry." Then, "Which w-way?"

7

Did he just apologize to me?

The question flashed through her brain, then disappeared just as quickly.

"Left or...r-right?"

"Left."

He yanked her arm to the left, walking down the short hallway to the open door of her bedroom.

"Where's..." His breathing was growing shallower by the minute, and if she wasn't mistaken, the grip on her arm was weakening. "...the bureau?"

"Just there," she said.

His fingers on her arm were starting to shake. "W-Where?"

"Umm..." If she continued to stall, would she eventually be able to overpower him? To run away from him? "Over there. To your right."

He tried to pull her right, but his fingers slipped from her arm just as another bolt of lightning lit up the room. Tierney turned to face him, staring into his glassy, ice-blue eyes. Her gaze slid up to his forehead, which was covered with beads of sweat.

Fever, she thought. *A bad one.*

Without thinking, she reached up with her free hand and laid it on his forehead, wincing at the scorching heat there. "You're burning up."

"Stop...arsing around," he said, jerking away, his breathing shivery and uneven. "Get the...f-fucking ph-phone."

He staggered forward, pushing her against the bedside table to the right of the bed, which crashed to the ground.

"Please, Mr...."

"*Brrr.*" He shivered, his body swaying before he fell backward onto her bed with a groan.

She slid away from him, keeping her back to the wall as she inched to the corner of the room, reaching for the phone on the edge of the bureau. She pulled it from the wall, cord and all, running her finger over the home button on the bottom and glancing at it as it came to life. *4:32 a.m.* A light-blue glow filled the room.

"I'm calling the police."

"No!" he screamed. "*Na dean sin!*" *Don't do that!*

Something in his tone—desperation, terror, maybe both—made her pause and look up. He wasn't exactly sitting up, but he was trying to.

"Why not?" she asked.

"P-Please. Don't."

"But…but you need an ambulance."

"*Uihm g-gardai,*" he groaned, his eyes at half-mast, his neck barely able to hold up his head. *No police.*

That's when Tierney saw the gun.

Still held in his shaking hand, he raised it, pointing it at her. "*Curr sin sios.*" *Put it down.*

"Okay. It's okay. No phone. No police," she said, holding up her hands and leaning back against the bureau. "Could you put the gun down?"

"No," he panted, shaking his head.

Tierney lowered her arms, glancing at the home screen on her phone and trying to remember the trick for calling 911 without dialing. But that's when she noticed something dire: she had no signal.

Her phone, which usually had at least two bars, had none.

She glanced out the window and realized that the house on the hill was just as dark as her cottage. Lightning must have hit the cell phone tower hidden in the barn by the main house. It had happened more than once before.

Shit. Fuck.

No. Don't panic.

Think, Tierney. Think.

She glanced at the bed, where the stranger still held a shaking gun trained on her, though she could see he was fighting to keep his eyes open. He was in bad shape and worsening by the moment.

"I won't call the police. I promise. Listen," she said gently, taking a step toward him, "you're obviously in trouble, but I don't want to hurt you…and I don't think you want to hurt me. Put the gun down and you can have my phone, okay?"

"Give it," he said, holding out his other hand, which shook as badly as the first.

"There's no signal," she said, scrunching her shoulders up around her ears as she handed it to him and he grabbed it.

"Fuck!" Clutching the phone in one hand and the gun in the other, he lay back on the bed, muttering, "I c-can't…d-die here."

With the phone resting on his bare chest, the blue glow illuminating his skin, Tierney noticed something else, something unusual and unexpected: a medal of St. Michael lying on top of his tattoo.

"Saint Michael," she murmured. The warrior angel. The patron saint of policemen.

"*Sceilig Mhichíl*," he breathed, drawing out the Irish

10

pronunciation with a hiss. "If he c-could…k-kill the d-devil, why…c-can't…I?"

"Mr.…"

"Burrrrrr," he murmured, and this time Tierney realized that he wasn't cold; he was telling her his name.

"Mr. Burr—"

"J-Just…Burrrrrr," he said, his eyes closed, his hands on his chest, still tightly clenched around his gun and her phone.

The adrenaline that had been pumping through her body had exhausted her, and as she realized that he was almost completely incapacitated, she relaxed a little, slumping against her bureau.

With two brothers her age, Tierney Haven had more than a little bit of experience reading men, but this one was throwing her for a loop. A St. Michael medal sitting on top of a tattoo that read, "Destroyer." Contradictions abounded.

Although he'd forced his way into her home, and his language and manner were rough, she didn't believe he'd come here to hurt her. In fact, since the moment he'd arrived, he'd been dogged in one pursuit: to use her phone.

Yes, he'd grabbed her hair to get her out of the corner of her living room, but he hadn't added a gratuitous slap or kick. Even when he'd touched her breast in an attempt to find her arm in the darkness, he hadn't lingered on it, hadn't copped an extra feel. And when he'd pushed her at the top of the stairs and she'd bumped her head, he'd *apologized* to her.

He's not here to hurt me, she quietly decided, relaxing a little more. But who was he? Where was he from? How did he get here? And why?

His feet were still on the floor, though the rest of his body was lying across her bed. She stepped to the edge of the bed, leaning over him just a little.

"Burr?"

He groaned softly, his eyes fluttering open. "D-Don't...g-go."

She gulped. His voice sounded so much like Ian's, she could almost close her eyes and believe he was her brother.

"Me?"

"You. D-Don't...want...to...d-die...alonnnnnne," he murmured, the last word drawn out like the word a*men* after the Our Father.

It did something to her heart, that terrible and simple request, and she cocked her head to the side, watching as he remained motionless on her bed.

After several minutes, she whispered his name again.

"Burr?"

He murmured in his sleep, groaning softly, but didn't open his eyes.

She sucked her bottom lip between her teeth as the screen on her phone went dark. The rain was finally letting up a little, and a faint lavender glow—a mix of moonlight and dawn—filtered into the room.

What do I do? What do I do now?

She backed away from the bed, looking out the window, and that's when she noticed his car. A little way down the road, outside the gate, the headlights and interior lights were on because the driver's-side door had been left open.

I should move his car, she thought, taking a concerned look at him before slipping quietly from the room.

She headed downstairs, grabbing an umbrella from the antique bucket beside the front door, and headed out into the rain, grateful that the storm had subsided. It only took a few minutes to reach the gate and punch in the entry code. Luckily the gates opened inward, because his car would have been in the way had they opened out.

It wasn't a fancy car—a blue Honda Accord, your run-of-the-mill city vehicle. Where was he from? Concord? No. Even in Concord, you'd need four-wheel drive to get around from October to March. Hmm. Maybe Boston? Boston was the biggest big city within a couple hours' drive.

Peeking into the car, the first thing she noticed was a blackish stain on the driver's seat where his shoulder would have rested. Oil? She leaned closer, pressing her finger against the moisture and drawing it away. It was dark red on the pads of her fingers. Blood? She didn't remember seeing blood on his chest or arm, but there'd barely been enough light to get a good look at him, and frankly, an injury would explain his slurred speech and obvious fever.

She slid into the car, leaning forward so she wouldn't touch the upholstery with her white nightgown. Too far back for her to reach the pedals, she adjusted the seat forward, then pulled the door closed, driving through the gate and up the road a little ways to her cottage. Pulling the car into her driveway, she shifted it into park and turned on the interior lights. A pink bubblegum air freshener hung from the rearview mirror, and an empty orange juice bottle sat in the center console. There was an open pack of wet wipes on the passenger seat, with several stained wipes littering the floor.

She opened the glove compartment, searching for clues about who he was, and found a sippy cup, two sparkly hairbands, ketchup packets, tissues, and the car's registration. The car was owned by someone named Suzanne Riley, whose address was in Dorchester, Massachusetts, a neighborhood located just south of Boston proper. Turning to look in the back seat, she found a balled-up leather jacket, a booster seat that had half a cup of Cheerios in the built-in cupholder, and a stuffed bunny slumped over beside it.

Who was this Suzanne? Someone's mother, obviously. But who was she to Burr? Wife? Girlfriend? Or was the car stolen? Maybe he had no connection to Suzanne at all. Had he hurt the mother and child taking their car? Whose blood was on the driver's seat upholstery? She let the question sit for a moment, waiting for a feeling of dread to overwhelm her, but it didn't. She didn't know Burr at all, but something—intuition, surely—told her that he wasn't a murderer. If he was, she'd already be dead.

With far more questions than answers, she closed the glove compartment and withdrew the keys from the ignition. About to go back inside, her eyes flicked to the rearview mirror, landing on the trunk. Hmmm. Scooting from the driver's seat and rounding the car, she unlocked the trunk and looked inside. She found a half-opened black nylon duffel bag, which she hoisted onto her shoulder, and a brown Stop & Shop bag. Opening the paper sack, she looked inside to find neat stacks of money filling the lower fourth of the bag.

It had to be thousands of dollars.

Why would he be driving around with that? What was he into? Drugs? Weapons? Her mind flitted back to the tattoo on his chest. Was he a gang member? From Boston? If so, how in the world did he end up outside her door tonight?

Shoving the paper bag back into the corner of the trunk, she slammed it shut and headed back into her cottage, closing the front door behind her. Motionless in the dark living room, she listened for a sound from upstairs but heard nothing. With his duffel bag still on her shoulder, Tierney made her way to the kitchen and grabbed a flashlight, matches, and two candles from under the kitchen sink.

She placed the candles on the kitchen table and lit them, then sat down with his bag before her. Curious to know what it contained, she gulped before unzipping it the rest of the way, then flicked on her flashlight, leaning forward to look inside.

On top she found a white T-shirt that was clean except for some bloody fingerprints, a pair of jeans, socks, boxer shorts, and some beat-up sneakers. Underneath the clothes, she found a pistol, a box of ammunition, a knife, a small pair of binoculars, a first-aid kit, two Kind bars, a small bottle of orange juice, and a pair of handcuffs.

Hmm.

The money in the trunk looked shady, yes, but the contents of the bag, coupled with the St. Michael's medal he was wearing, felt more like a cop's, not a gang member's.

But why would a Boston cop bang on her door in Moultonborough, New Hampshire, at four thirty in the morning? And why did he have thousands of dollars in his trunk and look like a gangbanger, with his shaved head and tattoos?

"Suze! Suzy!"

The anguished cry came from her bedroom.

Tierney zipped his bag shut, stood up, and turned to

the stairs, knowing she had an important decision to make…

Either she could walk back out her front door, get in her car, and drive to the Moultonborough Police Station, or she could go upstairs and check on her unexpected guest.

What surprised Tierney the most was that her choice was already made, even before she'd laid it out for herself.

Maybe it was the fact that tonight had been scary, yes, but also exciting, while life for Tierney, in general, had become fairly routine.

Or maybe it was that she sensed he was in trouble and she wanted to help. Tierney had two brothers she loved more than anything—one of whom had been in trouble many times—and maybe once or twice, someone else's sister had looked after Ian. Maybe this man, Burr, had a sister who loved him as much as Tierney loved Ian. Looked at in a cosmic context, this was her opportunity to pay back that kindness.

Or maybe it was as simple as her own damned curiosity. Was he a destroyer or protector? A villain or hero? Tierney loved reading mysteries more than anything, poring over the ones on her Kindle night after night from the safety of her bed. But here was a real, live mystery on her doorstep. If she turned him in to the police, she might never find out where he came from and how he ended up finding his way to her.

He still has a gun, she reminded herself.

But if he was going to use it, she reasoned, *he already would have.*

Clutching the flashlight to her chest, she turned away from the door and started back up the stairs.

CHAPTER TWO

Declan Shanahan had the gun pointed at Suzanne.

Fuck, fuck, fuck.

"Where is he?" demanded Declan's brother, Sean Shanahan, who stood inches from Suzanne on her front stoop.

"I haven't seen him in years," she said.

"Who is it, Mommy?" asked Brigid, peeking out from behind Suzanne's legs.

Burr clenched his jaw, his heart thundering into overtime. Get back inside, baby girl. Please, God, get her back inside, Suzanne!

Sean narrowed his eyes at Suzanne before squatting down before her daughter. "What's yer name, now?"

"Bridey Riley. What's yours?"

"I'm Mr. Shanahan."

"Shanahan. That's a funny name."

"'Tis, isn't it?"

Brigid nodded, grinning at Sean Shanahan, one of the most dangerous criminals in Dorchester.

"Hey, Bridey," he said, "where's yer Uncle Burr at, eh?"

Brigid frowned at Sean, scrunching her little shoulders around her ears. "I dunno. I never seen him."

Sean grunted at her, then stood up, running one hand through his graying hair. "Where is he, Suzy?"

"Please, Sean. We don't know."

"He's a fucking narc, ain't he?"

"I don't—" Suzanne's voice shook as she put her hands over Brigid's ears, drawing her daughter closer. "I don't know what he's up to. But 'narc' feels pretty unlikely since he was busted for drugs and kicked off the force."

You're doing good, *thought Burr, who was hiding in the dark shadows next to Mrs. Murphy's garage across the street. Sean Shanahan didn't kill women and children. Maybe he'd grill her a bit, then leave her be.*

"Yer dad must've had a coronary over that one, eh?"

Suzanne blinked at Sean, licking her lips nervously before shrugging. "My dad…he's retired. We don't—we don't talk about Burr much anymore."

"Well, Declan," said Sean, turning to the man standing on Suzanne's small patch of lawn, who had a discreet pistol aimed at Burr's sister, "I guess we got some bad information, eh?"

"Looks like it, boss."

Sean turned back to Suzanne. "You see your brother around, you let me know, yeah?"

"'Course, Sean," she said, and Burr watched her face, the way her features relaxed just a touch.

Burr relaxed a little too, holstering his sidearm as he watched Sean turn his back to Suzanne, heading to the stairs. Once Burr knew that Suzanne and Brigid were safe, he would deal with his own mess…and he'd start by figuring out which rat-bastard had revealed his true identity to Sean.

He glanced back at Suzanne, a bolt of longing making him breathless as he stared at his sister and niece. It had been three long years since he'd made contact with them, and he missed them fiercely. Maybe it was okay that his cover had been blown—it meant that his life as an undercover cop was over. And God knew he was long past ready to leave this life behind.

He watched as Sean lumbered down the four steps of the stoop, making eye contact with Declan, his lips thin, his eyes furious. The tip of his head was so subtle, anyone else would have missed it, but Burr had worked closely with Sean for years. Not only did he catch it, but he knew what it meant, and dread sluiced through his being.

Shit, shit, shit! Suzanne, run!

Thrump. *The sound of a gun with a silencer being shot registered in Burr's brain just as his sister stumbled back, falling in a heap on the floor of her open front door.*

"That'll get his attention," muttered Sean, opening the passenger side of the car as Declan turned back around and hustled over to the driver's side.

"Fuck! No!" yelled Burr, shaking himself from his shock and stupor to run down Mrs. Murphy's driveway, grabbing the gun from his holster. He fired it at Declan, who whipped around in surprise, pointing his gun at Burr.

A bullet smacked into his shoulder, and Burr distantly acknowledged the hot, tearing pain, but it didn't stop him. He fired again, hitting Declan in the chest before he could open his door. He fell back against the car.

Someone in the neighborhood must have called the cops, because the screech and cry of sirens split the night, drawing closer and closer.

Declan slumped against the side of the car as Burr approached, wondering why Sean, who'd made it safely inside the car, hadn't shot at him yet. But then he remembered, Sean Shanahan preferred fists to guns—he left the shooting to men like his brother, Declan.

Within reach of the car, Burr made eye contact with Sean through the window and raised his gun, aiming at his head, but Sean slid across the front seat, shifted into drive, and hit the gas before Burr could pull the trigger. The tires shrieked, and Declan's head hit the pavement as his brother's car screeched away. Even though Burr shot twice at the bulletproof glass of the back windshield, Sean disappeared into the night just as Boston's finest arrived on the scene. Their sirens didn't drown out Brigid's high-pitched screams as she knelt by her mother's unresponsive body.

"Shhh. Shhh. Stop thrashing now."

The voice was firm but gentle, just like his—"Mam?"

"No. I'm not your mother. I disinfected it," she continued, "but I should call a doctor. It needs stitches."

"Suzy?"

"No. I'm not Suzy either." She paused, then asked, "Is she your wife? Suzy?"

"Where…am I?" he asked.

His mouth was so dry, his lips stuck to each other when he made the "m" sound of "am." She pressed a glass to his lips, and he took a small sip of water.

"New Hampshire," she said.

New Hampshire? Why the fuck was he in New Hampshire? What the hell was going on?

"You're safe here," she said, offering him the water again.

He took another sip, but his eyes were still closed, too heavy to open.

They're at Suzy's.

They're going after Suzy.

He'd received the call last night around ten. He hadn't known who was on the other side of the line, because the caller disguised his voice, and the line went dead before Burr could find out. On his way to drop off his daily collection to Sean, Burr had done a U-turn in the middle of Roxbury, racing to his sister's Dorchester neighborhood and parking one street away. Cutting through the Koswalskis' backyard and hiding against the Murphys' garage, where he could see Sean talking to her. And then...And then...

"Suzy!" he screamed, opening his eyes wide.

The first thing he saw was...

Her: a young woman, midtwenties, dark hair, green eyes, glasses. Her face was close. She sat in a chair beside the bed where he was lying. Placing a glass of water on the bedside table, she looked into his eyes.

"Who are you?" he demanded.

"Calm down. You're safe here," she said again.

"Where the fuck am I?"

"My house."

"Where?"

"I already told you: New Hampshire."

My wife's family has a place on Lake Ossipee. Twelve Carlson Road in Freedom, New Hampshire. Go there. Stay out of sight. I'll be in touch.

"O-Ossipee?"

She shook her head. "No."

"Where?"

"Moultonborough," she said.

"Where the fuck is that?"

"About thirty miles away."

"East or west?"

"West."

He clenched his jaw, staring at her. "Who are you?"

"Tierney."

Her answers were maddeningly brief, telling him nothing.

"Tierney what?"

"Haven."

"Where's my gun, Tierney Haven?"

She dropped his eyes for a moment, then looked up again. "Safe."

Goddamn it. He took a shaking breath. "Get it."

"No."

"Now!"

"I can't do that," she said. She went to reach into her pocket, and he flinched, jerking back from her. She froze, looking at him curiously, then nodded in understanding. "I'm only reaching into my pocket for your keys." Moving slowly, she pulled Suzanne's keys from her pocket and placed them on the bedside table. "You're not a hostage here. You can go whenever you like."

He snatched the keys and fisted them, still staring at her.

"How did I get here?"

"You drove here."

"When?"

"Last night. Your car is in my driveway. I moved it from the road."

His memories of his drive north were spotty, at best. Before he left Dorchester in Suzy's car, his partner, Ray, had grabbed some painkillers from the paramedics who came to take Suzy to the hospital. They must have been pretty strong.

"Tell me what happened."

"You woke me up, banging on my door at four o'clock in the morning. You wanted my phone."

That made sense. He had given his burner phone to Ray so his whereabouts couldn't be traced, but finding out what happened to his sister would have been a priority. Was she alive? Dead? He inhaled sharply at the terrible thought.

"Did I call anyone last night?"

She shook her head. "No."

"Why didn't you call the cops once I passed out?"

"No service," she said, reaching into her back pocket and holding up a phone. "They're restoring it now."

"They?"

"AT&T."

He stared at her, still trying to determine if he was safe here or not, despite her reassurances. "You could have driven to the local police department when I passed out."

"Yes." She stood up and nodded, stepping away from him to lean against her bureau, her clear green eyes still fixed on his face. "I could've."

"Why didn't you?"

Her lips twitched and she pushed her glasses up her nose. "You asked me not to involve the police."

"I broke into your house at four in the morning waving a gun around—no doubt scared the shit out of you—and you didn't call the police or run to them the second you could?"

"You didn't *break in.* I opened the door."

"Do you always open the door to strangers?"

"I thought you were my brother."

Burr sighed. "And when you realized I wasn't…?"

"You were already inside," she said.

He shook his head, deeply annoyed with her. She was going to get herself killed behaving like this. "Stupid."

She blinked at him, cocking her head to the side. "You're calling me *stupid*?"

"You shouldn't have let me in. You shouldn't have

opened the goddamned door! Didn't anyone ever teach you anything about strangers?" he demanded.

"I guess they were too busy teaching me how to say thank you," she said tartly. She took a deep breath, her unsettling green eyes still trained on his. "I'm not afraid of you," she said softly.

You should be. I've been living with animals for three years.

She reached up and pushed a lock of dark hair from her forehead, which revealed a fresh bruise. Burr grimaced. "Did I do that?"

"Not on purpose."

Fuck! He'd hurt her?

"Why didn't you go to the police?" he yelled, furious at her for putting herself in danger. How the hell had she made it to adulthood acting like this? "You should have gotten help!"

"It's not too late," she snapped. "I'll get in my car right now and tell the whole county you're here. Why don't you come with me? We'll stop by the hospital on the way. Make it a real fine field trip."

Fuck it all, but she was sassy.

The reality was that he didn't know who in the Boston Police Department had betrayed his identity to Sean, but he couldn't risk seeing if Sean's tendrils reached as far as New Hampshire. Not to mention, Sean would be combing reports of emergency room patients from Portland to Providence.

"Is that what you want?" she prodded, schoolmarm tone on point.

"No. I don't want the police involved," he muttered, looking away from her. "I'm just saying…you should be more careful."

Until he knew what was going on or could get to Ray's house on Lake Ossipee, he couldn't risk letting anyone else know where he was, and that included local police and emergency rooms.

He shifted his gaze back to the woman, letting his eyes trail down her body and back up again. She was a sweet little package—rounded hips, small waist, big tits, long, dark hair and a pretty, if way too serious, face.

"Smile," he said, as surprised by the word as she seemed to be.

She flinched, narrowing her eyes with undiluted anger. "*Téigh dtí diabhail.*"

Fuck off.

He couldn't help the chortle of laughter that lifted from his belly. She looked like a goddamn librarian but swore as neatly as any of Sean's thugs.

"Ha! Damn."

"I'm not afraid of you," she said again. She turned toward the door, then glanced over her shoulder. "I'll bring up some soup. Stay in bed. Your shoulder's bad."

"Where's the john?"

She raised an eyebrow. "The *restroom*?"

It had been a while since Burr had needed his Catholic school manners. But duly chagrined, he nodded. "Yes, please. The restroom."

She hooked a thumb to the left. "Down the hallway."

And then she was gone.

He listened to the sound of her steps fade until he couldn't hear her anymore. What did she say her name was? Tierney? *Irish*, he thought. *Well, of course she's Irish. She curses like she was born there.*

25

Loosening his grip on Suzy's keys, he placed them on the bedside table beside the glass of water, his memories of last night starting to return—and with them, a wave of fear and sorrow.

Hiding in the blue-and-red tinged shadows behind Suzanne's garage, he'd learned from Ray that his sister had been shot in the hip, though the paramedics who arrived at the scene said they doubted, based on the way she was bleeding, that her artery had been hit. Suzy's husband, Connor, had been called home from his shift at the Dorchester Fire Department to take care of Bridey. Burr and Suzy's parents, Sheila and Frank (a retired Boston cop), had also been contacted, and were on the way to the Miami Airport.

After sharing this news, Ray had grabbed some gauze and painkillers from the ambulance, bandaged up Burr's shoulder best he could and told his partner it was time to go.

"I'm not fucking leaving, Ray. They shot my fucking sister! They could've hit Bridey too. Fuck, they could have—"

"You don't leave now," said Ray, grabbing Burr firmly by his uninjured shoulder, "and I give you less than twenty-four hours to live."

Fuck, but it had killed Burr to leave.

Suzy was shot because of *him*—or, more accurately, because of the person who'd sold him out to Sean and the rest of the New Killeens, where Burr had been undercover for almost three years—and if he wasn't by her bedside, the only place he wanted to be was hunting down the motherfucking traitor who'd put Suzanne O'Leary Riley in danger.

"Where's your car?" asked Ray.

"Over on Mulberry," Burr said, hooking his thumb toward the Koswalskis' house.

"Good. Leave it there. Take Suzy's," he'd said, gesturing to the garage. "My wife's family has a place on Lake Ossipee. Twelve Carlson Road in Freedom, New Hampshire. Go there and hide. Take care of that shoulder when you can. Stay out of sight. I'll be in touch."

Except Burr hadn't made it to Freedom. He'd gotten lost in the storm—the painkillers muddling his head, the hammering rain making it impossible to read highway signs—and somehow, he'd ended up thirty miles off course in…where was he? Oh, yeah. Moultonborough. Wherever the fuck *that* was.

He heard Tierney's footsteps approaching, and he took a deep breath, sitting up. He instantly regretted the movement, dizzy from the sharp and intense burst of pain it caused to move. She was right—his shoulder was bad.

"Soup," she said, stepping into the room with a tray. She crossed over to him, placing it carefully on his lap. "Split pea and ham."

Burr looked down at the lumpy green muck. He hated pea soup with a fiery passion. "Thanks."

"I made it myself," she said, pushing her glasses up on her nose, "with a leftover ham bone."

For the first time, it occurred to him that she might have a husband. None of the single girls he knew baked hams or made soup from scratch. That was a married-lady skill.

"You married?" he asked, taking a spoonful of the soup and finding it not as horrible as he remembered from his

27

childhood.

"No."

"Who'd you make the ham for, then?"

"Me and my brothers."

Brothers could be trouble.

"They live here too?"

"Not *right* here. Nearby."

Relieved, he nodded, taking another bite of soup. "This is good. I don't like peas. Usually."

"You've probably had them from a can. They're not very tasty that way," she commented, hovering by the foot of her bed.

"You can sit down if you want," he said, gesturing to the chair by the bed with a flick of his chin.

She obviously thought it over for a minute before accepting his invitation, but her back was rigid when she sat down, her unsmiling face quietly disapproving.

"Why do you have a gun?" she asked.

"Protection."

"From whom?"

"Better you don't know."

She pursed her lips. "How about the money in the back of your car? What's that for?"

The spoon froze halfway between the bowl and his mouth. He turned to her. "What do you know about that?"

"You left your car on the road. I pulled it into my driveway and found money in the—"

"Don't worry about it," he said, giving her a hard look before drawing the spoon to his lips.

"Well, I *am*…worried about it," she said. "I'm also worried about Suzanne Riley. The car's registered to her. Did you hurt her? How'd you get her car? You called out for her a lot last night."

Burr dropped the spoon into his bowl with a clatter and clenched his jaw. Her questions were hitting him in soft places, and he didn't like it, though he guessed she was entitled to some answers.

"*I* didn't hurt her…" he muttered, "but she got hurt."

"Will she be all right?"

"I don't know," he admitted, pushing the tray away. *Enough.* He looked up at her. "I need to go to the…restroom."

"Didn't you go before?"

He shook his head. "Hurt too much to sit up."

"I'll get you some more Advil," she said, standing from the chair and holding out her hand. "Want help?"

He stared at her for a minute, baffled by the fact that she was helping him, a frightening stranger who'd arrived at her door in the middle of a dark and stormy night. He couldn't think of another woman he knew who would act as she had, and he didn't know whether she was the stupidest or bravest woman he'd ever known.

"You're really not afraid of me, are you?"

She shrugged. "I told you…I have two brothers."

"Older or younger?"

"Same age," she said.

"You're triplets?"

She nodded as he took her hand, groaning as he swung his feet over the side of the bed and stood up. "You and two brothers, huh?"

"Yes. Me and two brothers. That's how triplets work," she said, leading him out of the bedroom and down a short hallway. She dropped his hand to push open the bathroom door. "Here you go."

"Thanks," he said, offering her a brief, miserable grimace that would have to pass as a smile. "You've been…" His words drifted off. She was allowing him to stay here and feeding him, and she hadn't called the police yet. For that, she deserved his gratitude. "…helpful."

"Who is Suzanne?" she asked again, hands on her hips.

"My sister," he said, figuring he owed her one true answer.

"Oh," she murmured, her face relaxing, her lips parting, her green eyes all the wider behind her glasses. "Your *sister*. You're someone's brother."

You're someone's brother.

The words hit him square in the chest and stole his breath for a moment, because he'd missed his family so damned much over the past three years, it ached. *Someone's brother.*

"Yes. I am," he murmured.

"And she's hurt?" Tierney's brows furrowed together. "I'm sorry."

"She's not *dead*," said Burr quickly, his voice harsher than he intended.

"No. Of course not," said Tierney. "I…that's good. I hope she…"

Her voice trailed off, and she turned around without another word, heading down the stairs and leaving Burr alone.

chapter three

His sister.

He'd been calling for his sister, *not his girlfriend, not his wife.*

Why this information made her whole being relax, followed by an unaccountable feeling of relief in the general vicinity of her heart, wasn't something Tierney cared to explore. In fact, it was something best left ignored…forever. What mattered was that someone in the world—Suzanne Riley—certainly loved this man as much as Tierney loved Rory and Ian, and Tierney would do what she could, on Suzanne's behalf, to keep her brother safe.

Tierney stood at the kitchen sink, washing out the soup pan she'd used to heat up Burr's lunch. Overhead she heard the toilet flush, followed by his footsteps and the creak of her bed.

Out the window, on the top of the hill, she could see the towers of Moonstone Manor, the historic Gish estate, known locally as "The Palace in the Sky." The electric company had already restored power, but the AT&T crew was still up at the barn working on the antenna concealed in the lookout tower. For that reason, among others—especially her rogue houseguest—Tierney had made an executive decision to keep the estate closed for today and was confident it was the right decision. As caretaker of Moonstone Manor, such choices were under her exclusive purview.

She liked being in charge of the historic landmark—being the official caretaker of the great house, outbuildings, and property—though she'd stumbled into the position in sort of an unconventional way.

Two weeks before graduating with honors from Dartmouth College six years ago, Tierney's mother had suffered from a debilitating stroke and been rushed from Summerhaven to the nearest trauma center in New Hampshire: the Dartmouth-Hitchcock Medical Center.

For the following two years, Tierney had remained in Hanover with her parents, helping her father care for her mother, shuttling her mother to therapy and doctor appointments, and willingly putting her own future on hold. Although she'd double-majored in classics and fine art as an undergraduate, hoping to parlay her education into museum work, she'd done little more during those two years than occasionally volunteer over at the local Shaker Museum in Enfield.

Tierney didn't mind putting her life on hold for her family. If anything, she looked at caring for her mother as a sacred responsibility and being useful to her parents as an honor. So it came as a surprise, after those two years, when her parents and Rory had staged a mini-intervention, the intent of which, more or less, was to tell her it was time for her to leave Hanover.

"Darlin'," started her mother, her speech still stilted by the effects of the stroke, "you've been…the best daughter…I could ask for." She'd paused. "But I'm gonna…get right to the point. Some baby birds…spread their wings one day…and fly away…because it's time. And others…"

Tierney had searched her mother's face, trying to figure out what she was saying.

"…need a push," finished Rory.

"A push?" Tierney had repeated, glaring at her brother before sliding her gaze to her father's ruddy, bearded face.

"…Out of the nest," added her father, laying a hand on his wife's shoulder. "Tierney, it's time for you to go live your life. You can't hide here forever."

"Hide?" she'd protested, feeling immediately defensive.

She'd spent two years driving her mother to medical appointments, in addition to handling all of the shopping, cooking, and housekeeping. How was that *hiding*?

"I'm so sorry that my services aren't needed anymore," she'd huffed, blinking back the unexpected sting of tears.

"Tierney Eileen…don't be like that," said her mother from her wheelchair. "You know…how much…we've appreciated you…bein' here."

"Being here? Or *hiding* here?"

"Tier," said Rory, pressing on with the tough love, "don't act like you have no idea what we're talking about. Remember when we were kids at Summerhaven? After all of our chores were done, Ian and I would go spy on the girls at the lake or head down to the Weirs Beach boardwalk to rustle up some fun. You'd…"

I'd go escape to the hammock at the far side of the lake and read, she'd finished for herself.

With a grim but knowing smile, Rory had nodded, watching as she put the pieces together.

But what was wrong with that? Was it so bad that she preferred her own company? Or that she wanted to be of

33

service to her family? Why was it bad for her to want to be with them? Couldn't they see that, barring time alone, she was most comfortable in their company? Wasn't that okay?

Apparently not.

With a heavy heart, she'd gotten her meager resume together and looked online to make a list of all the museums in New Hampshire that might be seeking a docent.

The day she'd stopped by Moonstone Manor to drop off her resume also happened to be the day after the previous on-site caretaker and lead docent had decided to quit. The preservation committee was convening in the visitor's center, trying to figure out if they should advertise for a new caretaker/docent in the Boston newspapers or online. In the meantime, they'd have to schedule round-the-clock shifts to man the ticket booth and tours, or they'd lose the valuable summer tourist traffic that made future improvements possible.

Smack in the middle of their meeting, Tierney had walked in, asking if they had any positions open. She'd never seen eight strangers smile with such identical combinations of surprise, relief, and warmth.

After they perused her resume—impressed that she'd attended Dartmouth and had volunteered regularly at the Shaker Museum—they'd offered her the job on the spot.

The rest was history.

Along with the fact that the tiny caretaker's cottage where she lived came with the job (and was a large part of the position's benefits), Tierney was her own boss. She managed all repairs on the estate, hired docent interns from area colleges to lead tours every summer, and—from October 30 until March 30 every year when the estate was closed to the public—hid out in her tiny cottage reading mysteries on her Kindle and readying the house or grounds for the occasional seasonal event.

The position, and her life, was perfect in almost every way. Her brothers, Ian and Rory, worked close enough to stop by once or twice a week for dinner, and her parents only lived two hours away. She loved the estate itself: the great house with north and south parlors; a ballroom, dining room, kitchen, six bedrooms, and servants' quarters; a barn/carriage, pool house, and aviary. She loved exploring the boxes of old letters and journals in the attic and occasionally creating a new exhibit in the entry hall based on her findings. She loved the autonomy. She loved her quiet little cottage. She loved her quiet little life…

…*mostly.*

Her hands were pruning in the sink, and she blinked, rinsing the soup pot and placing it in the drying rack.

Yes, she did. She *mostly* loved her quiet, solitary life.

Except…

Except lately, when Rory and his girlfriend, Brittany, came to family dinner together, she felt an ache inside—*deep* inside, where uncomfortable truths can mostly stay secret and unacknowledged. Only once did she force herself to look at said ache, and what she saw was a young woman growing older, growing older, growing older, growing *old*…all alone, hidden away from the world. It made her feel something that Tierney didn't feel very often: it made her feel *lonely.*

For what? A partner, maybe. Someone to love and love her back. Children, perhaps. She didn't know, really. She just knew the feeling, and she knew she didn't like it.

Suddenly her cell phone came to life in her hip pocket, dinging and buzzing, which told her that AT&T had been able to repair the tower and restore service.

She pulled the plug from the sink to drain the soapy water and dried her hands on a dishcloth before taking out her phone.

First, she checked out her text messages, starting with the text group that included her and her two brothers.

RORY: Tier, you okay? Bad storm out there tonight.

IAN: She's fine. Tough as nails, our girl.

IAN *(less than a minute later)*: You okay, Tier?

RORY: I thought you said she was tough as nails.

IAN: You don't have a monopoly on worrying about her, boyo.

RORY: If you need us, shout.

IAN: She's probably asleep.

RORY: I'll check on you in the AM.

Shoot. It was almost noon and the last thing Tierney needed was for one of her brothers to come by and find a strange car in her driveway and a tattooed stranger in her bed. Lord. Her fingers flew over the keys.

TIERNEY: Power and cell service got wiped out. Back on now. Museum closed for today. All is well.

RORY: Phew. You had us worried. Ian's on his way over.

Tierney's eyes widened as she gasped. *Shit. Shit. Shit.* Ian was coming over? Her brother Ian was more playful than their other brother, Rory, but he was also bigger. And there was *no* way he'd be okay with a strange man in his sister's bed.

Racing through the living room, she took the stairs two

at a time, turning left down the hallway and beelining into her room, where she found Burr flat on his back, the tray of mostly uneaten soup beside him.

"I need your car keys," she said.

"Why?" he asked, opening one eye.

"My brother Ian's on his way over. I need to put your car in the garage."

"Why?" he asked again.

"Because he'll beat you to kingdom come if he finds you in my bed," she answered.

"Nothing happened between us," he said, his eyes slipping to her breasts and lingering for a moment before sliding back up.

She ignored the sudden and surprising warmth in her belly. "Doesn't matter."

"Pfft. I can hold my own against your brother."

"You don't know my brother," she said.

"I don't need to," he said, cocky despite his injuries. "I know myself."

"You have a mangled shoulder and a fever. You're weak, Burr. Think again."

He looked supremely annoyed over her use of the word "weak," but reached for the keys and threw them her way. They clattered to the floor.

Tierney reached down and grabbed them. She ran downstairs, opened the garage, backed her car into the driveway, then pulled Burr's into the garage. Just as the garage door hit the ground, Ian pulled up.

She took a deep, calming breath and waved at him. "Hi!"

"Hey, Tier," said Ian, parking the car and sliding out of

the driver's seat. "Came by to check on you."

"I just got all of your texts."

"Power went out?" asked her brother, giving her a giant bear hug.

Her brother, Ian, had been sober since April 1st—132 days as of today—and he was mostly back to his hearty self. At six feet three inches tall and a little over two hundred pounds, Ian was muscular and burly, his face covered with a dark beard and his long, unruly black hair back in a man bun, both of which were at odds with the conservative cut of his dark-green Summerhaven staff polo shirt. But no matter how many times Rory asked him to shave his beard and cut his hair, Ian refused.

Tierney held on to him for an extra beat, remembering how she'd felt last night when she'd briefly wondered if Burr would hurt her and if she'd ever see her brothers again.

"Hey," he said, "you okay?"

"Yeah," she sighed, finally releasing him. "I'm just…it *was* bad storm last night."

"I'll say. Took out a couple of trees at camp. Rory and I were up at dawn with the axes and chainsaws."

"What group arrived yesterday?" she asked.

Summerhaven's camp schedule ran from Monday to Sunday, and since today was Tuesday, a new group was just settling in.

Ian waggled his eyebrows. "It's single parents' week. Lots of hot looks across the oatmeal this morning. I imagine more than one woman was 'comforted' by a new friend during the storm."

Tierney snickered. "Better watch it, or you'll be snagged by a cute divorcée."

"Not a chance, little sister."

Although *technically* Tierney was older than Ian by a few minutes—she'd come out between her two brothers—they always called her their "little" sister because she was so much smaller than they. At five feet four inches tall, she was almost a foot shorter than Ian.

"Oh, no?"

"Nah," said Ian, who used to be a notorious player. "At the risk of sounding like a self-important, new age asswipe, I'm still working on me."

"Very wise," she said, nodding her approval. There was plenty of time for Ian to meet someone once he was confident in his sobriety, and frankly, Tierney was vehemently against anything—*or anyone*—who might impede or derail Ian's progress.

Ian gestured to her house with his chin. "Aren't you going to invite me in for a cuppa?"

Stay calm. Stay calm. "Um…actually, I was on my way up the hill to see how AT&T was getting along."

"Ah," said Ian, nodding in the direction of the barn. "Sure. Right. I'll come along. Mind some company? I have thirty minutes before I need to be back."

"That'd be fine," said Tierney, using the keys in her hand to unlock her car. Except…the keys in her hand weren't the keys to *her* car, so despite three attempts, nothing unlocked.

Ian looked down at them. "Um. Whose keys are those?"

Shit! They're Burr's—uh, Suzanne's.

"These? Oh! Right! Ha. These are…I mean, I found them…in the road. No. Not in the road. Um, up at the barn?

Right? Probably. Yup. The barn. I guess someone left them there. Yesterday or…sometime. Tourist probably."

Ian gave her a once-over. "And why do you have them now?"

"I must have…um, dropped them, you know, when I found them. I brought them back here, and then I must have dropped them in the mud, and I just—well, I just found them again when you pulled up."

"But they're not muddy," he said slowly.

"Oh! Right. I rinsed them off…you know, in the, um, the spigot? Behind the garage. Scrubbed them—um, uh, off."

"Tierney?" said Ian, rubbing his beard with his thumb and forefinger as he narrowed his eyes at her.

"Yeah?"

"You know that weird, spazzy thing you do when you're lying?"

She stared at him, refusing to answer.

"You're doing it now."

"What?" she asked, slapping him lightly on the forearm. "You're crazy! I don't have anything to…I mean—stop, uh, teasing me. I'm just going to get my…yeah. I'll be back, um, in a sec!"

Hurrying inside, she took her car keys off the hook next to the front door and hung up the ones in her hand. Standing against the front door for a second, she caught her breath.

You'd best get a hold of yourself, she thought, flicking her eyes up to the ceiling, *or you're going to let the cat—erm, lion—out of the bag.*

She turned around and headed right back outside,

determined to stop acting like a freak. But damn it, Tierney wasn't good at lying. Never had been. Never would be. Especially not to her brothers, with whom she was exceptionally close.

"Got 'em!" she said, holding up her keys and pressing the button that unlocked the doors of her Jeep SUV. "Hop in."

Ian sat down in the passenger seat beside her, and Tierney turned the key in the ignition before glancing at her brother. "See? *My* keys. All mine. Only mine. Ready to go?"

"Something's up with you," said Ian, staring at her thoughtfully, his eyes slightly narrowed.

"Nope," she insisted. "Nothing. Nada. Nil. Niet."

"Humph," grunted Ian as she pulled out of the driveway. "Something's *definitely* up with you."

***

Damn. Tierney Haven's brother is big, thought Burr, watching the brother and sister talk in the driveway from the upstairs window. Thick-big. Like an Irish boxer. All muscled meat on a massive, sturdy bear-like frame. *Good man to have your back in a brawl.*

As Tierney's car pulled out of the driveway, he shuffled back to her bed. A stain about the size of a baseball sullied her snow-white pillow in varying degrees of red and brown. *Fuck.* He reached over his shoulder and felt the dressing she must have put over the exit wound. The skin around it was hot. And it hurt. It fucking burned like crazy.

The jeans he wore slung around his hips were still damp from last night's rain. He flicked open the button fly and slid them down his legs, kicking them off in a heap and easing his naked body back into Tierney's bed. He sighed as he

41

found a comfortable position on his good side, the scent from her pillow rising up around him as he rested his head with a long sigh.

Who was this girl anyway?

She had a backbone, that was for sure—she was all of five foot and change, but she'd stood there telling him she wasn't scared of him, and he could go fuck himself for asking her to smile, and they could take a nice field trip to the po-po if he didn't stop harping on her safety. He chuckled softly, thinking about the sharpness in her green eyes; she didn't miss a trick, this one. Her tongue was as barbed as any Irish granny's, and she wielded it like a weapon.

Brothers, he thought.

Growing up with two brothers the same age meant learning how to hold your own. And if her other brother was as big as that monster, Ian, holding her own *physically* wouldn't have been an option. It was verbal or nothing.

He sighed, his smile disappearing as he thought about Suzanne. He wondered how she was doing. Was she in a coma? Unconscious? How was Bridey? Jesus, it would scar the kid for life, remembering her mother crumpling to the ground like that, men shooting it out on her front lawn. Never in his wildest dreams would he have taken the assignment if he knew the price his sister would pay last night.

Burr and Suzanne had grown up in Dorchester, the kids of Frank O'Leary, a detective with the Boston Police Department, and Sheila Sullivan, an elementary school teacher. Their childhood neighborhood, where Suzy still lived, was chock-full of Carrolls and Farrells, Murphys,

Shanahans, Sheas, Murrays, Doyles, and MacGuires. Mass on Saturday nights. Big supper at two o'clock on Sundays. CCD on Wednesday evenings. St. Paddy's parades every March. Celtic Camp over in Canton, Massachusetts, for three weeks every summer, and a visit back to Limerick, in the "old country," every three or four years to visit extended family.

Like his father and uncle, Burr had applied to the police academy after receiving his BA from UMass in criminology and working part time for campus police during his junior and senior years. He'd been on the force for three years before he'd been called into Captain Donnelley's office at the District C-6 "Southie" station where he worked.

"O'Leary," said the captain, "you ever think about going undercover?"

"I'm open to it, sir."

"You have a good record. You come from a good family of cops. You know Dorchester like the back of your hand, but you've been stationed here in Southie. You'd be on loan to Dorchester."

"Okay." He nodded for the captain to keep going.

"You ever heard of the Killeen Gang?"

"Sounds vaguely familiar."

"It was a south Boston gang started by three brothers in the 1950s. Mostly active in the '60s and '70s. Bookmaking, loan-sharking. The occasional body would show up bloodied, or dead, when a debt wasn't paid. Fought it out with the Mullens and the White Hill mob. Whitey Bulgar ran with them for a while."

"Whitey Bulgar. Sure," said Burr. "I saw the movie with Johnny Depp."

"Killeen was defunct by the 1990s, mostly taken over

by White Hill."

"Okay…"

"But now they're back. Started up again in Dorchester over the last couple of years by two brothers named Shanahan—Killeens on their mother's side. Called their crew the 'New Killeens.' They're getting stronger. We need someone on the inside to start collecting evidence, so we can make a case against them."

"Me?"

"That's the plan."

"How?"

"We'll plant drugs in your car. Stage a bust. You'll leave the department in disgrace and reach out to Sean Shanahan, the boss. Tell him you want in. Tell him you want revenge against BPD."

"And then?"

"We'll pair you with Raymond Cooper. You know him?"

Burr had nodded. Sure, he knew Ray Cooper—they both went to St. Gregory's Parish. They'd been altar boys together there.

"You'll meet up with Ray once a week, give him photos, gang plans, names—whatever you get. He'll make sure it all goes to Sergeant Seth Gunn, your gang task unit contact. I'll keep an eye on things from this end too. Eventually, it'll be enough to take them down and then you can return to Southie."

"How long is 'eventually'?"

"Three years," said Donnelley. "Maybe four."

As a single, twenty-four-year-old man, the idea had appealed to Burr. It sounded exciting, and dangerous—a chance to flex his muscles and make a big difference in the city he loved. It would also fast-track his dream of making detective before thirty. If he could be instrumental in bringing down the New Killeens, he could probably write his own ticket later.

"So? What do you think?" asked Donnelley.

Burr only had one major misgiving.

"My folks and Suzy. They'll know that I didn't *really* get busted for drugs, right? I'll be able to tell them the truth?"

The captain had sucked in a deep breath and grimaced. "Sorry, O'Leary. For the story to fly, you're going to need to be disgraced, and your family's going to need to have a genuine reaction to it. They're known in Dorchester; their reactions to you will go a long way in cementing how you're viewed. I need Shanahan to *really believe* that you're not a good O'Leary anymore. Not in any way that matters." He'd paused, looking Burr in the eyes. "I'll be honest. It'll be safer for your family that way too."

It was then that Burr had understood the full scope of the job in front of him. He'd be "busted" for drug use, fired from his job, get a shithole apartment somewhere in Dorchester, "run into" one of Shanahan's guys, and wheedle his way into the gang.

And he wouldn't be able to make contact with his family for the next three or four years. It was a big price to pay. A *huge* price…especially because Suzy was pregnant with her first kid, and Burr wanted to be an uncle more than anything else in the world.

"I'm not gonna lie," said Donnelley, no doubt translating the play of emotions on Burr's face, "this is gonna be a tough job, O'Leary. You'll see some pretty fucked up things. It'll be dangerous. You may have to compromise your own morals now and then. But...you could also be the man who brought down Sean and Declan Shanahan and kept the New Killeens from rising to power again."

Burr had nodded in understanding. "Can I have a day or two? To think it over?"

Donnelley had nodded, but the reality was that Burr's decision was already made before he left the captain's office. He had joined the force to make a difference, and if it came in the form of going undercover to bring down the New Killeens, so be it. When he was standing on a stage receiving a medal from the mayor of Boston, his parents and sister would understand.

Except, fast forward three years, and Suzanne was lying in a hospital bed. Bridey, whom Burr had never actually met in person, was probably scarred for life. His parents, who hadn't spoken to him for years, no doubt blamed him. What a fucking mess. He knew what he'd signed on for, but he hated what had happened. And more than anything, he wanted out.

"How're you doing?"

Tierney Haven's soft voice broke through the misery of Burr's thoughts, and he looked up to see her standing beside his bed.

He cleared his throat. "You weren't lying. Your brother's a big guy."

"You look awful."

"Aw," he said, "stop flirting with me."

She shook her head at him, her hand landing on his forehead. "You're burning up. Burr, you need a doctor."

"No," he said. "No doctor. Just…if you don't mind, maybe you could disinfect it and rebandage it."

"You need antibiotics," she said, opening her bureau drawer and withdrawing a bottle of ibuprofen. She poured two into her hand and placed them beside his glass of water on the bedside table. "You need stitches."

"Forget it. Stitches mean an emergency room, and I can't—"

"Not necessarily," she interrupted. She sat down on the chair beside the bed. "I'll make you a deal. You agree to trust me to bring someone discreet to help you, and I'll tell you a secret. A *really* good one."

A secret? Why would he want to know one of her secrets? What kind of leverage was that?

And yet…staring at her pretty face, which held an expression of worry mixed with anticipation, he found he *did* want to know a secret of Tierney Haven's.

He reached for the pills and swallowed them back, chasing them with a sip of water. "Fine. What?"

Was it his imagination or did her lips tilt up in the smallest smile? It disappeared so quickly, he couldn't be sure.

"Say you'll trust me," she said.

"What choice do I have?"

"Please say it," she said, cocking her head to the side. "There's a way of doing this, and we both know it."

The English welshed.

The Scots welshed.

The Welsh *certainly* welshed.

But the Irish bloody well did not welsh on each other. Once a deal was struck, it was dyed in the wool.

"Fine," he said. "I trust you. Now, what's your damned

secret?"

She spoke quickly, the words tumbling from her lips like she couldn't bear to keep them inside for a second longer. "Your sister was in surgery last night, but she was moved to a regular room an hour ago. Her hip was fractured by the bullet, but not shattered, and it missed her artery. She should make a full recovery."

He was staring at her face, clenching his jaw so hard, it was starting to ache.

He blinked his eyes furiously, refusing to cry. He hadn't cried in three years—not since the day his father had hung up on him, after calling him a "corrupt, rotten, good-for-nothing addict. You're a disgrace to the name O'Leary and you're not my son anymore." But he wanted to cry now. Jaysus, Mary, and Joseph, he wanted to sob, he wanted to bawl, he wanted this strange woman to put her arms around him and let him cry for hours because he'd never known relief so sharp and so blessedly overwhelming.

He cleared his throat. "How do you know?"

"I called Mass General."

"And they told you all that?"

"I might have said I was Suzanne's little sister...and I might have pretended to cry a little. So yeah." She nodded, that very slight smile tugging at the corners of her mouth again. "It sounds like she's going to be okay. I thought you should know."

"Okay. Thanks," he said, knowing full and well that his mumbled words were inadequate, but he hadn't felt real gratitude in so long, he was out of practice at expressing it.

In fact, the sensation of deeply feeling *anything* was foreign to him. For years, he'd been hiding his real feelings;

he was a little out of practice at recognizing, processing, and expressing them.

He was beyond relieved that Suzanne was going to be okay, but now that he'd been reassured, an overwhelming feeling of exhaustion was kicking in. He was sick to death of the life he'd been living for the past three years. He was finished being one of Sean Shanahan's collection goon squad. He wanted his parents and his sister and his niece back in his life. He wanted to be normal again.

But unfortunately, he didn't know how to make that happen.

Now that his cover was blown, he wouldn't be undercover anymore...but unless what he'd given to Sergeant Gunn, via Ray, was enough to put Sean and his associates away for life, Burr would be looking over his shoulder for the rest of *his* life—and no one standing next to him would be safe. Fuck, even if Sean went to jail, it probably didn't matter. He had a network of men working for him, and one of them would be tasked with making sure Burr didn't live long.

What a fucking mess.

Closing his eyes, he took a ragged breath, holding it, even though it made his shoulder hurt more.

"Are you bad or good?" whispered Tierney, more to herself, perhaps, than to him.

"I don't know anymore," said Burr, opening his eyes to find Tierney Haven staring at him thoughtfully.

Her steady green gaze scanned his eyes, his face, something deep and strong swirling in the mossy, emerald depths. *What are you thinking?* he wondered. *What's happening behind those eyes?*

"Good, I think." She nodded slowly, then pulled out her phone and typed a quick message.

"Don't be so sure," he muttered, looking away.

Something about staring into her eyes hurt, almost; it was the same way he used to feel when he saw rich Harvard kids driving around Boston in their BMWs when all he could afford was a shitty secondhand Toyota. Something he couldn't afford. Something he couldn't have.

"Well, anyway…thank you for trusting me," she said as she stood up from her chair. "Someone's coming to help you. I just texted him. I'll bring him up when he gets here, okay?"

"Tierney, wait…" he started.

"Don't go welshing, now," she said, stopping at the bedroom door and turning around. "You promised to trust me."

"I *do* trust you," he said, surprised by the words, surprised that he meant them. But then, this woman, whom he'd only known for a handful of hours, had already proven herself extraordinary.

"Then…what?"

Thank you. Thank you so much. Thank you for everything.

"Nothing," he said softly, pursing his lips together to keep from saying any more.

"Okay, then," she said, her face softening just a touch as she nodded at him and slipped out the door.

chapter four

Tierney arrived downstairs just in time to answer the doorbell, offering a polite smile to the man on her doorstep.

"Hi John."

"Tierney!" he said, a broad smile lighting up his homely face. "What a *nice* surprise to hear from you today!"

John Stuart, DVM, was the Holderness-based veterinarian of the German shepherd that Ian had adopted earlier in the summer. He was also a frequent "surprise" dinner guest at the Wednesday and Sunday family suppers that Tierney hosted, leading her to believe that her brothers were not-so-subtly trying to set her up with the well-meaning, good-intentioned thirtysomething doctor.

A few inches taller than Tierney, John was so slight, she guessed that they probably weighed about the same. With reddish-blond hair, freckles, and brown eyes hidden behind thick glasses, John didn't exactly scream "dream lover." Her wild imaginings ran much more toward tall, dark, and dangerous than small, ginger, and chipper.

"Thanks for coming by, John. I really appreciate it. Come on in."

"Your mysterious text sure got my attention!"

With his hopeful smile and enthusiastic inflection, he reminded her of one of the golden retrievers he looked after.

Be nice, she thought. *You're about to ask for a big favor.*

"I've been meaning to call you and thank you for dinner on Sunday. That was some ham!"

"I'm glad you liked it."

"With my family all in Maine, it means a lot that I get to share yours."

Since she didn't want to encourage him to think of ways to "officially" join her family, she didn't smile at this comment. Keeping her face impassive, she just stared at him.

He laughed nervously, his cheeks reddening. "Rory and Brittany sure look happy lately, huh?"

"They do."

"Love will do that, I guess," theorized John, clearing his throat. "It actually got me to thinking, Tierney…I mean, well, maybe you and I could, um—"

Oh, God, no. "John, I need your help with something."

"Right. Yes. Sorry. We can talk about other things, um, later." He looked around her tidy living room. "Where's the patient? In the kitchen?"

She glanced at the ceiling. "Upstairs."

"You said it was a hunting accident. Did you find the poor fellow in a snare?" he asked, following her across the living room and up the stairs.

"Not exactly. He came to my door."

"Really? My!" John gasped dramatically. "It's very unusual for animals to seek help from humans in such situations, but it has been known to happen. You have such a gentle manner, Tierney, I just bet he—"

"He *banged* on my door," she clarified.

"Oh? How odd. Banged, huh? Are we talking about a larger animal? How in the world did you get it up the stairs—"

She paused at her bedroom door, standing back and gesturing to Burr, who sat up in the bed, bare-chested with his "Destroyer" tattoo on full display and a wary expression that would frighten any normal human out of his skin.

John blanched, turning to Tierney.

"That is *not* an animal."

"You haven't met him yet."

She stepped into the room.

"John, this is Brian. Brian, this is John. John is a, um, well, he's a veterinarian who treats my brother's dog. Juniper. I mean—Juniper is the dog. Ian is my brother. Obviously. Brian is, um…well, he's an old college friend from, um, from Dartmouth, where I went to college, and, um, well…anyway, Brian was out…last night, um…hunting. Yes, hunting! With, um—he was with some—some buddies," she said, crossing her room to stand beside Burr and shoot him a disapproving look, "…and—and *this* happened."

There, she thought with satisfaction. *I'm getting the hang of this lying thing, aren't I?*

She shot a triumphant look at Burr, expecting to see admiration on his face, but he was looking up at her like she'd lost her mind, while John still hovered in the doorway of her room looking bewildered. His glance slid to the white bandage that Tierney was pointing to, then back to Tierney.

John cleared his throat and adjusted his glasses. "*This*…being?"

"A bullet wound," said Tierney. "It went straight through, as far as I can tell, but it needs care. Stitches, for sure. I think it's infected."

"I see," said John, still frozen by the doorway. "May I—May I please speak to you in the hallway, Tierney?"

"Yes," she said, turning to Burr. "We'll be right back...Brian."

Burr, who appeared to be waffling between annoyed and amused answered, "You got it...Millie."

Her lips twitched as she turned and followed John out into the hall.

"Am I to understand that that man has been shot?"

"Yes," said Tierney.

"While hunting?"

"Correct."

"By whom?"

"I don't know." She blinked at him. "Um. He won't tell me."

"It's irrelevant to us anyway. He needs to go to a hospital and file a police report."

"John," she said, reaching out and placing a hand on his arm, "if he does that, he'll get his friend in trouble."

John pursed his lips, his expression sour. "As well he should! His friend shot him! And I suspect—from the looks of him...he wasn't an entirely innocent party in this debacle."

"John, please." She sighed, curling her fingers around John's thin arm and feeling a small sense of satisfaction when he flicked his eyes to where she touched him. "I need your help."

John scanned her face with a sigh. "Who—erm, who is he to you? This...Brian?"

"A friend," she said.

"An...ex-*boy*friend?"

"Does it matter?"

"I think it does." John lifted his chin. "Downstairs, I

was about to ask if you'd like to go out on a date with me."

Oh, Lord.

"And frankly, Tierney, it would be awkward for me to have the feelings I have for you and to help your friend, only to find out later that you and he…well, that you're romantically involved with him."

"I see," she said. "Well, we're not. Romantically involved."

John visibly relaxed. "Okay. So about that date…?"

Tierney removed her hand, cocking her head to the side. "Are you coercing me into a date with you in exchange for helping my friend?"

That wiped the overconfident smirk off his face. "No! No, no, no! Coercing? Please. That's the wrong word, Tierney. Trading would be better: something I want for something you want."

Yuck. This was a side of John Stuart she hadn't seen yet, and she didn't like it one bit. He wasn't a golden retriever, after all. He was a fox…or a rat.

"If the cost of stitching up Brian is to go on a date with you, John, then yes, I'll join you for dinner some evening."

John took a deep breath, obviously not completely satisfied with her answer, but somehow recognizing that pushing her further would be unwise. "Well, that would be—just terrific. Does Friday work?"

"It does," she said, without a hint of warmth.

"Then I will pick you up at seven," said John.

She gestured to her bedroom door. "Now that payment's been sorted out, can we get back to…?"

"Uh, yes," he said. "I'll need some clean cloths and hot water."

"I'm on it," she said. "Let me just talk to, um...Brian. For a second, huh?"

John pursed his lips, looking annoyed. "Sure."

"Be right back."

She slipped back into her room and closed the door behind her, then turned to face Burr, who stared at her with wide eyes. "Your old friend from Dartmouth? A hunting accident? Brian?"

"You seem dead set on protecting your identity."

"I am."

"So? I'm helping."

"Helping?" he clarified. "You're the worst liar I ever saw in my whole life. I mean, you bring bad lying to an art form. They could write odes to how badly you lie."

"Not even!" she said. "That time was *far* smoother than usual."

"It gets worse than that?" He pretended to shudder. "Amazing."

She decided to ignore him. "John's a vet. He's going to stitch you up and give you antibiotics."

Burr's eyes narrowed just a little. "...in exchange for a date with you."

"You heard?"

"You didn't shut the door," said Burr. His lips turned down. "He's a weasel."

Yes! He was exactly right—John wasn't a fox or a rat. He was a weasel!

"Seemed like a small price to pay."

"For what?"

"For you to be well," she said. "For you...to be safe."

His icy-blue eyes bored into hers. "Is my wellness

important to you, Tierney? My safety?"

Her cheeks flushed with sudden heat, and she crossed her arms over her chest protectively. Did his safety matter to her? The answer came quickly: yes. Why? Hmm. Because of Suzanne? Partly, yes. But helping Burr solely for his sister's sake wasn't totally accurate either, which bothered her because she had no further answers as to why she kept sticking her neck out for this virtual stranger.

"Why do you care?" he asked softly.

"I don't," she lied, flashing her eyes to his.

"Then how come…?"

"Jaysus, Mary, and Joseph at the manger! Didn't anyone ever teach you to just say thank you?" she barked, turning on her heel and opening her bedroom door. "He's ready, John. I'll go get the water."

She hurried downstairs, pressing her cool palms to her flaming cheeks as she sped into the kitchen, pulled out a pot, and filled it with water before placing it on the stove.

Why do you care? Why do you care? Why do you care?

The words circled round and round in her head as she leaned against the kitchen counter.

I don't, she thought…but it was a lie. She did.

He's injured, she reasoned. *Any Christian person with an ounce of charity would care.*

Fine, responded her conscience, *then why are your cheeks red? Christian charity shouldn't make you as red as a tomato.*

Her cell phone buzzed in her back pocket, and she retrieved it quickly, grateful for the reprieve from her puzzling thoughts…until she saw the text.

RORY: Ian said you were being weird.

TIERNEY: Ian doesn't know weird from last Tuesday.

RORY: What's going on?

TIERNEY: Mind your business.

RORY: Dinner on Wednesday?

TIERNEY: Of course.

She stared at the screen for a moment, wondering if she should tell Rory about "Brian" before Wednesday, which was tomorrow. If she didn't, and John mentioned him to Ian sometime today or tomorrow before dinner, her brothers might overreact.

TIERNEY: BTW, I have a friend from college staying.

RORY: What friend?

TIERNEY: You don't know him.

RORY: Him?

TIERNEY: I have to go.

Suddenly her phone buzzed in her hand with an incoming call from Rory. *Oh, for fuck's sake!*

"Hello?" she said.

"Who is he?" asked Rory.

"Brian."

"Brian what?"

"You don't know him."

"So you said. Who is he? Was he there this morning? Why didn't you introduce him to Ian? Damn it! He *knew* something was off with you."

"Nothing was off," Tierney insisted. "He was upstairs sleeping. That's all."

"Where upstairs?"

"None of your business."

"Tierney—"

"I'm an *adult*, Rory. I'm not answering your nosy-parker questions."

"I thought I knew all of your college friends," her brother grumbled. "I've never heard of a Brian from Dartmouth."

"Just because I didn't mention every friend I ever had doesn't mean I didn't have them."

"So where was he when Mom had her stroke?"

"In…Ireland."

"He's Irish?"

That's when Tierney heard it—just the slightest relaxation in her brother's voice. And since Burr *was* Irish, she didn't have to lie, thank God.

"Yeah."

"Huh. Does he speak it? Irish?"

He certainly understood what she said to him this morning when he patronizingly asked her for a smile. "As well as us."

"Huh," muttered her brother, and she heard it again— that "he's one of us" thread in Rory's voice that told her he was calming down a little.

Except that Burr wasn't "one of them" at all, Frankly, she still had no idea what he was, but he wasn't clean-cut like Rory or big and good-natured like Ian. He was intense and secretive, with fiercely beautiful eyes.

"Will that be all, Commandant?"

He sighed. "I'm not trying to be an asshole."

"Really? Because, wow, Rory, you're awfully good at it."

"Come on. You're my only sister. I just…I want you to be safe."

"I *am* safe," she said, "though I'm more annoyed by the second."

"What's he doing there?" asked Rory.

59

"Visiting," said Tierney. "Like I said."

"Where does he live?"

"Boston."

"What does he do?"

She had no idea. And unfortunately, if she started weaving some story, she'd end up doing her weird, spazzy-lying routine, so it was better that she get off the phone entirely. "I have to go, Rory. You'll meet him tomorrow at dinner, okay?"

"How bloody long is he staying?"

"None of your business."

"Fine. Ian and I will...I mean, we'll look forward to meeting him."

Oh, Christ. "Grand. See you then."

Before Rory could utter another word, she clicked "End" and pocketed the phone. Then she took the boiling water off the burner and headed back upstairs.

***

For the first few minutes they were alone, John had put on latex gloves, then peeled back the bandages on the front and back of Burr's shoulder, rambling on about some horse he'd looked at this morning that had a disgusting-sounding intestinal blockage.

Burr tried not to look utterly repulsed...not by the horse, but by the man.

Who was this fucking jackass, forcing Tierney to go on a date with him? He boiled over the thought of her having to endure a night of this guy's company. Burr paid his debts, and he would owe her big after that.

"How do you know Tierney again?" asked the vet, swabbing at the bullet hole with something that stung like crazy.

"Dartmouth," growled Burr, suspecting that Dr. Weasel was having a bit of fun at his expense as he dug into the wound.

"Right. That's in…Dover, right?"

"No," said Burr, glad he'd played regional hockey and competed at Dartmouth a time or two. "Hanover."

"Of course. My bad," said John. "Well, I guess she'll be back in a second. I'll give you a shot, then I'll sew it up. I hope my technique works for you. I've only addressed bullet wounds on animals, not people."

"Pretend I'm a doberman," growled Burr, sliding his icy eyes to John and letting his nostrils flare with distaste.

"The doberman pinscher gets a bad rap." John laughed nervously. "They're actually very gentle animals."

Not the ones that Burr had seen. Sean and Declan had two that they'd trained to tear a man's face off, and Burr had seen them in action more than once.

"How do you—I mean, don't get me wrong," said John, dropping his eyes to Burr's tattoo before taking off his rubber gloves with a loud snap. "You don't seem like the sort of company that Tierney would keep."

"Is that right?"

"Yes, Brian, that's right. She's quiet. Gentle. She takes care of the museum. She takes care of her family. She reads. She takes walks. You…you seem rather rough, frankly."

"Rough."

"No offense," said John.

"None taken," said Burr.

"So…you were hunting?"

"Sure."

"Where?"

Fucking weasel. Not man enough to just come right out and call him a liar. Weaseling around in his weasely manner. Burr fucking hated guys like this one.

"John, I get the feeling you don't approve of me," he said softly, the unmistakable flavor of "you're really starting to piss me off" in the taste of his voice.

John took a deep breath and sighed, finally gathering the courage to look Burr in the eyes. "I like *her*. I want what's best for her, and you're not it."

"Oh. And I suppose you are?"

"I'm steady and serious. I have a thriving business. Her brothers like me."

"Then maybe you should extort a date from one of them," suggested Burr.

John blinked, his eyes furious, his jaw tight. And Burr had a feeling he might have even come up with a decent comeback if Tierney hadn't walked back into the room at that moment.

"Hot water," she said, removing the glass of water from the bedside table and replacing it with a soup pot of steaming water. "I have clean washcloths in the bathroom. Will that do?"

"Fine," said John, his lips thin and angry.

Burr grinned at Tierney. "Thanks, *aisling*."

Her eyes widened, and her lips parted, and Burr—who couldn't look away from her if his life depended on it—had a sudden thought that she might look a little like that if he ever licked her cunt nice and slow.

Fuuuuuck. Where did that fucking idea come from?

Didn't matter. It was already there, indelible in his

mind, and his dick twitched under her covers, hardening at the idea of tasting her. He wondered if any other man had claimed that particular territory with his mouth before…and for some reason, he doubted it.

"You're…welcome," she said, her voice just a little breathless, making more blood race south to jack up his cock.

"*Aisling?*" muttered John, who was threading a needle. "What's that?"

Ah, but thank the good Lord for John. Here was an excellent use for him: killing a boner.

"Do you speak Irish, John?"

"Don't you mean *Gaelic?*" asked Dr. Weasel.

Flicking a glance at Tierney, Burr watched, rapt, as her lips tilted up—*up, up, up*—until her entire face was brightened from pretty to breathtaking, transformed with a smile so pure, so guileless, Burr forgot how to breathe. Hers was the face of an angel, of someone whose emotions hadn't been sullied by a dark and terrible world, and all he wanted was to have the privilege of making and watching her smile for as long as she'd let him.

After years of dirty smirks born of another's suffering, he could have basked in her smile all day—bathed in it, fed on it, become drunk on it. And the best part of all was that she was smiling because they were sharing something—just the two of them. They knew something that John didn't know—hell, that most of the world didn't know. But *they* did. It was profoundly intimate to share an inside joke with her. He couldn't remember the last time *anything* had felt so damned good.

For all that they were born in America, Burr and

Tierney shared a proud Irish American heritage. And they both knew that the only people who called it "Gaelic," were people who didn't know their *masa* from their *uilinn*.

Shaking her head at Burr, the look on her face a warning to stop being naughty, she turned and left the room.

"No," said Burr. "I meant Irish. We call it 'Irish,' not 'Gaelic.'"

"We?"

"Irish Americans. Like me. And Tierney."

"Huh." John cleared his throat, clearly displeased that Burr and Tierney shared anything at all, and positioned a syringe near Burr's shoulder. "I'm going to give you a shot of lidocaine around the area. Should numb it for the stitches."

Tierney returned with the cloths and placed them beside the pot of water.

"*Aisling* means, um…means 'friend,'" she said, answering John's question and giving Burr a stern look. He raised his eyebrows at her, but she pursed her lips, telling him to hush up and go along with it.

"Fine," Burr said, acquiescing to her. "*Aisling* means 'friend.'"

Even though it didn't. Not at all.

Aisling meant "dream" or "vision," and in Burr's opinion, it was one of the sexiest endearments in the Irish language, especially when it was directed at Tierney Haven.

Twenty minutes later, Burr had four stitches on the front side of his shoulder, twelve on the back, and clean dressings covering both.

"I can't give you an oral antibiotic. What I have with me isn't intended for human use," said John, removing his gloves and placing a small tube on the bedside table. "But I cleaned out the wounds, and I've covered them with a strong antibiotic ointment. I'll leave some here with you."

"Thanks, John," said Tierney. "You're a lifesaver. Truly. Can I offer you a cup of tea before you go?"

"That would be nice," he said. "I'll tidy up here and meet you in the kitchen."

Tierney looked at Burr for a moment before nodding at John and heading downstairs.

"Thanks, Doc," said Burr. "What do I owe you?"

"Are you asking what I want in exchange for treatment?" John stood up from the chair next to the bed, narrowing his eyes at Burr. "That's easy. Go back to wherever you came from."

Burr didn't respond. He just stared at Dr. Weasel long and hard—a glare that generally scared the shit out of other men. To John's credit, he straightened up to his full, measly height, standing his ground.

"I don't know you, Brian," said John, staring back at Burr, his eyes concerned, "but you seem like trouble to me. Hunting accident? No. I highly doubt it. That injury was made with the bullet from a revolver, not a hunting rifle. Probably a nine-millimeter gun. Possibly a thirty-eight." He waited a moment, then he lifted his chin. "You said I 'extorted' a date from her, which bothered me, but I'm man enough to admit you're right. I've liked her for a while now, and she's a catch no matter how you slice it. Did I press my advantage earlier to get her to say yes? I did. I don't know if that's playing dirty or not—they say all's fair in love and war, right? All I really know is this: I would never hurt her, Brian. I wouldn't put her in danger. Can you say the same?"

There was nothing to say. John had called him out with

honesty and—for a weasel—a surprising amount of man-to-man dignity, and while Burr still didn't like him, he felt the first glimmer of respect for him.

"Take care of yourself," said John, picking up his medical bag and leaving the room.

Burr grimaced as John's footsteps faded.

Worst of all, Dr. Weasel was right.

Being here, staying here, was certainly putting Tierney in some danger. No, Sean and Declan didn't know where he was right now...but it was only a matter of time, wasn't it? Burr couldn't stay hidden in this little cottage with Tierney Haven forever. And he'd sooner gut himself than see another innocent woman get caught up in his mess—or worse, hurt. Especially Tierney, who'd looked after him with little regard for her own safety. She deserved so much better than to be caught in the cross hairs of his fucked-up existence.

Tomorrow he'd leave here and head over to Ray's house on Lake Ossipee. On the way, he'd buy a burner phone, call Ray for an update, and then wait to find out what would happen next. And no one, least of all Sean Shanahan, would ever be any the wiser that an Irish angel named Tierney had shown him more kindness than he deserved, and—for a brief moment in time—been his safe haven.

chapcer five

Wednesdays in August were always busy days at Moonstone Manor, but when it was cloudy out? Attendance doubled. No one wanted to be boating and swimming in Squam or Winnipesaukee when thunderclouds loomed.

By eleven o'clock, Tierney had already led two tours, and her docent intern from Brown University, Anna, had led two more. When Shannon, another intern from UNH arrived, Tierney happily took her lunch break, driving back down the hill from the great house to her cottage.

When she'd left that morning, Burr was still asleep, splayed out on her bed and snoring softly. It was the first deep sleep he'd had since arriving at her home, and when she'd gently touched his forehead, she was relieved to find it cool despite the rising summer heat outside. He'd shucked off most of the covers in his sleep until all that remained was a white sheet, draped carelessly over his hips and legs, which made it abundantly clear that he wasn't wearing, well, anything.

She'd stood over him, staring at his body, examining it as a scientist might investigate a specimen. His collarbone intrigued her first, the strong lines creating a triangle with his neck, which was thick and corded with muscle. Her eyes trailed up and down the column, resting on the pulse that beckoned her like a beacon. She had a sudden fantasy of leaning forward to press her lips to it and closing her eyes as she felt his heartbeat under the sensitive skin of her lips. Breathing sharply, she'd jerked her eyes away from his throat, landing them on his lips, which were open slightly, perfectly pink in repose. His top lip was thin, but the bottom was almost plump, as though making up for the top. She imagined capturing it between hers, sucking on it, feeling the texture of the tiny ridges with her tongue as she tasted his skin.

Heat had pooled in her belly—like the sun, with rays fanning out to steal the breath from her lungs and make her heart skip beats—and lower, where she sometimes touched herself when she read a sex scene in one of her many books…she throbbed. Almost painfully.

Turning on her heel, she'd raced from her room, down the stairs, and into the muggy August morning.

This is madness. That man upstairs is not for you. Find someone your own speed.

Though she had two brothers roughly the same age as Burr and was comfortable around men, she had precious little firsthand *romantic* experience with them. Shy and awkward during high school, she'd never been anyone's idea of a dream date, and Rory had ended up escorting her to the high school prom.

In college, she'd had several male friends, but it hadn't taken much of her brain power to figure out that she wasn't the girl they were interested in; she was the girl they befriended as a conduit to the girl they wanted.

That said, she did have one college boyfriend, Malcolm McDonald, a brash Scottish exchange student whom dated for a few weeks in the first semester of her senior year.

She'd liked him very much—liked holding his hand and kissing him—but their relationship had run aground when Tierney shared that she wasn't ready for a sleepover in his dorm room after three weeks of dating.

Malcolm, who explained that men had "needs," had asked if there was anything he could do to make her feel more comfortable with him. But there wasn't. What Tierney had needed was time, and she desperately hoped he'd give it to her, as she'd give it to him, were their roles reversed. She told him that she liked him, but she wasn't ready to have sex yet and didn't know when that day would come. In turn, he told her it hurt him to let her go, but it hadn't stopped him from moving on...right before her eyes, in fact, with one of her friends.

Her experience with Malcolm, however, had taught Tierney something important about love. Someone who truly cared for her would have waited, and that knowledge had softened the blow of his rejection.

When her mother got sick six months later, part of her was grateful not to have to worry about meeting or dating someone. She could find usefulness in being a dutiful daughter and helping her parents. And of course, by taking the job at Moonstone Manor, which was custom-made for a recluse half the year, she'd fashioned a life for herself wherein meeting someone was difficult.

The fact of the matter was that Tierney was, like many Irish before her, a late-bloomer.

Possibly because she was a little scared of the world—intimidated by the beautiful, rich girls of her Summerhaven childhood, with whom she felt she could never compete.

Or possibly, it was because she didn't brush elbows

against the sort of men to whom she was attracted. Men like John Stuart, DVM? Solid, steady, gainfully employed citizens? Sure, she could attract them. But men like Burr? Beautiful, complicated and dangerous? They looked past Tierney, through her, over her and around her. They didn't see her at all.

Which sort of sucked, frankly, because lately, Tierney had started to feel like maybe—just maybe—she was actually, finally *blooming*. For the first time in her twenty-seven years, the idea of meeting someone and letting herself have feelings for him felt like a risk she might want to take. And Burr had swept into her life like a summer storm—growling and jagged, wild and dangerous, blinding in its intensity and darkly beautiful. He'd only been in her life for two days, but he was impossible to ignore.

Besides, like every other human female, she sorted most men into buckets upon meeting them: John had been sorted into the "friend" bucket right away, while Burr, despite her attempts to see him primarily as Suzanne's brother, had been sorted into the "temptation" bucket almost immediately. She couldn't help it.

Except she wasn't an idiot, and someone like Burr surely had a girlfriend back in Boston—someone confident and sexy, fashionable and edgy; someone as experienced in the bedroom as Tierney was not. That was the person he'd be returning to. And Tierney? Well, she had her Friday date with John to look forward to.

She forced herself not to roll her eyes as her car rumbled to a stop in front of her cottage.

John was kind to drop everything and come over yesterday, and while she didn't love the way he'd traded his services for a date with her, what harm had it done? Hell, she'd get a free dinner out of the deal, at worst. And at best? Well, maybe she could *try* to see something in John that she liked— that she would like in someone who was more than just a friend. She could give him one last chance, couldn't she? He deserved that. And if he still resided in the "friend" bucket after their date? Well, she could gently turn down any further overtures.

Resolved, she slipped from the driver's seat, her wellies crunching on the pebbles of the driveway as she headed into the house. And she couldn't deny it, though she would've liked to—her whole body practically quivered in anticipation as she inserted the key in the lock. She'd only been away from Burr for a few hours, but she couldn't wait to see him again.

No, he wasn't the man for her. She knew that on an intellectual level. But damn if she could make her body believe it too.

She stepped inside, closing the door behind her, and was surprised to find Burr, fully dressed in jeans, a T-shirt (the same T-shirt that she'd found in his duffel bag), socks, and shoes. His hair—not that there was much of it—was damp, and his face looked freshly scrubbed.

"Hi," she said, feeling suddenly wary.

It was the first time since Monday night that he'd been out of bed, and she found she didn't like it. She liked knowing he was upstairs, safe and sound under her eiderdown comforter.

Was he going somewhere? Her eyes flicked to the bag by his sneakers.

Oh, God, he's leaving.

71

She didn't expect the corresponding feeling of being punched in the gut—didn't expect it and didn't like it.

He scanned her face thoughtfully, then sighed, forcing a smile. "I'm feeling better. I thought it was probably time for me to get going, Tierney. I think it's for the best."

The sudden, thick lump that rose in her throat made it hard to respond. When she finally did, her words were stilted. "Oh. Oh. You, um, but you're—you're welcome here. You don't have to go. Your shoulder—"

"I've been fever-free since the doc fixed me up yesterday. Got a good night's sleep last night. Doesn't even hurt as bad," he said, shrugging his injured shoulder gingerly.

"But who will change the dressing for you?"

"I suppose I'll manage."

Such sadness.

It had been a long time since she'd felt such sadness.

It swirled inside of her, making her feel breathless and small. How had he come to matter so much to her over the last couple of days? He'd barged into her tidy life, turning it upside down, and yet…and yet, it was some of the most exciting fun she'd ever had. She didn't want him to go. Not even a little bit. Not even the parts of her that knew it was for the best for them to say good-bye because no two people on earth could be more mismatched, and she knew what would happen were he to stay: she'd end up infatuated with him, and he'd end up having to let her down easy.

But she couldn't help the way she felt: unaccountably grieved.

"I'm sorry to see you go," she admitted softly.

He took a step closer to her, his smile all but faded. "Part of me is sorry to go too, *aisling*. You've been awfully good to me."

"Then stay a little longer," she whispered, her heart clenching from the endearment. It was probably the last time she'd ever hear him say it.

"I can't," he said. "You asked if I was good or bad. I can't tell you exactly who I am or what I've done, because the less you know, the better. But I want you to know this: I was always on the good side, Tierney. I've always counted myself among the good guys."

"I can see that, Burr. I know there's good in you."

"I've been in a bad place over the last few years," he continued, "but you reminded me who I am, who I want to be."

"Did I?"

"Yes. You're the bravest woman I've ever met. Also, the most selfless and kind and..." He grinned at her. "Just the right amount of sassy too." He took a deep breath and sighed. "But my being here could put you in danger. I won't let that happen. I can't."

She gulped, overwhelmed by his compliments and gratified by the fact that he wanted to protect her, but grieved that he had to leave to ensure it.

"I need my gun back," he said.

She stared at him hard, then nodded, walking past him to the kitchen and returning with it a second later.

"Thanks," he said, tucking it into the back of his jeans, his crystal-clear, light-blue gaze meeting hers.

With his buzz cut and handsome face, he looked almost normal—muscular and masculine to beat the band, of course—but not so brutish. Just a beautiful, complicated man standing before her, saying good-bye. It hurt to look into his eyes, so she dropped her gaze to his chest where the word "Destroyer" was inked beneath the white cotton of his T-shirt.

He's not yours. And if he needs to leave, you have to let him go.

Tierney wasn't a stranger to disappointment; mustering a brave face was one of her many useless talents. She looked up at him with a grim smile. "Come back if you need to. You're welcome here, Burr. Anytime."

"Maybe I will," he whispered quickly, the warmth in his light-blue eyes surprising her. "Maybe this isn't the end of you and me, *aisling.*"

Her breath caught as he took a step toward her. Placing two fingers under her chin, he lifted it so that her face was upturned to his. Then, gently, so gently that tears bit at the backs of her eyes, he dropped his lips to hers, brushing against them tenderly.

She hadn't been kissed in years, and instead of winding her arms around his neck and leaning into him, she froze almost entirely, even holding her breath. Only her eyes moved, closing against the burn and swell of her tears. She felt his tender touch on the thousands of nerve endings in her sensitive lips, smelled her soap on his skin and tasted tea and honey on the warm breath that whispered over her skin. He filled her senses, making her long for things that weren't hers, that—realistically speaking—could *never* be hers.

And then it was over.

Way too soon, it was over.

"Bye, Tierney," he said softly, dropping his fingers from her chin.

By the time she opened her eyes, his body had already whooshed past hers, out the door, out of her life, leaving her utterly alone and lonesome beyond words.

***

As his sneakers crunched over her gravel driveway, Burr was surprised by how much it ached to leave her. He'd only known her for a couple of days, but a connection had been forged between them, and as he'd once read, connections formed under duress were often the most intense of all.

No kidding.

What he felt for her was surprisingly intense.

She was everything he would have wanted if his life had taken a different path: beautiful without knowing it, witty, smart, brave, and kind, but she could still swear in Irish or put him in his place with a well-timed barb. He didn't know her very well, but she checked a lot of his boxes. He liked her. A lot.

And his body—which he'd starved of female company over his years undercover, for fear that he'd speak out in his sleep one night if he got too close to someone, betraying secrets that could get him killed—was on fire for her as he threw his duffel bag in the back seat of Suzanne's car, then slid into the driver's seat.

She had no idea how tempting she was—just like her sweet, soft lips, he bet that the tips of her lush breasts would be warm, sweet, and soft in his mouth too. He'd explore them for hours, hardening them into stiff points, marking them, owning them, making her come with his mouth before he moved on to her—

"Enough," he grunted, pulling out of her garage with a massive hard-on. He maneuvered around her SUV, careful not to flick his eyes to the front door of her cottage, lest he catch a glimpse of her and go running back inside. "You can't have her. Not now. Probably not ever."

So why had he said that cheesy line about maybe coming back to her?

"Wishful thinking," he growled, speeding through the gates of Moonstone Manor and forcing himself not to look in the rearview mirror. "Good-bye, Tierney Haven."

Heading south on Route 171, he stopped at a gas station in Tuftonboro, filling up Suzanne's tank and buying a prepaid phone card and local map. He spread it out on the back of the car, scanning the tiny roads around Lake Ossipee for Carlson Road. After finding it, he made a quick mental note of how to get there, then headed for the pay phone around the corner of the service station.

Using the prepaid card, he dialed Ray's number.

"Ray Cooper."

"Ray," he said. "It's me."

"Burr! Shit! I've been worried about you, man. You okay?"

"Yeah," he said, relieved to hear his partner's voice. "What's going on down there?"

"Suzanne's doing okay. Bullet missed her artery. She should make a full recovery."

He already knew this, thanks to Tierney, but it was good to have it confirmed. "That's good. How's Bridey?"

"I saw her at the hospital yesterday. She was clinging pretty hard to Connor, but you know kids. They bounce back eventually."

Burr gritted his teeth. Once he was out of this fucking mess, he'd do whatever was necessary to be sure Bridey got the therapy she needed to heal completely.

"What else?"

"Declan's dead. You killed him."

Burr knew his bullet had hit Declan in the chest, but he wasn't certain the shot had been fatal. Now that he knew, he couldn't say he was sorry. By bringing down Declan Shanahan, he'd saved a lot of people from a lot of misery.

"What else?"

Ray sighed. "Sean's put out a hit on you."

Burr winced. "I'm not surprised."

"Big bounty. Fifty thousand to whoever gets video proof of your, you know…demise."

"Fuck," said Burr, clenching his eyes shut. "What else?"

Ray lowered his voice. "You still, uh, up at the lake house? The one I told you to go to?"

He was only a few miles away; as good as there. "Yeah. I'm up here. Lake Ossipee."

"Good. Good. Stay there. You need to stay there."

"I will. Ray…what's next? Should I call Sergeant Gunn? Or Captain Donnelley? I'm sure we gave them enough for an indictment. Maybe they could fast-track the charges now so that I could—"

"No! No, no. Don't do that. Don't, uh, don't call Gunn. Don't call Donnelley. D-Don't call anyone. Burr, man, think about it: we have no idea who ratted you out to Sean. Could've been someone who worked at Southie with Donnelley, or someone on the Gang Task Unit. Just, uh, stay put at the house, and in the meantime I'll do some digging."

"Come on, Ray. I'm…I mean, we know the guys on the GTU. It wasn't one of them. Besides, I want to come in. I want to resolve this. Fuck, man. I want my life back. I can't hide out in New Hampshire forever."

"You gotta give me some time." Ray paused. "A few

days. A week. Just give me a week to try to figure out who sold you out, okay? We need to plug the leak before anything else."

Ray was right.

While it was frustrating for Burr to lay low, it was the smart move, and besides, Burr didn't trust anyone at the moment except Ray. After Ray figured out who had betrayed Burr's identity to the Shanahan's, it would be safer to return.

"Okay," said Burr, running a hand through the stubble on his head.

"You won't call anyone," Ray confirmed.

"I said I wouldn't," said Burr. "Thanks, Ray, for everything."

"Of course," said Ray. He cleared his throat. "You'd do the same for me, brother."

Burr hung up the phone feeling frustrated. He wanted to get back to Boston…only to find out who had stabbed him in the back, and then do whatever he could to help Ray, Gunn, Donnelley, and the rest of the district attorney's office take down the New Killeens.

Patience, he thought, thinking of something his dad once said: *Ninety percent of police work is patience. The other ten percent is not getting killed.*

Burr wondered if Ray had told his parents anything about where he was and what he'd been doing, or if they still believed that his life as a thug had led to Suzanne's injury. Turning his car back out onto the road, Burr took some meager relief in the thought that he'd be able to come clean with his family sooner than later. After three Christmases and Easters spent all alone—or worse, doing Sean's dirty, filthy bidding—he was desperate to reconnect with his family.

He rolled down the window as he drew closer to Ossipee, entertaining himself by wondering what his parents and Suzy would think of Tierney if they ever met her. Not that he'd ever really have a chance with a girl as smart and classy as Tierney Haven, but he was pretty certain they'd like her. They'd be disarmed by the fact that she could speak Irish, and they'd appreciate the fact that she was quiet and smart, not loud and showy. His dad would get drunk and sing "When Irish Eyes Are Smiling" in a pure bad brogue, and Tierney might even crack one of those rare smiles for him.

She'd fit in well, he thought as the hot August sun tanned his forearm.

If she let him, maybe he'd take her to some of the places in Boston that meant something to him: the tall ships by the harbor and Faneuil Hall. They'd hold hands as they walked along the Charles River, and if she said yes, he'd take her to a game at Fenway. And maybe he'd even—

Pop. Pop, pop.

Ripped from his reverie, he pulled over to the side of the road, yanking up the parking brake and scanning the woods on the right side of the car. Leaning down, his cheek against the passenger seat, he pulled his revolver from the glove compartment and made sure the clip was full.

Either he was going crazy, or he'd just heard gun shots.

Hunters?

Possibly, but it didn't feel right. Burr wasn't a hunter, but he knew that animals, and therefore hunters, were most active in the early morning.

He leaned his head up to look out the window but

didn't see anything strange. Straightening to look out the windshield, he noticed a mailbox with a gold, reflective number 12 on the side. Ray's driveway. He was here. He hadn't realized that he was so close.

Backing up about a quarter mile on the road, he pulled his car onto a side street, making sure that Suzanne's Massachusetts license plate was hidden by shrubbery. Then he double-timed it up the road and into the woods near Ray's place. He moved quietly from tree to tree, slowing down as a large, beautiful cedar-shingle lake house came into view through the woods.

Huh. Ray can afford this? he wondered, then reminded himself that the house belonged to Ray's wife's family.

Crouching down behind a rotting log, he checked out the car in the driveway: a gunmetal-gray Escalade with Massachusetts plates was parked beside a weathered Ford truck with New Hampshire plates. A shiver went down Burr's back. Escalades were Sean's favorite vehicle, and many of his henchmen bought them to curry favor with Sean.

Suddenly the front door opened and a man in a shiny gray suit stepped out onto the front stoop, talking on a cell phone. It was "Fat" Billy Griffin, one of Sean's top guys.

"No, you're not hearing me, boss. The narc wasn't here. We capped the goddamned handyman." A pause. "He saw our faces, Sean. Didn't have a choice." Another pause. "Yeah. Yeah. We know what to do." Another. "I'm guessing your guy gave you bad intel. Yeah. This was a waste of fucking time. He's probably still in Boston, hiding out somewhere. Fucking O'Learys."

Behind Billy, two more men—slightly younger, dressed

in jeans and T-shirts—came out of the front door carrying a rolled-up carpet. One was Billy's son, Patrick, but Burr couldn't get a good look at the other kid. Probably a new recruit. There was little doubt who was rolled up in the carpet based on Billy's conversation with Sean.

"Put him in the back, pops?"

Billy nodded at his son, flicking a button on his key fob. The boys rounded the car and stuffed the rug in the trunk.

"I gotta go, Sean. Time to clean up this shit show. Yeah. I'll be back in town tonight." He tucked his phone in his back pocket and turned to the kids.

"Go find the guy's keys," said Billy to Patrick's friend. "Drive his truck to the state line, lock it up, and leave it at a rest stop. Hitch a ride back to Boston. Pat and I will handle the rug. You did good today, kid."

"Thanks, Mr. Griffin," said the kid, running back into the house to find the keys to the Honda.

As for Burr, he'd seen enough, and it didn't take a rocket scientist to put the pieces together. Someone had told Sean where he'd be, and Sean had sent Fat Billy and his kid up to knock him off.

He stayed on the ground behind the log, waiting until he heard the truck drive away, followed a few minutes later by the Escalade. After thirty or forty minutes had passed, Burr walked back to his car. Once he was sitting down, he tried to make sense of what had just happened, of what he'd just seen.

He added up the numbers quick, but his mind didn't want to believe the sum.

"Fuck," he whispered. "No. No. Ray wouldn't do that to me. No! *Fuck!*"

But the facts wouldn't be denied. Only Ray—his partner, his friend—knew where Burr was hiding, which meant that he was probably the one who'd ratted out his identity to Sean. In fact, he was probably the one who'd called him on Sunday night to warn him that they were going after Suzy.

"God damn it!" he cried, beating his fists against the steering wheel as he remembered his sister's body crumpling to the floor. "No! Come on, Ray! No! You were my family. My—my fucking brother!"

Ray had been Burr's lifeline over the past three years. Every bit of information that Burr had gathered on the New Killeens had been given to Ray. When had he sold out Burr? And Jesus, had any of the evidence Burr had risked his life to collect even reached Sergeant Gunn? Fuck. If not, the DA's office wouldn't have enough to indict Sean, and it would be years before Burr and his family would be safe…if ever.

"You were my partner, Ray. Why?"

My partner. The thought was a dagger slicing through his heart as he thought of everything he and Ray had been through. He gripped the steering wheel until his fingers ached. *It can't be true. It can't.*

But it was. Because no one else knew where Burr was hiding. Only Ray. And Ray knew better than to tell anyone…unless he wanted Burr to be found.

Taking a deep breath, Burr pulled his car back out onto the road and turned north on Route 153, his only goal to place space between himself and the Griffins, who were headed south, back to Boston.

As he drove, he backtracked, trying to think of times when Ray's behavior hadn't felt "right," but he came up dry, which made him wonder if Ray's betrayal had been a relatively new development. Trying to find clues or tells, he shifted his thoughts to their phone conversation an hour ago, combing through what he remembered of their exchange, and one part stuck out like a sore thumb: Ray's fervent advice that Burr *not* reach out to Gunn or Donnelley. He'd even gone so far as to posit that someone in the Southie station could've been the rat.

Maybe. But Burr knew better.

The rat was from Dorchester, and Burr had practically known him his whole damned life. The rat was Ray—fucking Ray, who was like a fucking brother to him, and it broke his fucking heart.

A green sign on the road said that it was fourteen more miles to a place called Conway that had food, lodging, and gas stations. He needed to call Donnelley as soon as possible and tell him to warn Gunn about Ray; he stepped on the gas and didn't let up until he got there.

Pulling into a service station, he parked on the side of the convenience store, near the pay phone, and used his phone card to call Donnelley's direct line.

"Yeah? Donnelley here."

"It's Burr O'Leary."

"Fuck." He paused, dropping his voice to a whisper. "You're alive."

"Barely."

"Don't talk."

Burr took a deep breath and held it, waiting for more instruction.

"Call me at 617-555-2121 in five minutes."

"Got it."

Burr hung up the pay phone and turned his back to it, looking up at the now cloudless blue sky and sighing deeply. It was getting hard to decide what was the worst part of his life right now: his sister getting shot, the price on his head, or his partner betraying him. The only bright spot in his life recently had been Tierney, but God only knew when he might see her again, if ever. None of it was good. All of it sucked.

After five minutes, he called the 617 number he'd been given, and Donnelley answered right away. "O'Leary?"

"Yeah."

"You're okay?"

"I'm…I took a bullet through the shoulder at my sister's place, but it was a clean shot. Got it stitched up by a vet."

"Where are y—No! Don't tell me. Just in case."

"What do you know?"

"I talked to Seth Gunn. Someone ratted you out. Sean and Declan went to Suzy's place to lean on her, but she didn't know where you were. Didn't stop them from shooting her. Heard someone suddenly arrived on the scene and shot Declan Shanahan, then disappeared. I assumed it was you."

Burr clenched his jaw. "I got a tip that they were at Suzy's."

"Someone in the New Killeens?"

"I don't think so. I think it was Ray. I'm ninety-nine percent sure the rat's Ray."

"Cooper?"

"He told me to hide out at his wife's lake house up in New Hampshire. I got delayed on the way. When I finally got there today, Fat Billy and his kid were dragging a body out of the house. The handyman. I heard Billy talking to Sean on his phone—they thought the poor bastard was me."

"Shit."

"Yeah," said Burr. "Close call."

"You think it's Cooper told 'em where you were?"

"No one else knew."

"I hate to say it, but it makes sense," said Donnelley, his voice thoughtful, like he was putting puzzle pieces together. "Last few reports I got in July and August were sloppy. Not in your handwriting either. I just thought Ray recopied them for some reason." He paused. "And worse, some evidence went missing yesterday."

"Fuck!"

Donnelley sighed. "Yeah. The slug they pulled out of Suzanne. We wanted to match it to Declan's gun and prove he'd shot her. But someone stole it from the hospital."

I saw her at the hospital yesterday. She was clinging pretty hard to Connor, but you know kids.

Fuck.

"It was Ray. He was there visiting Suzy."

"Shit."

"Captain, I need to know…what now?"

"Ah, son, we're a little fucked here. If Ray was tampering with your reports and evidence, it'll be hard for the GTU to make a case to the DA based on them."

Burr scrubbed a hand through his bristly hair. "But what about everything *before* July? What about my testimony? I can come back to Boston. I'll do whatever you need to put those bastards away."

"I'll talk to Gunn and see what they've got," said

Donnelley, "and yeah, your testimony will be crucial, but keeping you safe will be...well, Burr, you should know..."

"I already heard about the bounty," he said, looking beyond the little town of Conway to the jagged range of mountains that rose in the near distance. "I can stay put up here for a while."

"That's good. You can't show your face in Boston. Not until Sean and some of his guys are behind bars."

Burr took a deep breath. "You could..."

"You have an idea?"

"You could lean on Ray. Force him to admit that he's the rat. Wire him."

"Wire Ray? For what?"

"A confession that they killed the wrong guy at his lake house. You could get him for collusion in murdering the handyman, and maybe he could get Sean to admit that there's a hit out on me. Attempted murder of a police officer. That's life."

"Hmm. Yeah. And I'm pretty sure we can also get racketeering, loan-sharking, and bookmaking added on with your testimony. That'd put him away for a long time."

"Sounds like a plan," said Burr.

"You're sure about this?" asked Donnelley. "About Ray?"

It gave him zero satisfaction to answer, "Yeah. I'm positive."

Donnelley sighed long and hard. "You heard that Suzy's gonna be okay?"

"Yeah. Thank Christ."

Donnelley paused for a moment. "Hey, wait...how'd you hear? From Ray?"

"Well, yeah. But also, a friend of mine called in to check on her, actually. Before Ray."

"Wait. A friend of yours called Mass General?"

"Yeah. Why?"

"Aw, shit. No, Burr. That's no good. They're looking for you. Costs them almost nothing to pay off a hospital receptionist to make notes when any calls come in about Suzy. When Ray finds out you're not dead, they'll be chasing down any and all leads to find you. Who made that call?"

Shit. Shit, shit, shit. Tierney.

"Fuck," he said, "I gotta go."

"Wait! Burr!"

"Yeah?"

"Destroy the phone. Then they can't triangulate it. All they'll have is a New Hampshire phone number. Can't get too far with that."

"Unless they figure out who the phone belongs to!" cried Burr.

"They'd need cell phone records for that."

"The kind a dirty cop could get out of the system in no time," said Burr with a bite.

"Ray," said Donnelley. "You think they'll ask him who made the call?"

"If they haven't already. Fat Billy was on the phone with Sean over an hour ago. He knows I'm not dead. I imagine he and Ray are talking right now," said Burr, running a hand through his hair. "And if Sean's pissed at Ray, he'll do whatever he has to do to get a new lead on where I could be."

How far am I from Tierney? Fuck…how far away am I from her?

"I'm calling Gunn as soon as we hang up. We'll pick up Ray today," said Donnelley. "Now. Before he can trace that number for them. I'll do it myself if I have to, but I'll make sure he doesn't trace that number."

And I'll go straight back to Tierney's.

"Captain, I've got to go. I have to make sure—"

"Yeah. You go to your friend and warn him not to use his phone. I'll take care of Cooper. It'll be my fucking privilege to haul his ass into an interrogation room."

She. She's a fucking "she," and she's brave but tiny.

"Burr! Call me in two days on this line. Friday. At seven o'clock in the evening. I'll let you know where we stand with everything."

Burr nodded. "Thank you, sir. I will."

He hung up the phone and ran to Suzanne's car, praying to Jesus and God and the Virgin Mary and all the saints in heaven that the call Tierney made on his behalf hadn't been traced…and while he was at it, he promised to trade his worthless fucking life for hers if only God would keep her safe until he got there.

chapter six

After a quiet lunch, Tierney headed back up the hill to the estate visitor's center, manning the ticket booth and restocking the shelves in the small gift shop…and trying not to think about Bur—about Burr's rumbly voice, about Burr's lips on hers, about Burr driving away.

Maybe this isn't the end of you and me, aisling.

She thought about those words most of all, playing them over and over again in her head as Anna and Shannon ran the two o'clock, three o'clock, and four o'clock tours, and Tierney, who generally enjoyed leading tours, sat behind the ticket counter in quiet misery.

She glanced over, checking the time on the credit card machine.

It was almost five o'clock. Ian, Rory, and Brittany would be over around six thirty.

Maybe she'd host their weekly family dinner outdoors tonight. The stormy skies had long passed, the sun was out, and it looked like a lovely evening ahead. She could serve something simple like hamburgers and hot dogs with chips and homemade coleslaw. After work she'd make a quick trip to the supermarket in Center Harbor and be back in plenty of time to set the picnic table behind her cottage. One of her brothers could start the grill when they arrived.

Thinking about her brothers, however, made her groan.

Rory and Ian would start asking about Burr the moment they walked in and she dreaded it. She didn't want to talk about him. She didn't know if she *could* talk about him without embarrassing herself. In contrast to her usual stalwart self, she'd been on the verge of tears since he left, and her feelings confused her. It was like she had let something precious and beautiful fall from slippery fingers and crash to the ground. She felt sadness, of course, but that wasn't all. It was accompanied by frustration, and longing, and regret.

His beautiful face flashed through her mind, and she lingered willfully on the harsh planes and angles of his cheekbones before slipping her gaze to the pillowed softness of his lower lip. Her own lips tingled with the memory of his kiss, and she whimpered softly.

It wasn't just that he was handsome, though his dark good looks and ice-blue eyes certainly heated up her blood. He was protective and unexpectedly funny. He obviously loved his sister. And there was something else. He was struggling so terribly; he seemed to be fighting with himself—wanting to do the right thing yet somehow mixed up in something wrong. She wanted to see him triumph over whatever evil plagued him. She wanted to see the Destroyer victorious.

The more she put the pieces together, the more convinced she was that Burr worked in some sort of law enforcement capacity. The St. Michael medal aside, there was the small speech he'd made before leaving her: ...*my being here could put you in danger. I won't let that happen. I can't.* Hardly the sentiment of a seasoned criminal.

Still, she wondered who shot him and why, and worried

they'd try it again. Turning her thoughts to St. Michael, she said a quick prayer for Burr's safety: *Wherever he is, keep him safe.* She paused, then added, *And if it's your will, please send him back to me. Amen.*

"Tierney."

Her eyes flew open.

"Burr?"

Taphadh leat, Sceilig Mhichíl!

"Hi," he said, and his face, which was marked with worry, seemed to relax just a little, the lips that had kissed hers a few hours ago tilting up slightly as he scanned her face.

"Hi," she answered, feeling a smile split her face, followed by a little chirp of surprised laughter. "You left. What are you doing here?"

"You never showed me the museum," he said, glancing at the entrance over his shoulder. "I thought I should swing back and see it."

She shook her head at him. He was kidding, of course, but she didn't care. He was here. He was back. "Oh. Well, the last tour was forty-five minutes ago. You missed it."

"Shoot," he said.

"There'll be more tomorrow," she said, hoping she didn't sound desperate but aching for more time with him.

"How about a *private* tour?" he asked in a low voice, making goose bumps rise up on her arms under her cream-colored Irish-knit cardigan.

"Well, um…we can see about that—"

"Hey, can I borrow your phone for a sec?"

"Sure," she said, pulling it from her back pocket and holding it out to him.

He took it from her, smiling in thanks, before throwing it onto the slate-stone floor and jumping on top of it. She heard the screen shatter, but he didn't stop. He lifted one booted foot and smashed it again and again until it was shattered into a million pieces.

"Wait! What…?" He stopped and looked up at her. "Wh—What did you do that for?"

"You asked me to trust you yesterday, and I did. Can you do the same?"

Could she? Could she blindly trust him? She grimaced.

"I…I have too many questions. I think you're going to need to tell me what's going on," she said carefully. "I don't like being in the dark like this."

He pursed his lips, his eyes conflicted. "I really don't want to."

"I really *need* you to," she answered.

He leaned down to pick up the mangled pieces of her phone and throw them in a nearby garbage can, then he turned to face her. "I'm going to put Suzy's car back in your garage. Meet me down at the cottage when you're done here? We'll talk, okay?"

Her heart swelled. "Wait…you're staying?"

"For a little while." He nodded. "You said I was welcome, right?"

"Yes. Yes, you're welcome here," she answered, unable to hold back her smile for the second time in the five minutes he'd been back. "For how long?"

He cleared his throat. "I don't know yet."

"But you'll tell me everything?"

"Yeah. I promise." He looked around the small shop, his eyes landing on an expensive coffee table book called

Moonstone Manor: The Palace in the Sky. "Can I take one of these?"

"They're seventy dollars," she said.

He took out his wallet, withdrew a one-hundred-dollar bill, and placed it on the counter. "Keep the change. Is the gate by your place the only way in here?"

She nodded. "There were two other gates originally, but they were walled off years ago."

"Good," he said. "I'll see you back at home, huh?"

At home.

Oh, my heart.

"Mm-hm," she murmured. "I'll see you in a bit."

Holding the book at his side, he turned around and headed back out the main door. Tierney strained her neck, her eyes dropping to his ass for a second, and sighed before she forced them back up. She leaned over the counter to watch him slide into his sister's car and drive away. But not *away*-away. Not like last time.

And just like that, her whole mood shifted from miserable to elated, which should have clued her into something grave: her feelings for Burr—her sharp, intense infatuation, which had just received a booster shot—were growing. But she was too happy to notice anything but the fact that he was back and that each second that passed now drew her *closer* to him, not farther away.

At five o'clock sharp, she powered down her computer and turned off the lights in the gift shop.

"'Night, Ms. Haven," said Anna, walking through the visitor's center on her way to her car.

"Good night, Anna. Is the main house locked?"

"Yes, ma'am, but there are still a couple of stragglers

checking out the barn with Shannon."

"I'll get them moving. Have a good evening," she said, turning off the lights and locking the double glass doors of the visitor's center.

Walking around the building, she followed a brick path toward the barn but stopped and waved when she found Shannon walking toward her with a mother, father, and two teenage boys.

"Finishing up?" she called.

"Yes!" said the mother, walking up the path to chat with Tierney. "We're so glad we stumbled across this place! I could wander around here for hours. What a find!"

Usually, Tierney would offer to take the family on an extra, off-hours tour of the estate's attic or one of the outbuildings not on the regular tour, especially when they were as enthusiastic as this family appeared to be. But tonight, she had somewhere to be and she was eager to get there.

"We're so glad you took the time to visit," she said, then looked at her watch purposefully. "But I'm afraid we closed…three minutes ago."

"Oh!" said the mother, looking disappointed. "I guess that's our cue to go." She turned to Shannon. "Thanks, again, for a wonderful tour."

Shannon nodded, accepting the tip offered and waving good-bye as the family walked back to their car, one of only three in the parking lot. The other two belonged to Shannon and Tierney.

"Big plans tonight, Ms. Haven?" asked Shannon with a teasing smile.

"Just my regular Wednesday night dinner. But I need to

get over to Center Harbor for groceries. How about you?"

Shannon looked surprised by the question. "Yeah, actually. My boyfriend works as a counsellor at a camp up on Squam. We're getting together tonight at Walter's Basin for dinner."

"Sounds like fun," said Tierney, realizing that she almost never asked her employees about their personal lives; before now, she'd kept everything professional.

Or had she? Maybe calling it "professional" was a cop-out. Maybe what she was really doing, was sort of like hiding; keeping herself isolated from people as she used to at Summerhaven. For whatever reason, the realization bothered her.

"I hope you have a really nice time with your boyfriend, Shannon. Try the trout. It's amazing."

"Thanks, Ms. Haven!" called Shannon, heading over to her car. "See you tomorrow?"

"See you tomorrow, Shannon."

Maybe she could make a little more effort with the young women who worked for her. They were all several years younger than she, of course, but Tierney could certainly be a little warmer with them. Something to think about.

She waved to Shannon as she drove away, then looked over at her own car.

Usually she took the time to check the locks on the estate house and barn before heading home for the evening. But she quickly decided it could wait until later. Right now, all she wanted in the whole world was to spend a little of this borrowed time with the man waiting for her at home.

Racing to her car, she followed the family of four and

Shannon down the hill to the road, watching as they disappeared through the gate before closing and locking it for the day.

***

Burr didn't know if the book he'd purchased from Tierney was worth a hundred dollars, but it was pretty damned interesting. He'd spent the past forty minutes sitting in the late-day sun, on her doorstep, looking at the pictures, scanning paragraphs about the Gish family, and examining the foldout map of the extensive property.

Tomorrow morning, he'd walk the whole thing and familiarize himself with all possible entry points. If Sean somehow managed to trace Tierney's cell phone to her address, he wanted to know every vulnerability of the property where she lived. He might even invest in some cheap, but functional, cameras from RadioShack and install them at weak points so that he could check out the feeds on his phone at all times.

Looking up, he saw a car roll down the hill, followed by a minivan, another car, and finally, Tierney's Jeep, which paused at the gate. He watched her get out of her car and pull the gates shut manually before walking over to a keypad where she punched in a code, which, presumably, locked them for the day.

As she pulled into the driveway, he closed the book and stood up, reaching for her car door and opening it for her.

"Hey," he said. "That gate's locked now?"

She nodded. "Yeah. And automated. Anyone else who wants to get in needs a code."

"And there are no other entrance points?"

"No. Like I said, this is it."

He sighed, feeling a measure of relief, then held up the book. "I've been reading."

"And…?"

"Interesting place," he said, looking up at the tower on the hill. "The view from the barn must be spectacular."

Tierney followed his gaze, shielding her eyes and nodding. "It is."

"They originally built it as a lookout?"

"In part," she said. "But mostly for aesthetic reasons. Herbert Gish liked that it was clearly visible from Lake Winnipesaukee. Tourists from miles around were impressed and intrigued by the sheer scare of it. Made Moonstone Manor look like a palace in the sky. He was a bit of a blowhard, by all accounts."

"You know what they say," said Burr, grinning down at her. "Small salami, tall tower."

Two spots of color appeared in her cheeks as her eyes widened. "*Who* says that?"

"Everyone who knew Napoleon."

She rolled her eyes at him, the way the sisters of sometimes-cross brothers often do.

"Any towers at *your* house, Burr?"

"No, ma'am. I only require a very modest, one-story dwelling."

She laughed at that, shaking her head at him like he was naughty, and it blew him away how much he liked hearing her laugh. It was the first time he'd heard it, and it was throaty and deep, and unintentionally sexy. But she sobered up pretty quickly. "We need to talk."

Burr held back a groan. There was never, ever a good time for a woman to say those specific words to a man, and today was no exception.

"I guess we do."

"But I also need to go to the grocery store, so unless you want the talk to wait until after dinner, I think you'd better come with me and fill me in on the drive."

Frankly, he wouldn't mind waiting forever to tell her the truth about his life, but if he was going to stick around to look after her for a while, she deserved to know why. He walked around her Jeep, hopping into the passenger seat and watching as she hit the numeric code on the keypad. It took the gates twenty seconds to open. He'd keep that in mind.

"So," she prompted as soon as she turned onto the main road. "Who are you, Burr?"

He took a deep breath and exhaled, realizing the he hadn't told anyone—no one—the truth about who he was for three years. It took a moment for him to remember where to begin.

"My name's Burr O'Leary. And...in a weird twist of fate, my middle name's actually Brian, so that was a good choice."

"What? No!"

He nodded. "Yeah."

"Burr Brian O'Leary," she said, and he tried not to take so much pleasure in hearing her say his full name, but he failed. It felt nice to hear it.

"That's me."

"I like it," she said. "What else? What do you do?"

"I'm an officer with the Boston Police Department. For the last three years, I've been undercover with the New Killeens, an organized crime unit headed by the Shanahan brothers, Declan and Sean."

He said it quickly, like he didn't want the words sticking around in his mouth a moment longer than was necessary.

She gasped softly beside him, stopping at a red light and turning to face him. "Undercover? That's a real thing?"

Her question completely disarmed him, and he laughed softly. "Yeah. That's a real thing."

"So you've been undercover with these Killeens for a few years...doing what?"

Terrible things. Things I don't want to tell you about, aisling. *Things I never want you to know about.*

Burr clenched his jaw, dropping her eyes to look straight out the windshield. "Whatever it took to gain their trust."

Peripherally, he saw her lips part for a moment before she snapped them shut. The light changed, and she pressed down on the gas. "You did what you had to do. What else?"

Her pragmatism, and lack of judgment, was strangely soothing.

"Someone—and I'm pretty sure it was my partner—betrayed me to the Shanahans on Sunday."

"Betrayed you?"

He nodded, clenching his teeth together before continuing, a fresh onslaught of pain making his chest tight. "Told them that I was working undercover for the BPD."

"Your *partner*? Oh, God. No!"

"Yes. The Shanahans went to my sister's house to try to get information from her, but she didn't know anything. I haven't spoken to her in three years. Anyway, someone tipped me off anonymously that they were paying her a visit, and I got there just in time to see Declan Shanahan shoot her in the hip." He paused. He hated to tell her the rest, but he'd promised her the truth. "I was across the street, but I ran to help Suzy. Declan got me once in the shoulder. I got him in the chest, and I—I killed him."

"Oh, Burr," she whispered. "I can't imagine what that feels like."

"Confusing," he admitted. "He was a bad man, Tierney. He could've killed my sister. So yeah. Part of me is glad he's dead, but at the same time, I take no pleasure in killing someone. Does that make any sense?"

"It does," she murmured. Her breath was shaky when she inhaled. "Keep going."

"My partner told me to ditch my car and use Suzy's to drive up here. He told me his wife's family had a house on Lake Ossipee and that I should use it as a safe house. But…it—it was raining so hard that night, and I was on some pretty strong painkillers. Plus, the shock of the gunshot wound…I was losing blood, I guess. I got lost."

"…and came to Moonstone Manor instead."

"Came to *you*, Tierney," he said, surprised by the way his heart clenched, by the rush of intense feeling that made him want to touch her, to draw her into his arms, to—to— "And you…"

She pulled into the parking lot of Heath's Supermarket, cutting the engine and turning her whole body so she faced him. "I…what?"

"You're so damned brave. You gave me sanctuary," he said, staring into her green eyes and wondering if any woman in the history of time ever had eyes as beautiful as Tierney's. "You took care of me. You kept me safe. You…you were my safe haven."

She stared back at him, licking her tempting lips before

parting them. "I just…I just did what anyone would have—"

"No. Anyone else would've called the police. Anyone else would've been terrified. But you weren't. *Why* weren't you scared of me?"

"I was at first. But when I hit my head on the bathroom door, you said, 'Sorry.' And later, you asked me not to leave. You said you didn't want to die alone."

"Fucking dramatic," he muttered, disgusted with himself.

"No," she said, reaching out to place her hand on his arm. "No, Burr. It humanized you to me. Something told me you weren't all bad. Just…desperate."

"I was." He nodded, using all of his willpower not to cover her hand with his. "And I *do* know how to say thank you."

Miss Sassy returned instantly, pulling her hand away. "Is that right? Because I haven't seen much evidence of it since—"

"Thank you," he interrupted, looking straight at her. "Thank you, Tierney. For everything."

"You're welcome," she answered, her lips—those soft fucking lips that he'd kissed earlier today—tilting up just a tiny bit.

"You should smile more," he said.

She blinked. "*Téigh dtí diabhail*, Burr."

Damn, but she was surprising. "Ha! Fuck off, huh? Again?"

But she didn't say it with venom this time. This time it was almost like a private joke between them.

"I'll smile more when you give me something to smile about," she said. "Now, finish up. Why'd you leave this morning? Why'd you come back? And why on God's green earth did you smash my phone to smithereens?"

"I left this morning because if Sean Shanahan somehow tracked me down, I didn't want him to trace me to you."

"Okay," she said. "Then why'd you come back?"

"That call you made to Mass General to ask about my sister. You made it with your cell phone, right?"

"Of course. I don't have a landline."

"They have someone on the inside there. They're looking for any leads that could point them in my direction." He watched her eyes widen with understanding. "There's a fifty-thousand-dollar bounty on my head."

Her mouth dropped open, but she snapped it shut a moment later, schooling her expression from real surprise to faux. "You're worth fifty thousand, huh?"

He'd watched her use wit before to deflect something serious or troubling. But he needed her to understand the gravity of the situation they were in. "These guys are no joke, Tierney."

"You broke my phone," she pointed out. "There's no way to trace it now."

"But they could get your billing address from the number itself," he said. "These are bad people. They shot my sister, Tierney. When I left you earlier today, I went to the safe house—a house on Lake Ossipee that my partner *said* was safe. I got there just in time to see some associates of Sean Shanahan kill the handyman, thinking it was me." He scanned her eyes. He didn't want to frighten her, but he needed her to be aware of the potential danger that surrounded them. "If they find out you called about Suzy and trace back your number to a billing address, they could come after you too."

"That seems unlikely."

"Unlikely? Maybe. Possible?" He grimaced. "Yes."

She gulped softly. "Shouldn't we call the police?"

"The Shanahans have their dirty fingers in a lot of pockets. I don't know if they're connected up here."

"Is it possible?"

"*Anything's* possible," he answered, "except risking your safety."

She was holding her breath, her breasts and shoulders high, but she exhaled suddenly, her body relaxing a little. "I appreciate that."

"It's the least I can do, *aisling*," he said, reaching over to her and capturing a strand of jet-black hair draped over her shoulder. He fingered the silky softness between his fingers for a moment before letting it go.

When she took another breath, it was just the slightest bit shaky—from him touching her? From the story he was telling her? He wasn't sure, but suddenly he hoped it was the former. He fucking liked touching her, and he wanted it to affect her as much as it did him.

She cleared her throat. "So what happens now?"

"My boss—Captain Donnelley—is working with the gang task unit on an indictment of the New Killeens. As soon as it comes down, Sean Shanahan will be arrested. Once he's behind bars, you should be safe."

"And you?"

"I'll go back to Boston and testify against the bastard and his associates."

"Until then?"

He sighed. "Any chance there's an apartment above

your garage where I can stay awhile? I want to keep an eye on things here."

She shook her head. "Nope. Just a dusty storage loft."

Burr had no right to ask her if he could stay in her cottage; he'd already inconvenienced her, and her kindness had placed her life in jeopardy. He could stay in his car. Hell, it was summer. He could buy a tent and sleep outside in her backy—

"I have a guest room," she said.

It was his turn to blink in surprise. "Huh?"

"A guest room. In my cottage. I have one. You can stay there."

"I can't do that to you."

"What? Sleep in an empty bed in an empty room? You won't be putting me out, Burr."

"Are you sure? You wouldn't mind?"

"You can't live in your sister's car. I don't see what other choice we have."

"I could get a tent and—"

"You're not sleeping in a tent when I've a perfectly good—and empty—guest room."

He grinned at her tone because it reminded him so much of his mother and sister. *Don't argue with an Irish woman once her mind's made up.* But thinking about his family made his mind turn to hers.

"What will you tell your brothers about me staying with you?"

She gave him a look. "That tale's already spun. You're my friend, Brian, from Dartmouth, injured in a hunting accident, staying for a visit."

"Can I make a suggestion?"

"Sure."

"…because you're a terrible liar."

"Come on!"

"The worst I've *ever* seen."

"Thanks a lot."

"Working with what we have, I think we should make the story a little more truthful so you'll have less trouble sticking with it."

"Oh, please instruct me on the ways of deception, master."

He swallowed a grin, because he liked her sweet and breathless, but damn if he didn't like her sassy too.

"Brian works. That's my middle name, so it's not a lie. But instead of us being college *friends*, how about we just met there? We're the same age, and I played ice hockey at Dartmouth several times for UMass, so we were definitely there at the same time. We could say we met while I was playing hockey there one weekend and hooked up again over social media."

"I guess that could work," she said.

"And why don't we say that there's been some trespassing on the grounds here, which is true. I trespassed on Sunday, right? So I've come on as temporary security. Also true. That's why I'm staying."

"Yeah. That's good," said Tierney. "Even though I live in the cottage, it isn't mine. Technically it belongs to the Gish Trust. So it makes sense that another employee would be offered housing there too. It's plausible."

"See?" he said. "Way better. And I *will* be there for security, Tierney." *Yours.* "I'll die before I let anything happen to you."

"Don't die," she said, her eyes unexpectedly beseeching.

"I'll do my best." He cocked his head to the side. "A word to the wise: don't make big lies. It's more to remember and easier to get caught."

"You're good at lying?"

He thought back on the last three years of his life, starting with the lies told to his family so that they'd believe he'd turned bad. "I don't like it...but I've had to be."

"But not with me," said Tierney, reaching out and touching his arm again. "Don't lie to me."

This time he glanced down at her fingers. They were cool on his arm, small and white, with clean, short nails and a gold Claddagh ring, turned heart-out.

"I like your ring," he said, brushing it with his fingers. "I like the way you wear it."

When a woman wore her Claddagh ring heart-out, it meant her heart was available...though he reminded himself that she had a date with Dr. Weasel on Friday night. The thought made him glower.

She slid her hand from his arm. "What?"

"Nothing," he said.

"Burr?"

He looked at her—straight into her emerald eyes, making a thousand dreams that he had no right to take root in his stupid heart.

"Promise to always tell me the truth?" she asked. "I need that. Lie to whoever else you need to, but be honest with me, okay? About all things. All the time."

"I promise," he said, though he already knew there were things he'd never be able to tell her, that would only make it more difficult to say good-bye when it was time for him to go.

"Okay, then," she answered. "Is that everything?"

He nodded. "Everything I can think of."

"Good," she said. "Now help me get some stuff for dinner. My brothers are coming in an hour."

Oh, right. Dinner with her brothers. He'd forgotten about that.

"Speaking of your brothers...anything I should know? Like...is the second one as big as the first one?"

She had her hand on the door handle, ready to leave the SUV, but she turned back to him, her eyes wide. "Hmm? No. Rory's not as big as Ian."

"But you *are* their only sister."

She grimaced, nodding at him. "That I am."

As he accompanied her into the grocery store, he couldn't help feeling that telling Tierney the truth about his life was nothing compared to what he was about to go through meeting her brothers.

chapter seven

As Tierney set the picnic table, Burr mucked out the charcoal grill in Tierney's backyard, then refilled it, squirting a little lighter fluid over the black briquettes before lighting them. They'd be grayish-orange by the time her brothers and Brittany arrived in thirty minutes, hungry for hamburgers and hot dogs.

When they'd gotten back from the grocery store, Burr had carried the bags inside for her before taking his duffel bag back upstairs to the guest room. She couldn't deny the thrill that shot through her when he returned downstairs barefooted a few minutes later.

You're staying. You're staying. You're staying.

The words circled around her head, finally followed by these:

I have a chance.

But at what?

At making him like her? He already seemed to like her. He'd kissed her earlier today and touched her hair so tenderly when they were in the car. He'd pledged to keep her safe and told her he liked the way she wore her ring, heart-out. Those were all signs of…of…*something*, right?

These were the moments when Tierney wished she had more real-life experience or one good girlfriend with whom to discuss matters of the heart. Because honestly, her natural instincts weren't the sharpest where men were concerned. She hadn't had enough experiences to hone them.

Playing devil's advocate with herself, she countered that his kiss earlier today wasn't romantic, but merely a way to bid her farewell.

Similarly, touching her hair was a just a distracted, tactile gesture that meant nothing on an emotional level.

Keeping her safe was his job, not a personal mission.

And saying he liked the way she wore her ring could just be a reference to their shared heritage.

It could all mean *something*.

Or it could all mean *nothing*.

And she was much less likely to get herself hurt if she believed the latter.

Nothing it is.

He was grateful to her, as he'd carefully articulated, but protecting her probably had more to do with making up for what had happened to his sister. He was a policeman. He didn't want to see anyone else hurt.

No doubt he wanted a friendship with her and nothing more.

The wave of disappointment she felt made her chest tighten uncomfortably. *The role of friend will be played by...Tierney Haven! Again!* Except, when she looked at Burr, whom she'd placed without any ambiguity in the "temptation" bucket, she didn't feel or want mere friendship. Aside from having an intense physical attraction to him, she was quickly growing to genuinely like him. By all accounts, they were going to spend the next couple of weeks together. Could she accept friendship if that's all he was able or willing to offer her? *Would* she?

"I just realized…" he said, pouring ice over the beverages in the cooler, "you don't have any alcoholic beer in here."

She looked over at him from where she stood, setting the table. "No. My brother Ian is in recovery."

He was squatting by the cooler, but he looked up at her, impressed. "Wow. You're really supportive."

"Of his sobriety? Of course."

"How long has he been on the wagon?"

"Four months and change."

"Not long," said Burr, standing up to take the empty ice bag to the garbage can near the garage.

There was something about this tall, lean, muscular man standing in his bare feet on her bright-green grass that just about made Tierney moan with pleasure. The grass would be soft and cool this late in the day, and suddenly she longed to feel it too. She placed the last of the forks she held beside a waiting plate, then sat down on the picnic bench, reaching to unlace her white tennis sneakers. She set them side by side under the bench, then took off her socks, revealing feet so white, they were almost light blue. She tucked the socks neatly in her shoes, then stood up, letting the blades of grass sluice between her toes, wiggling them against the soft green.

"I haven't been barefoot in ages," she said, reveling in the almost-forgotten sensations against her skin.

He grinned at her. "Me neither. But I couldn't resist. Summer's a time for being barefoot, isn't it? I don't think Suzy and I ever wore shoes from Memorial Day to Labor Day."

His reference to his sister jogged her memory, and she remembered a question she had for him. "Can I ask you something?"

"Sure."

"Before, in the car, you said that you haven't spoken to your sister in three years."

His grin faded fast, and he nodded, stepping over to the graying coals and checking on them.

"But you seem really close to her," continued Tierney. "You talk about her. You love her. That's obvious."

"She's my sister," said Burr softly, pushing the briquettes around for a moment before looking up at her with troubled eyes. "Of course I love her."

"That's why I don't understand."

He sighed, keeping his gaze trained on the grill. "My captain thought it would be more believable for me to leave the department in disgrace before hooking up with the New Killeens. They staged a drug bust. Found enough cocaine in my car to put me away for years. But instead of an arrest, presumably to save the department from embarrassment, they 'let me go' dishonorably. The story I fed the Shanahans was that I felt betrayed by the BPD and wanted revenge." He shrugged. "They bought it."

She glanced at the table, set for family dinner with her brothers, then slid her eyes back to Burr. "So…oh, God…so, you haven't seen or spoken to your family in—*in three years*?"

The idea was utterly obscene to Tierney, who saw her brothers twice a week, visited her parents once a month, and talked to all of them once a day or more.

His face was tight. His eyes sad. "Cost of the job."

"Big price to pay," she said softly, her heart aching for him.

He nodded. "I've missed them. My father—well, he pretty much disowned me after the fake bust. He was also in the BPD before retiring. The idea of having a delinquent son was unbearable to him. My mother stopped talking to me. Suzy tried to reach out, but I didn't return her calls, and eventually she stopped trying." He paused. "You know, of all the things I had to do to get in with the Killeens—and there is some dirty fucking shit I've seen and done, Tierney—that was the worst part. By far."

Tierney rounded the table, needing to be closer to him, to offer him comfort if she could. "It was a means to an end."

"Part of me thought it would be glamorous," he said, looking into her eyes, his expression stupendously grieved. "What a stupid fucking kid."

She reached out to him, her fingers landing on his arm. "It's almost over now. You'll be able to tell them the truth soon. And they'll understand, won't they? They'll…welcome you home again?"

Suddenly his arms were around her, and she was drawn against the strong, solid wall of his chest. He held onto her, clasping her to him, clinging to her like a life raft in a terrible storm. Caught unawares, she let him hold her, adjusting to the warmth of his surprise embrace.

"I hope so, Tierney," he murmured near her ear. "God, I hope so."

Winding her arms around Burr's waist, she rested her head on his chest and hugged him back, thinking about Rory and Ian and remembering how much it had hurt when Ian was on one of his famous three-month benders and wouldn't call her back. She couldn't imagine being out of touch with him for three years. She felt terrible for Suzy, who must still grieve the loss of her brother every day, and terrible for Burr, who was forced to give up his family in order to serve his city.

"You're a hero," she whispered. "You're so brave."

"I'm not," he grunted, his voice gravelly with emotion.

"You are," she insisted, the words slightly muffled against his T-shirt. "You made a tremendous sacrifice for the greater good. That's the definition of a hero."

"You don't know what I've seen…what I've done…"

"I know that the New Killeens will be under indictment any day now. And that's because of you. Countless lives saved, Burr, because of you."

"Tierney," he sighed, his arms tightening around her as he pressed his lips to the top of her head. "Where did you come from, *aisling*?"

His words made goose bumps rise up on her arms, and she leaned into him for warmth. While she usually wore a cardigan sweater at the visitor's center because the air conditioning was always on, she'd taken it off in the car and only wore a thin, dark-blue tank top over crisp white khaki shorts. She could feel his body everywhere—his chest against hers, his heart under her ear, his hands clasped together on her lower back. And she wished she didn't love the sensation of being held in his arms, but she did. So much. Too much.

In the not-so-far distance, she heard the sound of car wheels on gravel and Burr's arms loosened around her. She looked up at him, and the expression on his face was so intense, she half-wondered if he would have kissed her again if her family hadn't interrupted them.

"I think your brothers are here," he said softly.

Tierney gulped. "Yeah. I think—um, I'll be right back."

She stepped out of his arms, walking around the house to stand in the driveway and wave hello to her family. Her cheeks were probably flushed, but the late-summer sun was still high and strong, so she hoped they wouldn't be suspicious.

"Hey, Tierney," said Brittany, her brother Rory's girlfriend, running over to her with a bouquet of wild flowers and a plate of brownies.

Tierney accepted both, looking at the brownies with cautious interest. "Did *you* make these?"

Brittany's skills—or lack thereof—in the kitchen were legendary among the Havens. She'd once tried to make a frozen dinner with the cellophane still on the container.

"I did," she said, grinning at Tierney, her wavy blonde hair picture-perfect in a black-and-white-gingham hairband, "with Chef Jamie's help. Don't worry."

"Oh! I wasn't worried!" she said, grateful for the skills of Rory's head chef.

"Yeah, right," said Brittany. "I'm never going to live down my first few weeks in Rory's kitchen, am I?"

Tierney cringed, then shrugged. "Give us a little more time?"

Brittany rolled her eyes with a cheerful giggle, then leaned forward conspiratorially. "What did I hear about some guy staying here with you? Rory's a mess. I need details!"

"Rory *is* a mess. And we *all* need details," said Rory from behind his girlfriend. He leaned forward to kiss Tierney on the cheek. "Is he here?"

Tierney nodded. "And I'll thank you not to be a jerk to him."

"A jerk to who?" asked Ian, slamming the back door, stepping over to the group, and giving his sister a peck on her other cheek.

"Whom," corrected Tierney. "Bu—uh, Brian. Brian, is my houseguest. I mean, employee. Here. At Moonstone, uh, Manor."

Rory and Ian shared a look.

"She's doing the lying thing," said Rory.

"In spades," observed Ian. "I told you she was being weird."

Rory nodded. "Yeah. I can see."

Brittany turned around, her back to Tierney and her hands on her hips. "No ganging up on Tierney, you two! So what if she has a guy staying here? Good for her, I say!" She backed up, facing the Haven brothers as she put her arm through Tierney's. "Brian, you said? Let's go find him. *I* can't wait to meet him."

"Great," said a voice from behind the ladies, "because here I am."

Tierney looked up at Brittany, watching her pretty brown eyes widen just a touch as she saw Burr over her shoulder. "Oh. You must be…"

"Brian," said Burr, his voice warm and low.

Brittany extracted her arm from Tierney's to shake hands. "Hi."

"Brian," said Tierney, "this is my brother's girlfriend, Brittany Manion."

"Manion like the hotels?" he asked.

"Exactly like the hotels," said Rory, pushing Brittany's

115

hand away from Burr's and taking it into his. "I'm Tierney's brother, Rory." His tone was unfriendly. "And you're Brian from Dartmouth, huh?"

"Actually, I went to UMass," said Burr, pumping Rory's hand.

Tierney watched Rory's face—the tight clench of his jaw, his unsmiling lips and narrowed eyes.

"And this is Ian," she said. "My other brother."

Rory dropped Burr's hand, and Ian took it, his knuckles whitening. She watched as Burr increased his own pressure, until his knuckles were the same color as Ian's. *Oh, for fuck's sake.* Men were so damned stupid.

"My friend John told me you went to Dartmouth," said Ian.

"I did," said Burr, his voice level, not unfriendly, but not trying too hard either. He took back his hand from Ian. "I played ice hockey there a few times. Met Tierney one of the weekends I was up there."

"Huh. I played a little ice hockey myself," said Ian, taken off guard by this information. Ian had been an all-star in ice hockey at Boston University and coached at the high school level for a few years before his drinking habit had overtaken his life. He put his hands on his hips, sizing up Tierney's guest. "You say you played for UMass?"

"Yep."

"What position?" asked Ian.

"Left wing. You?"

"Defense."

"When did you graduate?" asked Burr.

"Six years ago."

"Me too. Boston had a great team."

"So did UMass." Ian rubbed his beard. "We probably played each other. I bet I slammed you into the boards a couple of times."

Burr scoffed. "Like you could've caught me. You defense guys are ass-draggers."

"Whoa, son! That sounds like a challenge."

"You name the rink, I'll bring the heat," said Burr.

"Done deal," said Ian, grinning like the Cheshire cat. "Saturday afternoon. Four thirty. Gilford Arena. You and me."

"I'll be there," said Burr. "Care to make it interesting?"

"*Damnú*," growled Ian, nodding appreciatively at Burr before glancing at Tierney. "Yer man here's got a death wish."

"*Téigh dtí diabhail, a thóin mór,*" said Burr. *Fuck off, fat ass.*

"Jaysus, he speaks t' Oirish like a feckin' native," said Ian with a heavy accent, blinking at Burr in surprise.

"Limerick," offered Burr.

"Killarney," said Ian.

"Fifty bucks on Ian," said Rory, stepping forward. "And I'll referee."

"Oh, that'll be fair," deadpanned Burr, looking back and forth between the brothers.

"I'll make sure it's fair," said Brittany, slipping Rory's arm around her shoulders. "Now let's put our genitals away, boys. Tierney's making dinner."

As the three men and Brittany made their way around the house to the backyard, Tierney sighed in relief. *Well, that went...okay. For now.*

Talk turned to college days and sports at the grill, and unsurprisingly, the Haven boys and Burr got along pretty well, all things considered. Or they did until Rory started getting all protective again. As Tierney handed Burr a plate of raw hamburgers to place on the grill, Rory asked, "What did Tierney mean about you being an employee here?"

"There were some poachers here last weekend," said Burr. "I've been hired as security."

"Don't you have a real job?" asked Ian, his tone only half joking.

"I was between things," said Burr.

"What does *that* mean?" asked Rory.

"Rory," said Tierney. "Let it be, huh?"

Burr took his time placing the burgers on the grill, then closed the lid, looking squarely at Rory. "Why don't you trust your sister?"

"I—I trust her. What's *that* supposed to mean?"

"Tierney's wicked smart," said Burr, glancing at her and making her warm all over. "She's thoughtful too. Mature. Sensible. Brave. She's not some dopey kid who doesn't know her ass from her elbow. How come you're giving her such a hard time about me being here?"

"I'm not," said Rory, hands on his hips, lips thin with anger. "In fact, I'm not talking to *her* at all. It's *you* I'm talking to. You met Tier up at Dartmouth. How'd you reconnect?"

Tierney just about had enough. "For fuck's sake, Rory. On Facebook."

Rory kept his gaze trained on Burr. "How long are you staying?"

Burr took a deep breath, which broadened his chest. "As long as Tierney needs me."

"And how long'll that be?" Rory asked his sister.

"'Til the end of the season," she said, taking a step

closer to Burr.

"Staying *where*?" demanded Rory.

She glanced up at the guest room window, then slid her narrowed eyes to Rory. "Here."

"Absolutely *fucking* not," growled Rory. "You met him years ago when he played hockey one weekend. You don't even *know* him."

That was it.

She snapped.

She grabbed the spatula from the hook on the grill, took a step forward, drew it back, and slapped Rory on the ass with all her might. He yelped, covering his ass with his hand and looking at her in shock. "*God damn it*, Tierney, I'm only trying to—"

"He's staying because *I say* he's staying," she yelled, raising the spatula again as Rory backed up in retreat. "And he's staying in the empty bedroom owned by the Gish Trust that's located down the hallway from mine because he's an employee here. Unless you plan to buy this estate from the state of New Hampshire and change the rules to fit some antiquated ideas you have about my goddamn virtue, boyo, then you are out of luck. This cottage is *not* under your purview, Rory Kavanagh Haven, and for that matter…nor is *his* bed, nor is *mine*. Yes. It's none of your damned business. *An dtuigeann tú*?"

Rory stared at her, his mouth gaping, one hand still resting on his smacked buttocks.

"Do you understand?" she repeated in English, wielding the spatula with as much fury as her mother used to wield the spoon.

"Fine," said Rory, glaring at Burr for a moment, before

nodding once at his sister and muttering, "*Go dtachta an diabhal tu.*" *The devil take you then.*

As Rory walked away, toward the woods behind Tierney's cottage, she threw the spatula on the ground and stalked into the house, her eyes burning with tears. How dare her brother act that way? How dare he embarrass her like that?

Resting her hands on the sink, she took several deep breaths, then splashed her face with cool water and dried it with a paper towel.

"You like him."

Tierney turned to find Brittany standing behind her.

"What? Who?"

"Brian. Your…houseguest."

"I like him. Yeah," said Tierney, sniffling softly. "What's not to like?"

"He's good looking," said Brittany, "and nice."

Tierney scoffed. "I'm not stupid enough to fall for him. Why would I break my own heart?"

Brittany took the paper towel from Tierney's hands and gently dried her face. "Break your heart? Nah. He likes you too."

"Unlikely."

Girls like Brittany, who were wanted by every man who ever set eyes on them, didn't understand what it was like to be Tierney, the girl most likely to be cast as the best friend.

Brittany grinned. "The only thing standing between Rory's face and Brian's fist was you."

Tierney gulped, still furious with her brother. "Rory had no right to act like that. I've always been the good one, the quiet one, the responsible one. He has no right to treat me like a child!"

"He loves you," said Brittany gently. "And you're right. You've always been good and quiet, strong and sweet, shy and solitary Tierney. Having some guy here? *Staying* here? This is new for Rory and Ian. You don't generally have men coming and going. And now...well, now you do. Coming, I mean, not going. Oh! Not...not *coming*. I didn't mean it *that* way. I just meant...Oh, Lord."

Every so often, society-girl Brittany shocked the hell out of the Havens, blurting out some unexpected, and generally inappropriate, word or phrase.

Tierney giggled softly, grateful that Brittany's blunder had eased some of the tension in the room. "I—I know what you meant."

Brittany's cheeks were pink, but she grinned at Tierney. "Either way...good for you."

Now Tierney's cheeks heated up as she thought about Burr and *coming* in the same breath. *Think of something else. Think of something else. Like...Rory.*

"I whacked him hard on t'arse. Is he okay?"

"Who? Rory?" Brittany walked over to the window. "Well, Brian's flipping burgers at the grill with Ian...and Rory's...hmm, where is he? Ah! There he is. Rory's coming back now. Reaching down to the cooler. Grabbing a beer. Ian's getting the top off for him. Hmm. He's saying something that looks vaguely like, 'If you hurt my sister, bloodhounds won't find your body...' and...ah-ha! *Sláinte!*'

Crossing the kitchen, Tierney stood next to Brittany, watching her brothers and Burr clink their bottles together and sighing softly with relief as they drank.

"You know...Rory's got a mean grease stain on the

back of those khakis," observed Brittany.

"He deserved it," said Tierney, but her lips twitched with more laughter.

"Yes, he did," said Brittany, putting an arm around Tierney and hugging her as they watched the boys from the kitchen window. "Indeed he did."

***

The Havens were pure Irish. Clannish to the core.

After dinner, they lingered, helping Tierney clean up until she announced that she still needed to lock up the great house and outbuildings at the top of the hill. Rory and Ian jumped at the chance to drive her up the road, but Burr stepped in, telling them that he would accompany her. With a look caught somewhere between annoyance and acceptance, Rory shrugged, grunting at Ian and Brittany that it was time to go.

"Well…that was interesting," said Tierney, sighing deeply as she stood next to Burr on the driveway, watching the gates close behind her family.

Burr put his hands on his hips. "You want to hear something surprising?"

"Sure."

"I liked your brothers."

She turned to look at him, her green eyes wide beneath her glasses. "You did?"

"Yeah," he said, glancing at her and nodding. "I mean, I almost took a swing at Rory when he was grilling you like a drill sergeant, but I understand where he was coming from. Some guy they've never heard of shows up at their sister's place, staying indefinitely. My sister's husband, Connor? Man, I gave him a tough time before they were married."

"I've got my keys," she said. "Go get your shoes on and then tell me about Connor while we walk up to the great house."

He ran into the house and returned a moment later. They turned from the gate to walk up the long driveway, the twilight soft and magical as crickets chirped and cicadas sang their timeless songs. It had been a long time since Burr had spent any time in a place that smelled as clean as Moonstone Manor. He soaked up the evening sounds, letting gratitude fall over him, despite how shitty his life might look to an outside observer.

"So…" said Tierney, falling into step beside him, "why didn't you like him?"

"Connor? Nah! I loved him. He's a great guy. Redheaded and freckled. Built as strong as a Mack truck—like yer man, Ian. He's a lieutenant in the Dorchester Fire Department. Known Suzy since they were kids. He's good for her."

"Then why'd you give him a hard time?" she asked.

"Well," said Burr, chuckling softly at his memories. "I liked him fine before he was—well, for lack of a better word—*boinking* my sister. Once I found out they were getting it on? Yeah, I gave him hell. I didn't want her mistreated, you know? Or taken for granted."

"Yeah. I know." Tierney nodded. "You're all Neanderthals."

"A little," he agreed. "We're possessive, the Irish. We look out for what's ours."

"When did you let up on Connor?"

"When he put a ring on my sister's finger. Then I couldn't care less if they screwed all over Boston. They were legit. He'd taken responsibility. He'd done what was right."

Tierney stopped walking beside him, and when he realized it, he turned around to look at her. She stood in the dying light, her hands on her hips, a pissed expression on her pretty face. "What?"

"Do you have any idea how reactionary that sounds?" she asked him.

"Wha—"

"*He took responsibility*," she barked, adding a sour laugh. "*Done what was right*. Are you kidding me with that stuff?"

He shrugged. "Not really."

"You and my brothers are straight out of Victorian times. It's ludicrous."

"Because we want to keep the women in our lives safe? Happy? Free from harm? That makes us…reactionary Victorian Neanderthals?"

"You can't smother us in Bubble Wrap, Burr. Believe it or not, we can think for ourselves, speak for ourselves, and take care of ourselves. We don't need you idiots—"

"Hey, now," said Burr, placing his hands on his own hips in a mirror image of her. "I didn't say you couldn't take care of yourself. Hell, woman! I've seen you with a spatula, and that shit was terrifying." He sighed, taking a step toward her, wanting her to understand that he was talking about old-fashioned values in a modern world, and frankly, he hoped there was room for both. "I'm saying…when we care for someone—for a woman, be she a mother, a sister, a girlfriend, a lover, a wife, a daughter—we can't bear to see her heart get broken. We'd rather have both our arms and legs snapped in half than see her cry. Or better yet, we'd like to beat the stuff out of the guy who hurt her."

Her expression softened just a touch, but she cocked her head to the side. "I think it's less about loving someone and more about posturing…and ownership."

"Then you're crazy," he answered, thinking about his mother as he turned and started walking again. "When I was young, my mam would shake her finger at me as I left the house in the evenings. She'd say, 'One, use your head. Two, use your head. Three, picture my face.' Let me tell you…picturing my mother's face kept me from doing a lot of stupid or dangerous things. Couldn't stand to upset or disappoint her."

"Mmm," hummed Tierney beside him, not convinced.

"Or take the time Father Jim called my mam because I wouldn't stop crying at school."

"Why?"

"Why was I crying?" He chuckled. "Okay, here's the story. So the father calls her in and there I am, weeping all over my pressed Catholic school shirt in his office w' Sister Mary Grace wringing her hands in the chair next to me. My mam comes in and Father Jim says, 'Well, Mrs. O'Leary, young Burr has been emotional all morning, and we can't get to the bottom of why. Felt we needed to call you in and apprise you of the situation.' My mother rounds the desk to stand next to Father Jim, her face thunderous, and Sister Mary Grace takes my hand in hers as though to protect me. 'Well, son?' asks my mother, no-nonsense, arms crossed over her chest. And there I am, crying even harder now that she's there. 'Have you been hurt, my child?' asks Sister Mary Grace, all concerned about my well-being. My mother scoffs, rolling her eyes. 'Burr Brian O'Leary, you tell the sister and Father Jim why you're crying. I have groceries waiting in the car. Quick, now.' And I look up through tears—mind you, I've been crying for over an hour, so my eyes are so swollen, I can barely see—and I wail, 'I s-smoked one of my d-dad's cigarettes l-last night b-behind the h-house...' I pause there to catch a breath. 'Yes, son?' says Father Jim, frozen with anticipation, ready to hear I'd endured the beating of the century, with strips of my flesh still lying all over our backyard, right? And I finish off by adding, '...and now mam's d-d-deeply d-d-d-disap-p-pointed w-with me!'" Burr looked askance at Tierney, watching as a dimple dented her cheek, and feeling victorious. "No one had laid a bloody hand on me. I'd stolen a cigarette, smoked it, and gotten caught. And I'd been crying all morning because my mother was *deeply disappointed* in me."

"Guilt and shame," said Tierney. "Every Irish mother's favorite weapons."

"I've heard the spatula's making a comeback," said Burr, purposely knocking into her gently with his elbow.

"All right. All right. So you love your mother and your sister."

"And your brother loves you," said Burr. "No mistake, I would've popped him if he'd kept going, because I didn't like what he was insinuating about you. But I still respect him."

Tierney shook her head. "You're all impossible."

"Will you come on Saturday? To see me skate?"

The question surprised him because he hadn't thought it over before asking, and frankly, it was a blessed relief, because it had been years since he'd felt comfortable enough and safe enough to speak before thinking.

"Probably," she said. "Though I could be out late on

Friday night and exhausted come Saturday."

"Oh, yeah? Why?"

"Have you forgotten? I have a hot date."

Hot date? Burr scrunched up his face. *What am I missing?*

"With John," she added.

Oh, shit. That's right. She has to go out on a date with Dr. Weasel on Friday night.

"Aw, forget him. I'll take you out instead," he offered, keeping his voice level, though the thought of Tierney going out with the fucking vet made bile rise to the back of his throat.

"A deal's a deal," she said, reaching in her pocket for the keys as they approached the visitor's center.

"Says who?"

"The stitches on your back and front."

"I'll pay him."

"With the Shanahan's dirty money? I don't think so."

Burr reached out, placing his hand on her arm, just over her wrist. "Don't go, *aisling*."

She pulled her arm away gently. "I have to. You know I do. It's what's right."

He sighed, running a hand through his hair. "Anyone ever tell you that you're stubborn, Tierney Haven?"

"About a million times." She checked the door of the visitor's center, then continued around the building with Burr traipsing, annoyed, behind her.

The door to the great house was unlocked, but she locked it quickly before turning down another path that led to the barn and watchtower.

"Want to see the inside?" she asked over her shoulder, and unless he was mistaken, there was a thread of hope in her voice, like maybe she'd like to show it to him.

Yes, he did. He was dying to see the view from the watchtower. And no doubt the sunset over the lake would be spectacular, but the problem was that if he stood up there, on top of the world, he'd want to kiss her again. And kissing Tierney wasn't a good idea.

Burr meant it when he said that he liked her brothers and understood their misgivings where he was concerned. He wasn't interested in disrespecting their sister by making cheap moves on her when his reason for staying a Moonstone Manor was solely for her protection. No matter how appealing she was—and she beat out any other woman on his radar—she needed to be off-limits. At least for now.

"Not tonight."

"Oh," she murmured, two patches of pink appearing in her cheeks. "Okay."

"Another time," he said, trying to soften the blow. He leaned against the side of the barn as she closed the double doors and locked them. "I have work to do…studying, the, uh, the property maps. I'll walk you home and check on the gate before bed."

A heavy silence descended between them at the mention of bed, the click of the lock behind her key somehow punctuating the word. *This cottage is not under your purview, Rory Kavanagh Haven, and for that matter…nor is his bed, nor is mine.*

Her bed.

Damn, but he'd sure like to see it again someday…with her in it.

His cock twitched and he shoved himself away from the barn, into a shadow cast by the high red walls.

You're here to protect her, not romance her, he reminded himself again, though the heat in his groin increased with every beat of his heart, sending blood to his dick, which hardened behind the zipper of his jeans. He wanted her. Christ, this was a mess. Falling for Tierney Haven was the sort of thing that could get him distracted and get them both killed.

You need to stay away from her, boyo. As far as you can in that tiny cottage.

"Well, then I guess we're done here," she said softly, turning away from the barn and heading back up another path toward the visitor's center.

And Burr, who was ever more drawn to her by the moment, stayed a respectful distance behind her until he'd gotten himself under control. But their easy camaraderie was done and gone, and they walked the rest of the way back to her house in silence.

chapter eight

Whether it was her imagination or just the adjustment of living with a man under the same roof, Tierney felt like Burr was avoiding her.

When she woke up at seven thirty to shower, dress, and walk up to the great house for work, he was already gone, a rinsed mug on the drying rack and a note on the kitchen table informing her that he was on patrol.

When she returned at one for lunch, there was evidence that he'd been back to make himself something to eat, but no follow-up note about where he was and when he'd return.

And at the end of her workday, she missed him again, this time leaving *him* a note of her own, saying that she was attending book club in Sandwich and wouldn't be back until later.

When she returned, he was sitting on the couch in the living room, studying maps of the property, and her heart took flight. Soared through the sky to the watchtower and back, only grounding itself again when she realized that he didn't look up at her as she closed the door and locked it behind her.

"I'm home," she said, feeling stupid announcing herself when he obviously heard her walk in.

He didn't look up. "Uh-huh."

"All good?" she asked, awkwardly.

"Huh?" he muttered.

"Hi," she said directly.

He finally looked up. "Hi."

Her cheeks colored because his tone was abrupt, and he immediately looked back down at what he was doing. Was she *bothering* him? Because it sure felt like it.

"Is everything okay?"

"So far, so good."

"Did you have dinner?"

"Yeah. I heated up some leftover soup."

She held out a plastic wrapped paper plate of leftover cookies, just under his nose. "I brought these from book club. Thought you might want one."

"Great. You can leave them there," he said dismissively, gesturing to the corner of the coffee table. "Thanks."

What was going on with him?

On Wednesday, it felt like she and Burr were at the start of something—the way he called her *aisling*, the way he'd kissed her good-bye, the way he'd held her so tightly before the barbecue, the way they'd chatted so easily walking up to the great house after dinner.

And now? He felt like a stranger—even more than he did the night he arrived. What had changed?

"Did I…?" She swallowed, biting her lower lip as she stared down at his bristly head.

"Hmm?"

"Have I offended you, um, somehow?"

"No," he said, still staring at his damned maps.

Fine, she thought. *I'm not going to beg you for attention.*

"I'm going out tomorrow night," she threw over her

shoulder as she headed for the stairs.

"Yeah. I remember."

She paused and turned around. "Aren't you going to tell me to have a good time?"

"No, I'm bloody well not," he answered grimly. He didn't look up at her, but she saw the tic in his jaw that indicated he was clenching it.

Hmm. Okay. So he wasn't completely immune to her. Was he upset that she was going out on a date with another man?

"You know," she said, taking a chance that this was the problem, "I'm not *into* John. I'm only going out with him because I promised to. You know that, right?"

His neck snapped up, and he looked at her, his eyes stormier than they'd been a moment before, his voice terse and low. "You *should* be into him. He'd be a good choice for someone like you."

"Someone like me?" She recoiled as though slapped, then straightened her spine and demanded, "What's that supposed to mean?"

"He's stable and settled and…and…and *sensible*," he bit out. "Perfect for you."

"Well, maybe I don't *want* stable and settled and sensible," she snapped, her fingers curling around the newel post at the foot of the stairs. "Maybe I want *un*stable, and—and *un*settled, and…*wild!*"

He blew out an exasperated breath, like she was being ridiculous.

"Don't patronize me," she warned him.

He rolled his eyes. "Then stop acting like a child."

"Says the person who's been avoiding me all day."

"I haven't been *avoiding* you, Tierney."

"Yes, you have. Why?"

"Because I'm *bad* for you!" he growled. As soon as the words left his mouth, she saw that tic in his jaw again, like he was grinding his teeth together to keep from saying anything else. After a moment, his face relaxed and he delivered a speech: "I'm sorry if I sent you mixed signals yesterday. It won't happen again. You don't need someone like me. You need someone like John. And I need to stay focused on your safety...and nothing else."

She blinked at him, trying to decide if she was hurt or insulted. Or both.

Both, she decided. There was nothing she liked about what he was saying, but her humiliation was sharp enough that she didn't want to discuss it further.

"I see," she said. "Then I'll stay out of your fucking way."

"Come on," he muttered. "Tierney, wait..."

His voice trailed off as she hurried up the stairs, her eyes burning with stupid, useless tears. Why should she care what this man thought of her? Why should she care if he thought she deserved someone like pasty, wheedling John Stuart? It didn't matter. Not one bit. Not at all.

Slamming her door shut, she locked it for good measure, then sat down on the edge of her bed, looking at herself in the mirror over her bureau. Her dark hair was back in a severe bun, she wore no makeup, and the dim light in her room bounced off the lenses of her glasses, obscuring her eyes. She took them off, folding them carefully and placing them on her bedside table, then took her hair from its bun and shook out the long straight, dark mane. It fell around her shoulders in black curtains, making her pixie-like face appear smaller and slimmer.

I'm not bad-looking, she thought, tilting her head to the side. *Am I?*

Tierney had never put much effort into her appearance.

Makeup felt heavy on her sensitive skin and made her break out. And fashionable clothes made her feel conspicuous when all she really wanted was to hide or blend in. She kept herself neat and clean, but she didn't try to make herself more or less attractive than she was naturally.

But now? Now she considered herself in the mirror, wondering what feminine wiles she might use if she *wanted* to stand out, if she wanted to be noticed. Feeling bold, she pulled her plain black T-shirt over her head, then cupped her breasts and pushed them together to make a swell of cleavage. Then she tossed half of her long hair over her shoulder, so the dark, blunt ends hovered just over her nipple. Hmm. Some lipstick. A little black dress.

Ignore me then, she dared the universe, lifting her chin.

Knock knock. "Tierney?" *Knock knock.* "Can we talk?"

She dropped her hands and frowned at the door.

She remembered having the "let's be friends" conversation at college more than once, and she could already hear it in his voice. She knew what was coming. He wanted to soften the blow of his rejection by offering her his friendship as a consolation prize.

Well, forget it. I'm not interested.

Which begged the question: *What* do *I want?*

She gulped, trying to form a quick and snappy answer, but her thoughts were cloudy and disjointed. There was only one thing she knew for certain: though Burr had only swept into her life a few days ago, she already knew that friendship wasn't what she wanted from him.

With some people, when they walked into your life, you knew—*you just knew*—that there were some roles they *could* play and some they *couldn't*. And Burr O'Leary could only be her friend if he was a friend she could also touch and kiss and reach for, a friend who wanted her with the same burgeoning intensity that she wanted him.

The problem with accepting his friendship was that it would eventually break her, because her attraction to him was *already* too great; she wanted things from him—the dark flash of his eyes, a reprisal of his lips upon hers, his strong arms encircling her body. She wanted to have a right to those things, and if she compromised her own desires by settling for friendship, she'd be subjugating them. If she agreed to a friendship with Burr, she'd be ignoring the whisperings of her heart and the fierce longing that had already taken root in her body.

So no. She didn't want to hear what he had to say.

She didn't want to have to nod and smile when he told her that a friendship between them would be for the best. Mostly because one, she didn't believe it, and two, she simply didn't want it.

"Not now," she said.

"Tierney, please…"

"No." *I can't buy what you want to sell me.*

She heard a deep breath and sigh, followed by the muffled thump of something hitting the door. His palm? His forehead?

"I'm sorry," he said softly.

Me too, she thought, disappointment engulfing her.

"Good night, Burr," she said firmly, reaching for the light on her bedside table and turning it off. A moment later, she heard his retreating footsteps and the slamming of the guest room door.

Lying back on the bed still partially clothed, she watched as the branches outside her window made shadows on her ceiling. If he wasn't interested in her, that was his right. But not accepting a friendship with him when she longed for the *possibility* of something more was hers.

Tierney was tired of being—*how had Brittany put it?*— good and quiet, strong and sweet, shy and solitary. Part of her would always be those things, she supposed, but she'd felt herself growing and changing this summer, readying herself for passion, for love, for something more than all she'd known so far. And frankly, she'd rather take two steps forward with someone else than three steps backward with Burr.

Which led her to thoughts of John.

Hmm. She sighed, rolling to her side, her whole body slumping apathetically against her comforter.

He wasn't her type physically, she didn't exactly love the way he'd coerced her into tomorrow night's date, and the way he sometimes waxed on about the intestinal problems of his livestock patients, didn't exactly scream romance. But he'd shown some initiative in blackmailing her into a date, which—strangely enough—showed a bit of spirit she could admire. Maybe she'd misjudged him. Maybe she needed to put her best foot forward tomorrow night and do her part to find what she wanted with someone who actually wanted her back.

And as for Burr?

Well, Burr O'Leary could keep his offer of bloody friendship or take it to the devil.

***

Up for the second morning at the crack of dawn, Burr walked the entire perimeter of Moonstone Manor before Tierney left for work, taking care not to return to the cottage until after she'd left for the visitor's center.

It took willpower not to meet her downstairs for breakfast or "coincidentally" end up at the cottage for lunch at one when he knew she took a break from work at that time. But he didn't need feelings for her clouding his purpose. Was he attracted to her? Fuck, yes. Did he like her? Yes, again. A lot more than he should. It didn't change the fact, however, that indulging those feelings, on any level, was a recipe for disaster.

Maybe one day, once Sean Shanahan and his associates were in jail, Burr could reach out to Tierney again. He'd ask her out on a proper date and bring her a bouquet of roses when he picked her up. He'd hold her hand and kiss her sweet lips as much as she'd let him, and he'd wait as long as she needed to invite him into her bed. And once he was there, he'd show her all the ways he'd dreamed of having her. But there was simply no space for such feelings right now.

He didn't want to hurt her by backing away. Seeing the look on her face last night when he told her that he was "bad for her" had squeezed his heart. He'd gone upstairs hoping to offer her a friendship—*something instead of nothing*—even though it would have been a pretense since his attraction to her was growing daily.

But she'd turned him down—the conversation and, he

suspected, the friendship too. The chemistry between them, however new, was palpable. It was just *like that* with some people. It didn't matter how short a time you knew them; they were sorted into the "something more" category practically upon meeting, and anything else—including some sham, bullshit platonic friendship—wouldn't work out anyway. It would just destroy the potential for something else later.

But after what happened with Suzanne, Burr refused to be distracted.

Refused, no matter how much it sucked.

The doorbell of the cottage ringing at seven o'clock sharp was, in fact, a fairly brutal reminder of that very suckage.

Burr opened the door, staring at John without welcoming him inside.

"Brian? Huh. Hello. Are you still here?" asked John, straightening his glasses with a nervous twitch.

"Yeah."

John craned his neck, trying to look around Burr's muscular body, which took up most of the doorway. "Um. Can I come in, please? I'm here for Tierney."

When Burr had returned to the house after his sixth perimeter walk today, he heard her upstairs. First the shower, then a hair dryer, then some soft music while she put herself together. For another fucking man. A *weasel*-man. And Burr got a front row seat to the whole torturous thing.

"She's upstairs," he grunted, opening the door a crack more.

John sidestepped into the living room, then turned to look at Burr, and Burr was reminded of how physically small the veterinarian was. Almost as short as Tierney, but not half as good looking, he wore pressed khaki pants, a short-sleeve light-blue dress shirt, and loafers. He looked like a do-gooder come to sell bibles and salvation.

"How long are you staying?" asked John.

"A few weeks," said Burr, crossing his arms over his chest.

"That long?" John's eyebrows rose. "I didn't realize."

"Yeah. I'm working here now."

"Working here?"

"Security," said Burr.

"Oh." The sound was sour. "And where are you living?"

"Here."

John's chin dropped in surprise, though his eyes held Burr's. "Here. With Tierney?"

Burr sighed. As much as he didn't like this guy, he wasn't going to let him think poorly of Tierney. "In the spare room."

John's features relaxed just a touch. "I see."

"So, Doc," said Burr, "where are you taking her?"

For a split second he thought John was going to say "None of your business," but at the last moment, he must have decided that sharing details of their impending date would be a better form of torture. "There's a great restaurant in Meredith called the Lakehouse Grille. Nicest place for miles around. Great views of Winnipesaukee. Fireplaces. Candlelight. Live music. Great food. It's pretty romantic."

"Is that right?" growled Burr, clenching his arms tighter to purposely pop his biceps.

"Y-Yes, it is," said John, adjusting his glasses higher up

on his nose. His expression was veering into nervousness, like he realized he'd overplayed his hand, when his eyes suddenly slid to something—or *someone*—over Burr's shoulder. His lips parted, his face overtaken by a look of such stunned admiration, Burr couldn't help but follow his rival's gaze.

Standing on the stairs behind him was a woman who looked vaguely like Tierney Haven—but an entirely different version of the woman he'd gotten to know. She stole his breath. Just standing there, she fucking sucker-punched every ounce of oxygen out of his lungs. His lips parted. His eyes widened. And he ogled her like he'd never seen a woman before in his whole bloody life.

And maybe he hadn't.

Certainly not one who looked half as beautiful as she.

Burr already knew that she was pretty, but beneath her frumpy work clothes, severe hair, and thick glasses, Tierney Haven was a fucking stunner.

Dressed in a short black cocktail dress that fit her body like a glove and ended just above her knees, her surprisingly long legs were on full display in high heels. Sliding his gaze back up, he felt his jaw tighten at the plunging V neckline of her dress. His eyes stuttered at her throat for a moment where he paused to check out the gold and emerald Celtic cross she wore between the plump cleavage of her full breasts. Finally, he lifted his eyes to her face and felt his nostrils flare with Neanderthal lust. Her porcelain skin was white, but her lips were cherry red and her eyes had been darkened. Long, black lashes framed her glasses-free emerald eyes, and her dark hair—parted in the center, with two sections swept over her shoulders—made his fingers twitch with longing.

Her lips tilted up in a slight, triumphant smile as she caught his eyes.

"Don't you have a sweater?" he demanded, his voice gritty and irritated.

Her smile vanished. "It's seventy-five degrees out."

"That's—that's fucking chilly," he growled.

"No," she said, stepping down the rest of the stairs, "it's not."

"You take my breath away, Tierney," said Dr. Weasel, stepping forward and reaching for her hands.

With his fingernails curling into his palm, Burr had to stand by and watch as John pulled her close and kissed her cheek. When she drew away, she smiled up at John, her eyes glimmering in the dim evening light, her whole body smelling lightly of flowers or some other girly shit that made his blood hot and his dick hard.

Tierney turned to look at Burr, lifting her chin, and the warmth she offered John drained from her face. "Don't wait up."

"Oh, I *will*," he answered, giving John a hard look. "Out of respect for your brothers."

"My—? What a crock." She rolled her eyes at him, snorting once before turning back to John with a warm-honey smile. "Ready?"

"Absolutely," he said, pulling open the door for her and pulling it shut behind.

And Burr, who watched her go, could do nothing but smash his tight fist into his other hand and wish *he* was the one taking her out to dinner at a fancy candlelit place…the one who had a right to kiss her cheek or hold her hands. But he wasn't. And the phone call he needed to make reminded him of just how much danger he'd brought into her quiet life.

He pulled a burner phone from his back pocket and dialed the number Donnelley had given him on Wednesday.

"O'Leary?"

"Yes, sir. Any news?"

"You were right about Ray. I'm so goddamned sorry."

"He confessed?"

Donnelley cleared his throat. "Gunn had his own suspicions. They had his office phone tapped, and they overheard him talking to Fat Billy, giving him your whereabouts."

"Fuuuuck." *Why, Ray? Why?* "Did he say why?"

"Nah. They pulled him into an interrogation room and he folded as soon as Gunn mentioned the tap. According to a guy I know over there, he started crying at one point, saying how sorry he was about Suzy."

But not about the hit on me, thought Burr, rubbing his chest with his free hand.

He didn't want to waste his energy thinking about his rat-partner. "Now what?"

"He agreed to wear a wire when he next meets with Shanahan, but the problem is that *you* were the conduit between Ray and the New Killeens. It might spook Sean if Ray asks for a meeting. We have to wait until Sean approaches Ray."

"Sean's gotta know I'm still alive by now."

"Which could also make him suspicious that Ray's been found out," observed Donnelley. "But sooner or later, if Ray goes about his life like nothing's changed, Sean'll reach out.

And then we'll wire Ray and, hopefully, get a confession."

"Could take some time," said Burr.

"Yeah," said Donnelley, "but it's foolproof. A hit on a policeman? We need it, Burr. Gunn gave your reports to the DA, but unfortunately, because Ray was your partner, the reports aren't admissible."

"Fuck!" All those years of working with the fucking Shanahans down the drain? *Fuck you, Ray. I better not ever be face-to-face with you again.*

"Yeah," sighed Donnelley. "I know. But wiring Ray and getting a confession would implicate Shanahan and Griffin. Your testimony on the stand will help too. And of course Gunn and the other GTU guys can testify as to what they've witnessed. It might be enough for a conviction. But we *need* the attempted-murder rap. That's the coup de grace."

"Lean on Ray. You've got to get Sean's confession."

"We'll do our best."

Burr took a deep breath and sighed. "Any chance Sean tracked down the call my friend made to the hospital?"

"No way to know," said Donnelley. "But best stay put wherever you are. Look after your friend."

Burr nodded. He wasn't going anywhere until he knew that Tierney was safe. "When should I call you again?"

"Gimme a week, huh? Call me after the Labor Day weekend. Hopefully I'll have some news by then about a possible indictment."

After telling him that Suzanne was set to be discharged in a few more days, they hung up. Burr scrubbed his hands over his bristly face, falling down onto Tierney's couch with a groan. Dirty cops weren't exactly a novelty in Boston, but Ray's betrayal fucking hurt. It made Burr feel stupid too, like he should have seen the signs, like he should have known.

The clock over Tierney's fireplace chimed once, and he looked over at it. Seven thirty. He wondered if they were at the restaurant yet. With that eat-shit look she'd given him on her way out the door? She knew what she was doing. She wouldn't be back for hours. He bet she'd even draw out the evening to make it harder for him. Fuck, she *saw* the way he looked at her, like he wanted to taste every inch of her skin and kill any man who wanted the same. If she'd been uncertain about his hunger for her, she wasn't anymore. The way he'd looked at her left no room for ambiguity. He wanted her. Bad. And she knew it.

"I need a fucking drink," he muttered.

He stood up, beelining into the kitchen. He knew that she didn't serve alcohol on Wednesday out of respect for Ian, but maybe she had a little nip of something hidden away, and *damnú*, but he could use a dram tonight.

It didn't take long to uncover a mostly full bottle of Jameson Irish whiskey in the back of a cabinet over her refrigerator. *I'll buy you another bottle*, he thought, grabbing a crystal lowball glass from the adjacent cupboard and pouring himself a sip.

He knew about a hundred Irish toasts, but bearing in mind the changes he hoped were coming, pending Shanahan's indictment, he chose a short one, because it somehow seemed fitting: "*Go maire sibh bhur saol nua.*" *May you enjoy your new life.*

He downed the contents of the glass, then poured himself another before screwing the cap back on the bottle.

New life. New life.

That's what he wanted most of all—a *new* life.

He couldn't be the Burr O'Leary he was before going undercover with the New Killeens—he'd seen too much that he couldn't unsee; he was no newb cop anymore—but he was desperate to leave the last three years behind and move forward to something better.

Burr's official job with Sean's gang had been collecting money owed to the New Killeens, with Brody Halloran along as Burr's extra muscle. Burr asked for the money; Brody broke their fingers and toes if they didn't have it. If Burr and Brody had to return a second time, their faces were bashed in. If a third round of collection was required, Brody would bring a baseball bat. Brody relished his job, and Burr didn't "have a stomach for it." So Burr stood by and watched as Brody inflicted mass destruction on these poor fucks, every cell in his body wanting to arrest Brody for assault, his conscience protesting the gruesomeness of his fucking life.

Though he'd never been sent out on a hit, Burr had heard Sean order them. And he'd been there when big holes were dug in the woods outside of the city; fuck, he'd been holding the shovel once or twice when another one of Sean's associates arrived with something—*someone?*—ready to be buried in a big black plastic tarp.

Every Sunday morning, just as the church bells rang out for mass, Burr would write up his report for Ray: who owed Sean, who'd been hurt for owing Sean, how much money he'd collected, what deals were going down, who'd been murdered and who was next.

He swallowed back the Jameson, uncapped the bottle, and poured another glass. But this time he opened the cupboard, put the bottle away, and walked back into the

145

living room. Another drink or two and he'd get drunk, something he didn't especially like.

It had been three years of hell, but at least—while he was working—he'd taken some comfort in the knowledge that the information he sent back to the GTU would result in Sean's arrest and the dissolution of the New Killeens. Now? Fuck. Now those reports were all compromised because fucking Ray was a fucking informant. And the only way to take the New Killeens down was to wire Ray and use himself as bait.

Fine, thought Burr. If that was the price to have a new life, then that's what would happen. He'd wait it out in New Hampshire until Donnelley called him back to testify, and then, hopefully, they'd put Sean and his crew away for life.

He put his glass on the coffee table and lay down on the couch, which smelled like Tierney, and closed his eyes.

Tierney.

Beautiful fucking Tierney, who he wanted like he'd never wanted anyone. Besides the fact that he hadn't had a woman in three years, he just fucking liked her. A lot. She was strong and spirited, and because she was Irish, she had felt instantly familiar. She knew who she was—she wasn't one of these eejit kids on their phones all the time, posting selfies and more concerned about their Facebook statuses than their actual lives. She knew how to swear in Irish and put her brothers in their places with a spatula, and damn it, but when her green eyes flashed with protest or pleasure or anger or want, he could feel it all the way to his heart. All the way to the tip of his cock.

After the things he'd seen and done, he had no right to someone as clean and fine as Tierney Haven, but more and more, his mind replaced the ugliness of his life with the Shanahans with fantasies of a life with her.

One day. One day.

Someday.

It was the front door closing that woke him up. When he opened his eyes, the first thing he saw was Tierney, standing over him, what was left of his whiskey in her hands.

"Hi," she said, pausing with the glass at her lips, her green eyes holding his blue as he slowly sat up.

"What time is it?" he asked.

"Late," she answered.

Her lipstick wasn't as bright as was when she left, and all he could think was that he desperately hoped the reason for that was food and drink, not John's fucking weasel lips on hers.

"*Sláinte,*" he said softly, watching as she tilted the crystal glass back and took a long sip of the amber liquid before handing the glass back to him and joining him on the couch.

Positioning his lips over the exact place where hers had been, he took a sip too. Then he sat back beside her, shoulder to shoulder, both of them staring straight ahead. She toed off her shoes and put her feet up on the coffee table, and he did the same, staring at her little white feet next to his, which were so much bigger and darker.

"Don't you want to hear about my date?" she asked without looking at him.

"Nope."

"Isn't that what *friends* do? Sit around and talk about their dates?"

"I don't know," said Burr. "I haven't had a real friend in years."

"Me neither," said Tierney after a moment, her voice soft and thoughtful.

"Besides," said Burr, his voice rough with longing, "I'm *not* your friend. It's a little more complicated than that. Don't you think?"

"Huh. Are you sure? Because last night I'm pretty sure you were going to give me the 'Let's Be Friends' speech."

"Last night I almost made a big mistake," he said gruffly. "It's not that I don't want your friendship. I do. But I want other things too. By itself, it wouldn't be enough."

"Oh," she murmured. She took a deep breath, crossing one ankle over the other before exhaling slowly. "What are you going to do about it?"

"Right now? Nothing." He hated the answer, but it was the only fair one to give.

"Okay. Rephrasing. What do you *want* to do about it?"

"So many things," he half-whispered, half-growled, his tone managing to be dirty and reverent at the same time. But his admission came with a caveat and she deserved to know what it was. "But my hands will stay tied until Sean Shanahan is behind bars. I can't be distracted. I won't risk your safety, Tierney. I can't."

For the first time since sitting down, Tierney turned her head to look at him. He felt her gaze, the way her eyes studied his face, and it took all of his strength to stay still and not to turn to her too. If he did, his lips would be millimeters from hers and it would be im-fucking-possible not to kiss her.

Finally, she faced front again, her breasts rising softly in her sexy fucking dress as she took another deep breath. "I can wait."

His neck jerked to face her, and while she didn't turn back to look at him, she lifted her chin, her bloodline showing—all the strength of one little green island jammed into that one simple gesture.

"Wait?"

"For you," she said.

"*Wait* for me?" he murmured.

She nodded once, crossing her arms under her breasts, which made them swell against the V of her dress. "We'll wait until Sean Shanahan is in jail and then we can…" She cleared her throat. "Well, we can see what happens. Between us."

"It could take some time," he said, but his heart was already racing, thumping with hope and excitement behind his ribs.

"I have plenty of time," she said. "There's only one of you."

"You don't have to do this."

She set her jaw and scoffed softly. "Been a long time since I did anything I didn't want to do."

"Tierney—"

"Burr." She stopped him with a single word, a single sound, his name on her tongue the key to trading his will for hers. She turned to look at him, cocking her head to the side. "Don't dangle a steak in front of me, then tell me to eat dog food. Don't tell me you want me, then tell me to move on, because I can't. I won't. My mind's fixed on you. If things don't play out between us, I'll always wonder."

My mind's fixed on you. She took his fucking breath away. Zero artifice. Zero games. Her frankness and honesty were everything he craved after years of lying and treachery.

"Me too," he said, his breathing shallow and jagged as he lifted his eyes to hers. "I'd always wonder. I'd always wish that we'd...I don't know...given each other a try."

"Regret is the worst hell there is," she said.

"*Is fhearr fheuchainn na bhith san dui,*" he whispered. *I'd rather try than only hope.*

She nodded at him. "So let's not wonder. Let's just...wait. Together."

"And in the meantime...?" he asked, not even certain what he was hoping for.

"We're not *friends,*" she said, her inflection on the word *friends* making it clear how she felt about it.

"Agreed," he said, dropping his eyes to the swell of her breasts before lifting them again. "What else?"

"No more dates with Dr. John," she promised.

He smiled at her. "Thank Christ."

She grinned back at him, her smile so much easier now than it was when he first arrived, and fuck, in that moment, he wanted it to be the thing that started and ended every last one of his days.

"And I'll put this dress in the back of my closet for now."

"Small mercies," he muttered, then added, "But keep it safe for me?"

"I will."

"So what do we *call* this?" he asked.

"Nothing." She shrugged. "*Us,* I guess." Leaning forward, she took another tiny sip of whiskey before standing up. "Now that that's sorted, time for bed."

"Bed," he growled, watching the way her body moved as she stood up. And suddenly he couldn't bear it that she was leaving his sight. On impulse, he grabbed her hand, holding it, staring at where his flesh touched hers. He rubbed her soft palm with his thumb in slow circles, the pad lingering on the band at the back of her Claddagh ring, dragging out the moment, the contact; wishing that he could swoop her into his arms and carry her to her bed.

When his cock was thick and long, straining against the denim of his jeans, he half-whispered, half-grunted, "*Oiche mhaith, aisling.*" *Good night, sweetheart.*

Her voice was low and breathless when she gulped before answering, "*Oiche mhaith, m'Burr.*"

Good night, my Burr.

Then she slipped her hand from his, leaned down to pick up her sexy shoes, and walked slowly up the stairs.

CHAPTER NINE

Tierney sat huddled in the bleachers next to Brittany, both women in winter coats with empty cups of hot cocoa on the bench beside them.

"Whoo! Go Brian!" yelled Brittany, hoisting one fist in the air as Burr gained possession of the puck and raced across the ice, the blades of his skates *whooshing* as he chased it toward Ian's goal.

"Ian's coming! Go faster!" screamed Tierney, jumping to her feet, unable to look away as Burr paused just beyond the center line, stilled the puck, drew back his stick, and *whack!*

The puck sailed across the ice, straight into the netting of Ian's open goal.

"Five to four! Game shot!" yelled Rory from the center of the ice.

"Yes!" cried Brittany, jumping up and down next to Tierney. "He won!"

Tierney waved at Ian, who gave her a good-natured grin from the ice, shrugging his massive shoulders as his skates *kish-kished* over to Burr to shake hands.

While Ian and Burr had been playing for the last hour, Burr hadn't spared many glances up at the stands—he'd been totally focused on the game, and Tierney, who'd attended plenty of boring hockey games in her life, had been totally riveted. Watching his raw talent was exciting, but his intensity made something inside of her tighten and quiver. Did he commit that sort of dedicated concentration to *everything* in his life? And if so, and if they made it to the day that Sean Shanahan was imprisoned, would he focus all of it on her? The very thought made her shiver as Brittany looped her arm through Tierney's and pulled her down the bleacher stairs to the ice.

Burr and Ian high-fived, then Burr skated over to the boards while Ian went to retrieve the puck. As Burr approached, he finally looked up at Tierney. His face glistened with sweat, but his eyes sparkled when he unclipped the helmet from under his chin and took it off. He grinned at her, then closed one eye in a sexy wink. And Tierney? Lord, Tierney felt that wink all the way to her toes and everywhere in between.

M'Burr. M'Burr. Mine.

"What'd you think?" he asked, his body slamming into the boards as his skates *whooshed* to a stop.

"I never enjoyed hockey so much," she confessed.

He swiped the sleeve of Ian's borrowed Bruins sweater over his sweaty brow. "Been a little while since I played."

"Couldn't tell," she said, feeling a swell of pride at the way he'd held his own against her brother.

"Son, that slap shot was *insane*!" said Ian, thumping Burr on the back. "Never saw a shot that good 'cept by a guy in college...shit, what was that guy's name? Oh, fuck! I think he went to UMass too. You probably *knew* him!"

"Lots of good guys on the team," said Burr, his smile fading a touch.

"Nah," said Ian. "This guy was *epic*. Um...Fuck! What

was his name?"

Rory skated up. "Do we need to put away the goals or anything?"

Ian shook his head. "Lou does it." He looked up, over Tierney's shoulder, and when she followed his eyes, she found the rink manager approaching. "Done here, Lou. Thanks for the ice time."

"Tough break, Ian. I saw that slap shot," said Lou. He shifted his eyes to Burr. "You local?"

"Nah. Just here for a little bit. From Boston."

"Huh. Well, if you're ever local, we could use you."

"League play?"

Lou nodded. "Local league…yeah. But it's serious. Ian knows."

Ian nodded eagerly. "Oh, yeah. It's no joke."

"Well, you're welcome to use the showers," said Lou, gesturing to the locker room door with his chin. "I gotta get the ice cleaned up for disco night."

Burr locked eyes with Tierney, lowering his voice to a hum. "Wait for me, *aisling*?"

She nodded, feeling warm all over. "Definitely."

"Burr O'Leary!" bellowed Ian. "Burr *O-fucking* Leary! That was the guy's name. Fast Irish fucker. *Wicked* slap shot. From UMass. Fuck! I *knew* it would come to me!"

Burr was stepping through the gate, but he froze as Ian yelled his real name, whipping his eyes to Tierney.

She licked her lips, turning to Ian. "Burr O'—*what*? What kind of, um, name is that? *Burr*. Like 'Brrr, I'm cold'? Or, um, burr, like—like Mom's accent? Or—"

Burr stepped forward, purposely knocking into her. His arm shot out around her waist to steady her, his bulky glove digging into her hip and telling her to stop blathering. She looked up at him, her eyes meeting his.

Stop, he mouthed.

"No," said Ian from behind them. "Just Burr. It was his name."

Burr's eyes slipped to her lips for a second before he released her gently, looking over his shoulder at Ian. "Yeah, I remember him. Sort of a cocky bastard."

Tierney chortled, then disguised it as a cough.

"Maybe so," said Ian, "but he had a hell of a slap shot."

"Yeah," said Burr, winking at Tierney a second time before walking passed her, headed for the locker room. "I guess he was okay."

Burr followed after Ian, and Rory after Burr, stopping for a moment to press a quick kiss to Brittany's lips. "What's next?"

"Dinner?" she suggested. "At the Mug? Burgers?"

"Sure," said Rory, looking vaguely disappointed, like he wouldn't mind if "next" was one-on-one time in Brittany's bed.

"Ew," said Tierney, turning away from the happy couple to watch as the Zamboni started its rounds. "Get a room, you two."

"Go hang out with the boys for a few minutes, huh?" Brittany asked her boyfriend. "Give me and Tierney some girl time. We'll meet you guys in the lobby."

"Yeah," said Rory, kissing her again. "Okay."

As Rory headed off to the locker room, Brittany grabbed Tierney's arm. "So? I need an update!"

Suddenly Tierney remembered what she'd said to Burr last night about not making a new friend in a long time, and she wondered if she'd been wrong. Brittany Manion, for all her intimidating beauty and wealth, was gaga for Rory and kind to Tierney and Ian. Maybe Brittany could be the new friend Tierney so craved. In fact, maybe she already was.

"We had a talk last night."

"A *talk*? Ooo. Okay. Good or bad?" asked Britt, steering them toward the lobby of the arena.

"Good," said Tierney. "I think."

"But…you're not sure?"

She was *pretty* sure, based on the giddy grins she and Burr had been trading all day. Starting this morning, they'd shared coffee and breakfast together, then taken his first perimeter walk together. And later, when it had been too busy for her to return home for lunch, he'd walked up the hill with a sandwich for her.

No, there'd been no hand-holding or kisses. But he was back to calling her *aisling*, and there was an easiness, almost a relief, between them after their talk last night, and Tierney felt more excited, more happy, than she'd felt in a long, long time.

"It was *good*," she said firmly, grinning at Brittany.

"Wait a second!" Brittany gasped. "Is that a *smile*? I didn't know you had so many teeth, Tierney Haven!"

Her silliness only made Tierney smile wider, shaking her head as she looked down at her shoes. "What can I say?"

"You can tell me what you guys talked about!" Brittany screeched.

"Shhhh! Oh, my God, they're going to hear you," said Tierney, shooting a glance at the locker room door as they passed by.

"Pshaw! They're in the shower," said Brittany, pushing

open the doors that led to the warm lobby. "Now tell!"

She looked askance at her brother's ~~gir~~—no, at her *~~friend~~*—wishing she could tell Brittany everything.

"He's really, um, well…he's really serious about—oh, yes!—um, sorting out the security issues for Moonstone Manor. Once he's done with the—the, um, job, and we don't work together anymore, we'll…you know…give things a, um, try." She nodded to add punctuation to her lies. "That's, um—that was our talk."

"Gosh, that sucks," said Brittany. "Is there a rule about dating where you work?"

Oooo! That was a good one.

"Yes," said Tierney, "there, um, is, and it's a serious offence, so…"

Brittany scrunched up her nose. "So that's it? You're…waiting?"

"Until the end of the season." Tierney shrugged, hoping that her white lies were convincing. "Yeah."

"*How?*" demanded Brittany, her voice veering into shriek territory. "How can you do that? It's got to be torture! You totally want each other, and you're living in the same house!"

"I'm…" Tierney bit her lip. She was about to say that part of her was grateful for the time because she was so inexperienced, and she wanted to be comfortable with Burr before things progressed physically between them. But she was worried about what Brittany would say if she confessed that she was a twenty-seven-year-old virgin.

"You're what?" asked Britt, a sweet smile on her face as she cocked her head to the side and gently pushed a lock of Tierney's dark hair behind her ear.

"I've never…" She cleared her throat. "I've never been with someone…like—like Brian."

"Oh," said her friend, nodding conspiratorially. "I get it. He's…*really* intense, right? But the intense ones are—"

"No," said Tierney quickly, shaking her head. "No. I mean…I mean, I've never been with *anyone.*"

Her friend's eyes widened. "Oh."

"It's weird. *I'm* weird."

"No, it's not." Brittany insisted. "No, you're not."

"I'm twenty-seven."

"I know, but—"

"So it's *super* weird," said Tierney, pressing her still-cold hands to her heating-up cheeks. "He's…I mean, I'm…"

"You're a virgin," Brittany blurted out. Then she shrugged casually. "So what? We were all virgins at some point, Tierney."

"How old were you when—"

"Doesn't matter."

"How old, Britt?"

"Nineteen."

Tierney's shoulders, which were up around her ears, fell a little. "Eight years younger than me."

"Who cares?" asked Britt.

"I do. It's freakish."

"I don't think so," said Brittany thoughtfully. "In fact, if I could go back in time and not sleep with Travis and not sleep with Ben? If Rory could have somehow been my first?" She sighed, her smile small and wistful. "I'd give a lot for that. I'd give a lot for Rory to be my *only.*"

Tierney was generally grossed out by the image of one of her brothers in an intimate scenario, but she was too comforted by Brittany's words to care. "Really?"

Brittany nodded. "Yeah. Nobody's ever loved me like Rory." She held up her hands. "I know that you and Brian aren't—aren't, you know, *in love.*" She shrugged again, folding her hands on her lap. "But...to be with a guy who really cares about you the first time? That's the best."

In love? Even the words sounded ridiculous.

"We barely know each other!"

Brittany took a deep breath. "Over Valentine's Day, the *Boston Globe* did this really cool article about these four couples who'd all met and married within four weeks of meeting each other and who were still married after forty years. It was called 'Four and Forty.' One of the couples met at the wedding of mutual friends. Another met on line at Hardee's. Another at a water park where they both had summer jobs. And the last when she got a flat tire, and he stopped to help her. And I remember reading it and just thinking to myself, I*t's luck.* It's all about luck. It's about the teeny, tiny everyday choices you make on your journey...like saying yes to a wedding invitation or deciding to grab a hamburger after work or applying for a summer job at a water park or—oh, my God, sometimes it's not even up to you! The fourth woman drove over a nail on her way to Easter dinner at her sister's house one town over. And *bam*! This guy stops to help her and something just...*happens*!

"There are seven and a half billion people in this world. Seven and a half *billion.* Finding *that* person? *Your* person? It has so little to do with how you meet them and where you meet them and how long you date. You know I was married before, right? Did you know that Travis and I went to kindergarten together? We did. But our marriage only lasted for three years. Why? Because I wasn't the right girl for him, and he wasn't the right guy for me. And you know what? Thank God! Because he was part of the journey that led here. To Rory. And Tierney? *Bam!* Rory's it. He's the love of my life. He's the one I never knew I was waiting for."

Tierney stared at Brittany, loving her confidence and faith, and weighing it against her own notions about the world and luck and fate and love. And she found that despite any fears she had about opening her heart—and body—to love, they were mitigated by her growing feelings for Burr, which overshadowed everything, which, despite their short acquaintance, couldn't be denied.

"You girls ready to go?"

Rory's voice jolted Tierney and Brittany from their tête-à-tête, and as her friend jumped up to grab Rory's hand, Tierney shifted on the bench and looked straight up…into the light-blue eyes of Burr O'Leary.

And…*BAM!*

She felt it everywhere—that breathtaking, heart-squeezing, full-body feeling that he was the missing puzzle piece of her. And she had a sudden and overwhelming notion that spending a day—any day—without seeing his face would be the saddest day she could ever imagine.

She didn't know what this feeling was; a week ago, she would have said that love at first sight was a myth—a *ridiculous* myth. But now? Looking into Burr O'Leary's beautiful eyes? She wasn't sure of anything except that forty years from now, she still wanted to feel like this.

"I'm starving," he said, stopping in front of Tierney and running his knuckles gently against her cheek as he searched her eyes.

"Me too."

"You ready, *aisling*?" he asked, grinning down at her.

I'm getting there. Fast.

She nodded at him, feeling her smile break out across her face as she looked into his beautiful blue eyes. "I'm ready."

***

The Mug was the sort of local pub-style restaurant where Burr felt most comfortable. Cold beer. Good burgers. A couple of pool tables in the back. And the owners obviously knew Rory and Tierney, whom they greeted by name, asking about Ian and their parents before seating them at a table by the windows.

Ian had declined their invitation to dinner, heading back to Summerhaven to manage the final-night dinner/dance for the single parents' week. Because Ian wasn't in attendance, Rory had ordered two pitchers of cold Sam Adams Summer for the table. After he poured the four glasses, Burr slid his own glass closer and sat back, watching as Rory lifted his beer and intoned:

"Seo sláinte an tséitéara, an ghadaí, an trodaí, agus an óltóra!

Má dhéanann tu séitéireacht, go ndéana tú séitéireacht ar an mbás,

Má ghoideann tú, go ngoide tú croí mná;

Má throideann tú, go dtroide tú i leith do bhráthar,

Agus má ólann tú, go n-óla tú liom féin."

Tierney and Burr lifted their glasses with a murmur of "*Sláinte*," about to clink and dink, when Brittany stopped them.

"Wait!"

All eyes slid to Rory's girlfriend, who looked

exasperated. "Sorry to be the odd one out here, but I have no idea what Rory just said!"

Burr chuckled softly. "It was all good. I promise."

"I want to *know*," insisted Brittany. "Translation, please!"

"If you cheat," said Rory, his eyes tender as he regarded his girlfriend, "may you cheat death."

"If you steal," said Burr, grinning at Tierney, "may you steal a woman's heart."

"If you fight," said Tierney, sliding her eyes to Rory, "may you fight for a brother."

"And if you drink," said Rory, turning to Brittany with a look of complete devotion, "may you *always* drink with me."

"*Now* let's drink. *Sláinte*," said Brittany softly, a smile on her lips as she clinked her glass with Rory's and raised it to her mouth.

Burr took a sip of the cold beer, humming a satisfied "Mmmm" before placing the glass back down on the table. Rory leaned forward to give Brittany a quick kiss on the lips before they turned back to Burr and Tierney.

"So…how long have you two been together?" Burr asked them.

Brittany smiled. "Since May."

"Memorial Day to be exact," said Rory, winking at Brittany before turning back to Burr.

He would have guessed longer—they looked so damned happy together. "Only three months."

"Yeah," said Rory, "but we knew each other when we were teenagers. Brittany went to Summerhaven as a camper."

"…and basically tortured him all summer because he

wasn't allowed to date her," added Tierney from beside him.

"I wonder what that's like," Burr deadpanned, giving her a look. "To be tortured by a woman."

Her cheeks flushed as she turned back to her brother and Brittany, quickly changing the subject and asking Rory what group was arriving tomorrow for the final week of the summer.

Part of Burr felt like he'd struck a deal with the devil last night, agreeing to—to—hell, what exactly had they agreed to, anyway?

To live together while he protected her from any possible New Killeen threat.

To mutually want each other on a near-painful level while denying themselves.

Only to act on that longing when Sean Shanahan was behind bars.

As if my life wasn't messy and sucky enough, he thought, taking another sip of beer. *Now we can add extreme sexual frustration into the equation as well.*

Tierney shifted a little closer to him on the bench they shared until her hip grazed his, and he inhaled sharply at the contact. This woman. Damn, but keeping his hands to himself was proving impossible. At the ice rink, he'd rammed into her to stop her fibbing-diarrhea, but he couldn't deny the benefits of his quick thinking. Even through layers of hockey gear, she'd felt perfect against him. And later, in the lobby, when she'd looked up at him like he was a god come to life? Yeah. He couldn't resist reaching out to touch her cheek. But if he kept it up—these little touches—it would be a slippery slope.

Self-control, boyo. Self-control.

Hopefully, the next time he called Donnelley, Sean would already be in custody.

The waitress arrived with a huge plate of nachos and took their dinner orders just as his stomach let out a bellow. It had been a while since he'd played hockey, but knowing that Tierney was watching meant that he'd pulled out all the stops and skated his damned heart out. And now he was *beyond* hungry.

"So Brian," said Brittany, sliding a gooey clump of cheesy chips to her plate, "I guess you'll still be here for Labor Day weekend, huh?"

He nodded as he wolfed down some chips and chased them with beer.

"Are you coming to the party at Summerhaven?" asked Brittany.

He shifted inquiring eyes to Tierney. *What is it, and are we going?*

Tierney wiped her mouth before speaking. "It's one of two annual parties that Rory hosts at the camp. One at Memorial Day and another at Labor Day. He opens up the campground to all of the local towns. There are games for kids, boating, swimming—"

"Are *you* going swimming?" he interrupted, remembering how she looked last night in that dress with the plunging neck.

She chuckled. "Probably. Do you swim?"

He reached for more nachos. Whether or not *he* swam was completely irrelevant. All that mattered was seeing *her* in a bathing suit. "Yeah."

"It's a really fun day," she added, her eyes sparkling.

"There are fireworks too," said Brittany, sliding a

suggestive smile to Rory.

"And a barn dance," he added, his voice gravelly.

Tierney made a gagging noise. "My food's gonna come up if you two don't give it a rest."

Burr laughed looking back and forth between Rory and Brittany. "Need a room much?"

"Yeah," said Rory at the same time Brittany said, "No!"

Deciding that maybe her brother and his girlfriend needed a little alone time, Burr nudged Tierney. "Any chance you play pool?"

"Pool?" she asked, her lips twitching. "Um, yeah. I may have played once or twice."

"Table over there's free." When she didn't answer right away, he nudged her again. "Come on. I can give you pointers if you need…"

"Yeah, Tierney," said Rory, looking at his sister with a grin that somehow managed to border on sinister. "He can give you some pointers."

Burr's glance rested on Rory for an extra second, wondering what he meant by that, but Tierney sliding off the bench beside him distracted him.

"Have fun," said Rory in a singsong voice, waggling his fingers at Burr before turning back to his girlfriend.

Over at the pool table, Tierney was racking the balls with precision. When she was finished, she stood staring at the pool cues like they weren't all crappy restaurant sticks that had seen better days.

"You playing, Tierney?" asked an older gentleman at an adjacent table.

She nodded, winking at him. "Sure am, Bobby."

Bobby looked at Burr, stroking his gray beard. "You

ever played her before?"

Burr glanced at little Tierney, who'd finally chosen a cue and was chalking the tip like her life depended on it.

"Uh…no." *What in the world am I missing?*

"Heh heh," cackled the old timer, turning to his buddies. "He ain't never played Tierney Haven before."

"Is that l'il Tierney Haven?" asked one of the other two men at the table. "Well, hell. Lookit you. How's your folks doing?"

Tierney turned to them, smiling at the men like she'd known them all her life. "Real good. How's Norma doing?"

"She's down in Portsmouth with the grandchildren this weekend."

"Give her my best?" asked Tierney.

"Will do!"

"Who, eh, who you playing against here, Tierney?" asked Bobby, flicking a derisive look at Burr.

"This is Brian," she said, offering him a sheepish grin before looking back at the three older men. "He's visiting."

"Brian, huh?" Bobby nodded at him. "What do you do there, Brian?"

"Security," he said, absently grabbing one of the pool cues that Tierney had passed over. "Up here for a couple of weeks giving Tierney a hand."

"Huh."

How he managed to say, "Not impressed," in one mumbled syllable was a feat, thought Burr.

"He beat Ian on the ice today down in Gilford," said Tierney, hands on her hips, giving the old codgers a look that said, "Back off."

"That right?" Bobby lifted his chin, nodding in

appreciation. "Guess you're not all useless, then. Ian's good on skates."

"But Brian's slap shot was *wicked*," said Tierney, lining up the cue ball. She turned to Burr. "You want to break? Or should I?"

Hmm. She'd racked the balls, chosen her cue, and chalked it. Now she stood at the head of the table, hip cocked and eyes waiting. Between her brother's eat-shit smile and these old fellas giving him a hard time? Maybe Tierney wasn't some billiards babe in the woods.

"Go for it," he said.

She grinned at him. "Have any tips for me?"

He could kick himself for suggesting she needed any. "Nope. None I can think of."

She chuckled softly, lining up her shot before smacking the cue ball in an almost-perfect break shot that sent the striped-yellow 9 and the striped-blue 10 into the side pockets simultaneously.

"Oh," she said, looking up with a wide smile. "Did you want to play stripes and solids or…?"

"Yeah," he said, stepping up to the table. "That's fine."

She lined up her next shot, sending the striped-red 15 ball into the left corner. Chalking her cue, she stared at the table for a second before sitting on the edge with her cue behind her back. As she looked up at Burr with a cheeky grin, the cue tip hit the white ball perfectly and the striped-green 14 ball rolled into the right corner.

"Now you're just showing off," he said, amused by her antics.

This was a side of Tierney he hadn't seen yet—all confident and teasing—and he had to admit, it was pretty fucking sexy to see a woman who knew her way around a pool table like she did. Petite little beauty knocking balls into pockets like she was born to do it. Damn. Badass and tempting all at once.

Bobby cleared his throat. "Son, Tierney here was the All Lakes Champ five years running. She's a regular shark, this girl."

"So I see," said Burr, glancing at the table before lifting his eyes to Tierney. "You want to finish up here so we can have our food or what?"

"Don't *you* want to play?" she asked all innocent-like.

"My guess is that you're going to nail the 13 into the side, the 11 into that corner, and bounce the 12 off the side and dunk it in the other corner. Right?"

"Maybe I'll mess up," she said as she sank the 13 exactly where he said she would.

"Five-year champ? I don't think so," said Burr.

"You never know," she said, knocking the 11 into the opposite corner with a sassy grin.

Burr chuckled at her, enjoying the views of her body leaning over the table, the way she confidently lined up her shots and sank them. He imagined her at one of his local haunts in Boston, the two of them playing Suzanne and Connor, and everyone surprised that his small, mostly soft-spoken girlfriend was a pool shark too.

Girlfriend.

Huh.

Wouldn't *that* be something? For Tierney Haven to end up as his girlfriend?

Wouldn't that make up for the last three lonely years living in the gutter with rats?

Wouldn't that be something to live for? To wake up next to and fall asleep beside?

Tierney Haven…all his?

"Eight ball," she whispered in his ear, jerking his thoughts back to reality as her soft breath kissed his skin. "Left corner."

Crack. Slide. Plop.

She won the game with every solid ball still left on the table, exactly where they were when she broke less than ten minutes ago.

"What a woman." One of the men at the table beside them sighed.

I couldn't agree more, thought Burr.

"Sorry I didn't warn you," said Tierney after hanging up her cue. "But you sort of set yourself up with that 'pointers' comment. I couldn't resist."

"You're a woman of hidden talents," he said, placing his cue on the rack next to hers.

"Nah," she said, looking shy again now that the game was over. "Just good at pool."

"You're good at a lot more than that," he said, gazing into her emerald-green eyes, and wishing with all of his might that Sean was already in jail.

"*Now* who needs a room?" chirped Brittany, who suddenly appeared beside them. "Come on. Food's getting cold."

Tierney turned to follow Brittany back to the table, and Burr said a silent prayer that he'd have enough patience to keep her safety a priority no matter how surprising, no matter how tempting, no matter how completely *wonderful* she was.

chapter ten

Over the following week, they settled into a groove together—sharing meals, taking long walks around the grounds of Moonstone Manor, visiting with Tierney's brothers and Brittany on Wednesday night, and spending quiet time together in the evenings, watching TV or reading.

Tierney was a balm for the upheaval of Burr's soul, which had been tried and tested, burned and battered over his long years in the service of Sean Shanahan. Like a soldier returning home after a long and gruesome battle, Burr desperately craved the well-ordered gentleness of Tierney's quiet life, and to his everlasting gratitude, she shared it with him selflessly.

On their early morning and evening walks, often hand in hand, she'd point out flowers (she *said* her favorites were asters, but she always bent down to pick buttercups as they walked), or points of historical interest. There was a wishing well at one far corner of the property, and she still brought a penny to throw in every time. And hidden in a quiet copse, there was a stone bench with the initials LCG (Lily Christopher Gish) engraved on it. Almost completely overtaken by wild lilies, he was fairly certain it was Tierney's favorite place on the entire estate because she smiled so broadly whenever they passed it.

He'd finally seen the view from the lookout tower,

which was sweeping and grand, showing the entirety of the New Hampshire Lakes Region, but it didn't hold a candle to Tierney's smile as she took it in, wisps of her black hair blown back from her cheeks as she grinned at him. "Beautiful, right?"

"Never seen anything more beautiful," he'd answered, looking straight into her eyes.

It was hell not to reach for her, not to touch her and kiss her, and at night, when she closed her door and turned off her light, his deprived body longed for hers, ached for hers with an unholy level of arousal. He'd taken to long walks in the dark, followed by cold showers before bed. It didn't help much. He wanted her. Bad.

But perhaps even more important, he'd begun to realize that he needed her—Tierney Haven was bringing him back to a place of hope after a long sojourn with the damned.

Was it possible to spend three years in hell and leave it behind?

It had always seemed so unfair to Burr that names became inextricably bound in the world of crime. *I say Hinckley, you say Reagan. I say Oswald, you say Kennedy.* Why should murderers have the legacy of their names being bound with men of honor? They didn't deserve it, and he hated that it was so. And now, he wondered, would his name—Burr O'Leary—be bound to the New Killeens for life? Would both be spoken in the same breath forever?

You've heard of Burr O'Leary! They guy who brought down the New Killeens thirty years ago!

No tale of the New Killeens would be complete without mentioning Burr O'Leary, the Boston cop who lived undercover with them for three years and...

If it isn't Burr O'Leary, yer man who knocked off the New Killeens!

He didn't *want* that legacy. In fact, he hated it. Passionately.

Burr knew he had done his job and done it well, but he had not come back from the battle unscathed. And he didn't know how to bear a life wherein he was reminded—good-naturedly, but at every turn—that once upon a time, he'd done something good that had required him to see and do terrible things. He'd watched as men had their limbs broken, lives destroyed, and unmarked graves filled. He never wanted to think about the New Killeens again as long as he lived.

And being with Tierney made that possible.

She didn't ask much about his life in Boston, outside of questions about his family, and that was fine with Burr, because he really didn't want to discuss his work. Her life—her sweet, serene life—was a throwback to simpler times, eons away from the gritty streets of Southie and the treacherous corners of Dorchester.

He'd checked online, and there hadn't been one murder or robbery in Moultonborough since before 2004. Well over a decade. Not that there wasn't some violent crime here and there, but compared to the rest of the country, or—for fuck's sake—Boston? It was practically nonexistent. It was a different world than his, and part of him—a *growing* part of him—coveted it.

"Summerhaven party tomorrow," said Tierney as they walked the south path, the last rays of dying sun filtering through the trees in gold and orange.

They'd been over to her brother's camp this morning to help set up, and once again, Burr had been struck by the love and loyalty between the Haven siblings, which inevitably made him think of Suzy. He'd considered calling her once or twice, from a pay phone or his burner, just to check on her. But he figured it was better to wait. As soon as Sean and his gang were arrested, Burr could return to Boston, explain everything to his family, and hopefully resume his place in their lives. He desperately wanted to be a son and brother again, and—for the first time, thank you, Lord—an uncle too.

"Yeah. What time do you want to go?"

"We can leave here around one thirty. As soon as I'm done here, okay?"

"Sure thing."

Tierney had explained that as of Labor Day on Monday, Moonstone Manor would only be offering tours at nine, ten, eleven, and twelve o'clock every morning—and only on Fridays, Saturdays, and Sundays. Her free days and September afternoons would be spent readying the estate for the long winter ahead.

It had been almost two weeks now since he'd arrived on her doorstep and just about as long since she'd made that fateful call to Mass General. By this point, Burr was almost positive that either one, her phone call to the hospital hadn't been traced, or two, if it had been, and they'd tried calling her number, received an out-of-service message, and considered it a dead end. The New Killeens worked quick, and they would have shown up by now if they had her address. That said, he still wouldn't leave her until he was one hundred percent certain that her safety was assured.

While lying in bed at night, trying *not* to think about Tierney, he'd processed some of his feelings about Ray's betrayal. He still didn't understand how Ray could sell him out like that. For three years, Burr had considered Ray his best friend, his lifeline to his old life; almost a brother. But somehow, Ray had been behind Suzy's shooting and Fat Billy's unsuccessful hit on him. Why? Money? Power? Burr didn't know, and mostly he didn't fucking care. It didn't matter. Ray was a rat. The rest was just noise.

But knowing that Ray, someone Burr had trusted implicitly, could so casually betray him made him feel unsettled. Would he ever be able to trust another partner? How could he do his job effectively in the future if he couldn't let down his guard around a future partner? It bothered him. It worried him. His job was not just his livelihood but a large part of his identity, and if he couldn't do it well, who *was* he?

"Penny for your thoughts," said Tierney, taking his hand in hers and braiding their fingers together.

He welcomed her touch. It made it harder for him not to want more, but it also soothed the riot of emotions inside of him. "Just…thinking."

"Exactly. Ergo the offer of a penny."

"Bad deal for you," he said. "They're not worth a penny, *aisling*."

He just didn't want to talk about Ray or the New Killeens or his job. The closest he could come to talking about any of it was mustering up a question about his hometown.

"You ever been to Boston?" he asked.

"Many times," she answered. "To the museums. To Broadway shows. Shopping for a first communion dress with my mother. Once for the Saint Patrick's parade."

"What did you think?" he asked.

"About the parade?" she murmured, hedging the question. "Well. I…um…"

"You didn't like it?"

"Not at all. I was terrified," she confessed. "There were so many people, and everyone was drunk and rowdy, bumping into each other and getting into fights. I…I don't know. They were drinking green beer and yelling 'air-inn go braw' in butchered Irish, and I—I guess I just didn't get it."

"Probably because you're Irish every day," he said. "You don't need a parade to celebrate it."

"Maybe…but no," she said, "it was more than that. I think it was just too much for me. The city. The craziness. I'd prefer a family dinner of corned beef, mashed potatoes, and cabbage. An Irish blessing before. A long walk after."

He chuckled softly at her quiet idea for the perfect St. Paddy's Day celebration, so different from the way Boston celebrated—and yet so completely appealing.

"Yer puir Oirish, Tierney."

"Guilty," she said.

"So you've only been to Boston as a tourist," he confirmed, dropping the accent.

She nodded. "Yes. I've never lived there. I've never lived anywhere but New Hampshire."

"Never visited friends there? During college? Stayed in a dorm for a weekend?"

"Nope. I've never stayed longer than a night, and frankly, I was always relieved to come home." She chuckled softly. "Unless you haven't noticed, I'm a country mouse, not a city mouse."

He'd noticed. Of course he'd noticed. It was one of the

most appealing things about her: that she didn't seem to require the modern conveniences that most of the woman in her generation took for granted.

"I saw you got your phone replaced."

"I did. Someone broke it."

"Sorry about that."

"Ah, it's all right. I only use it to talk to family."

"I never see you on Facebook or Instagram or anything," he said as they headed down the hill, back toward her cottage.

"I have accounts on both," she answered, "but I'm bad at keeping them updated."

"You don't care about them?"

She sighed. "Not really. I mean, everyone I care about is *here*. I see them. They see me. Why would they need to look at my Facebook page? Actually…maybe that's a little selfish. My mom might like it—to see the boys and me at family dinner or enjoying a day at Summerhaven—but I share pictures with them when I visit them, which is at least once a month, so…no. You're right. I guess I don't care about Facebook or Instagram. Life isn't lived on a computer. It's here," she said, spreading out her free arm, "all around us."

Was it any wonder this unique woman had so captured his imagination?

He squeezed her fingers gently, thinking about the fact that sooner or later he'd need to go back to Boston. His life was there—his job, Suzy, everything. Not only would he have to go back to testify against Sean and the New Killeens, but he needed to mend fences with his family. Not to mention, there were friends there he hadn't seen in years. He should catch up with them, right?

Soon he'd leave her and go back to Boston.

…which sounded awful.

He comforted himself by remembering that she'd promised to hold on to her feelings and wait for him, but right now, he was having a hard time imagining where Tierney would fit into his real life, and it troubled him. How could they give things a try if he needed to be in Boston and she couldn't stand it there?

"What about you?" she asked, as though reading his mind. "What do you love so much about Boston?"

"Ah," he said. "I'm sixth-generation Boston proud. Fourth-generation cop. My sister's there. My aunts, uncles, cousins, friends. My father and mother are in Florida, but they used to come back up once a month and at least for three weeks at Christmas and in the summer. I don't know…" His voice trailed off. "I don't know if they still do that, but I assume they do."

"You'll find out soon," she said, adjusting their hands so that her palm was flush with his. "They'll be so proud of you once they understand everything."

He wasn't as certain as she.

He'd done his job, sure, but there'd been collateral damage in Suzy's injury, and it felt like a betrayal of sorts. His sister hadn't signed up for the risks he'd taken; it seemed unfair that she'd paid such a high price. Would his parents and sister forgive him? He hoped so. He desperately hoped so. But he'd understand if they needed time. He'd wait years if that's what it took. One day, they'd be ready to accept him again, and he'd be there, in Boston, waiting.

Far, far away from Moonstone Manor and the sweet,

soothing presence of Tierney Haven.

They were approaching her cottage, which was lit by the moon, and his heart felt like lead, and he let go of her hand at the door.

He liked her so much—more every hour of every day. It was going to hurt to say good-bye. He wasn't bound to her, but he was firmly attached, and it hurt when attached things were forced apart. It would be painful for both of them, and if he wanted to spare them that pain, it would be best to leave quietly as soon as he found out that Sean had been arrested. It would be best to leave in the dark of night, without a word, without the torture of good-bye.

He knew this, and yet he couldn't bear to imagine it, so he forced it from his mind, leaning down to tenderly brush his lips against her forehead as his heart tried to imagine a scenario in which they could stay together.

"Thanks for walking with me," he murmured, his lips lingering against her skin.

"I love our walks," she whispered, her voice soft and low, her breath dusting his throat and making him shiver.

"Thank you for letting me stay here with you, Tierney," he said, knowing that when he returned to his life, he would have her to thank for any healing that had taken place—both physically and emotionally—while he'd been away.

"You're protecting me," she said, her voice breathless.

"You're letting me," he murmured.

His lips grazed her skin again, gently dragging against the warm softness, his hands fisted by his sides as he fought against pulling her into his arms. He closed his eyes, breathing in the light scent of her shampoo, and he realized he wasn't sure who was protecting whom anymore. He was vigilant in making certain that the property of Moonstone Manor wasn't breeched, but she had given him sanctuary here, and there was a part of him—a strong and growing part—that she'd guarded in her own gentle way.

"I'm going to check on the gate," he said, drawing away from her.

"Yes. Right." She cleared her throat and pushed up her glasses. "And my Kindle's waiting for me."

"*Oíche mhaith, aisling,*" he said, his voice reverent and low as he looked down at her, trying to memorize every moment he had left.

"Good night, Burr," she answered, backing up against the door, turning the knob, and walking inside.

***

Tierney sat on a blanket beside Burr, their hands clasped inconspicuously between them, while Ian sat on Burr's other side, and Brittany sat beside Tierney.

Fireworks lit the sky, and the small crowd on the point *oohed* and *aahed* their appreciation.

Tierney turned just a touch to see bright white reflected in Burr's eyes, his lips upturned as he glanced at her quickly before training his gaze back at the sky for more magic.

It had been a pretty perfect day. Tierney had led her four morning tours, then locked up the estate; packed a bag with towels, a bathing suit, and a change of clothes; then given her Jeep keys to Burr to he could drive them up to Summerhaven. On the way, Jason Mraz' song "I'm Yours" had played on the radio, and she had grinned at Burr, who sang along in a pleasing tenor and occasionally looked over at her, as though he was singing to her:

So I won't hesitate no more, no more. It cannot wait…I'm yours.

Her cheeks had bloomed with pleasure, but her chest had tightened with the swift reminder of how much he'd come to mean to her in the short time she'd known him and how much she wanted her feelings to have the chance to grow. Except that every day they spent together was also one day closer to them saying good-bye.

When she'd agreed to "wait" for him, they hadn't discussed what that would look like when they were finally free to explore their feelings for each other. But the closer that day came, the more she forced herself to face the implausibility of it. She lived in New Hampshire, where she was happy—she loved her job and her cottage and being so close to her brothers. And from everything he'd shared with her, he was—in his own words—"Boston proud," a fourth-generation police officer.

Would they have some kind of long-distance relationship that relied on technology, keeping in touch over the phone with occasional visits? Was it possible to sustain a long-term relationship that way? She wasn't sure. She'd never tried it before, though she felt strongly that texts and phone calls were no substitute for reaching for someone, kissing them as well, or holding them after a bad day.

And what if—against all odds—the feelings they had now only continued to grow? Would he expect her to move to Boston? Would she expect him to move to New Hampshire? Which of them would have to make the sacrifice of leaving their family, their home, their life? Because she didn't love it that either of them would have to uproot themselves from a life they'd chosen and built.

It was premature for these questions on one hand, but Tierney was a sensible person; she wasn't going to leave the scenario for dating Burr unexplored in her head. Her bottom lip slipped between her teeth, and she snuck another look at him. Watching the sky, his profile was strong and handsome—high cheekbones; dark hair, brows, and lashes; the shadow of a black beard highlighting his strong jaw. Her attraction to him was extreme, but her body wasn't the only thing affected by Burr; more and more, her heart was on the line too.

Would something emotionally intense, but ultimately temporary, be worth the heartache later? Because she couldn't picture herself living happily in a big city, and she couldn't picture him leaving it for a girl he barely knew.

The grand finale rent the starless sky, decorating the firmament like the most brilliant-ever Christmas tree...and then, with a handful of wistful bangs, the show was over, the dark sky left empty and forlorn.

"Ah, that was great," said Burr, turning to her with a wide, easy grin. "Fireworks make me feel like a kid on the Fourth of July!"

She wanted to smile back at him, but she found herself a little stuck in her head, which still whirled with unplayed scenarios and troubling eventualities.

"Hey *aisling*," he said, still grinning at her, "how about a smile?"

"*Téigh dtí diabhail*," she answered softly, unable to keep herself from giving him a small smile, because he was incorrigible, and it delighted her to no end.

"Fuck off, huh?" He beamed at her. "Someday you're going to give me another answer."

"Don't count on it," she said, letting him help her up.

"So? Wasn't it beautiful?" Brittany asked Burr. "We

181

watched them from the roof of a cottage last time."

Rory, who had his arms around Brittany from behind, leaned forward and kissed her neck. "I'm going to help Doug get everyone out of here, and then I'm taking you to bed, *mo mhuirnín*."

"Gross. You feeling sick, Tier?" asked Ian, proceeding to gag.

"I just threw up in my mouth," she muttered, covering her lips with her hand.

"You know what, Ian?" said Rory. "Why don't you keep your salty comments to yourself and go help Doug so I can take my woman home?"

Ian nodded, still looking queasy. "Sure. Whatever you need. Anything to get these images out of my head."

Brittany swatted Ian on the arm. "Sure it's not jealousy, tiger?"

"Might be," said Ian, winking at her.

Tierney gave Ian a hug before he took out his flashlight and disappeared into the night to help people find their way to the parking lot at the top of the path.

"Guess that's it for us, too," said Tierney. "Need us to come back tomorrow and help clean up?"

Rory shook his head. "Got me, Ian, Doug, and Mrs. Toffle on cleanup."

"And me!" said Brittany.

"Oh, yeah. And one heiress from Boston."

"She's a damn good worker," said Tierney.

"Copy that," said Rory, sliding his eyes to Burr and offering him a hand. "Good to see you again, Brian."

"You too, Rory."

"Going to be at Tierney's on Wednesday?"

"Should be," he said.

"I'll see you then."

Brittany stepped out of Rory's half-embrace and put her arms around Burr's neck, giving him a squeeze. "Tierney looks happy with you," she said, loud enough for Tierney to hear.

When Brittany let go and backed away, Burr looked down at Tierney, his eyes soft. "It's the other way around. I'm happy with her."

Brittany gasped then sighed. "Aww. You two!"

"Enough about them. You. Me. Bed," said Rory *a la Neanderthal*, grabbing his girlfriend's hand and tugging her away. "'Night, Tier!"

Tierney giggled as Brittany looked back and waved cheerfully before letting Rory pull her home.

"They're good together," she said, turning to Burr.

"They are."

"Ready to go?"

"I have to make a quick phone call," he said.

"Can you make it in the car?" she asked, holding out her hand for her car keys. "I can drive home."

He pulled the keys from his pocket and handed them to her. "You don't mind?"

"Not at all."

Five minutes later, as they followed a parade of cars from the Summerhaven parking area, Burr withdrew his phone and dialed a number.

"Captain? Yeah, it's me. Uh-huh. Oh, wow. Yeah. It worked, huh? Good. Good. Um…okay. Well, I don't give a shit about that…Uh-huh. He can go fuck himself. Right. Tell me what you got."

Tierney concentrated on the pitch-dark back roads that led from Sandwich to Moultonborough, trying not to be obvious about listening to every word.

"Whoa. Really? Holy shit! Did he know you were coming?" Burr ran his free hand through his hair. "Jaysus, that was risky. Yeah, well. Those guys have balls of steel. Then what?"

She got the feeling that he was getting a play-by-play of some sort of "bust" or something and desperately wished she could hear the other side of the conversation.

"Wednesday? God. So fast. Okay. Yeah. Yeah, I can be there. For sure." He cleared his throat. "No bail, captain. I'll say whatever I have to say. Those fuckers need to stay in jail until their fucking court date."

Wednesday? What was happening on Wednesday, and where did Burr need to be?

For the first time since he'd started his conversation, her curiosity was outpaced by a surprisingly strong feeling of dread, and her thoughts during the firework show rushed back to her. Would this be their final night together at Moonstone Manor? Because damn it, but she wasn't ready to change gears yet. She liked having him live at her cottage. She liked seeing him first thing every morning and before she closed her door for bed every night. She wasn't ready for their quiet time together to be at an end.

But another thought occurred to her that swept all others from her mind.

My hands will stay tied until Sean Shanahan is behind bars.

Her heart beat faster as she realized that if he'd gotten the news that Sean Shanahan had been arrested…that meant her promised wait would be, well, over. Which meant kissing and touching and…and—Oh, God—

Her heart fluttered, and warmth pooled in her belly making her want to squirm in her seat.

—*sex.*

"Uh-huh. Yes, sir. No problem. Yep. Tomorrow afternoon." He paused, glancing at Tierney quickly before looking away. "I'll see you then. Thank you, sir. Good-bye."

Pulling the phone from his ear, he hung up the call and shifted in his seat to put it back in his pocket just as Tierney rolled down her window to punch in the gate code at home.

Without saying anything, she pulled into the driveway, cutting the engine but sitting in the dark quiet with her hands still on the steering wheel, waiting for him to say something, to say anything. She needed to know what was happening and what it meant for them.

"We need to talk," he said.

She couldn't manage much but a soft, "Mm-hm."

"How about I make a fire and you get us two beers?" he asked.

"O-Okay," she whispered, wishing she could take a deep breath, but only managing a shallow one.

The thought of Burr leaving hurt her heart, but the wall coming down between them turned on her body, making her hyperaware of him and of everything they'd put on hold until…until…*now.*

She opened her door without looking at him and beelined for the house, unlocking the door and stepping inside. Alone in the darkness, she leaned her head back against the door and closed her eyes, forcing herself to take a deep breath.

Are you ready for this?

For what, exactly?

For whatever lies ahead, she thought. *Being with him. Losing him. Whatever is about to happen.*

Oh, God, I hope so.

Shoving away from the door, she threw her bag on the sofa and walked to the kitchen, taking two cold beers from the lower shelf and popping off the caps. She kicked off her sandals and opened the back door, stepping outside to find him lighting the small fire he'd built in her copper fire pit.

She held out the beer, and he took it from her, clanking it against hers.

"Sean's been arrested. He's in jail," he said. "For now."

Still standing about a foot away from him, like a deer in headlights, she watched as he pulled an Adirondack chair a little closer to the fire. Then he kicked off his shoes, sat down, put his beer on the grass, and looked up at her.

"Come here. Come and sit with me."

"*W-With* you?"

He didn't smile. His unblinking eyes didn't slip away from hers. His arms rested on the arms of the chair. Finally he nodded, his voice firm. "*With* me."

Her heart pounded with anticipation as she closed the distance between them, her eyes cast down, her hands almost shaking. Was she supposed to straddle him? N-No. Surely not. Maybe she should turn around and back up onto his lap, but her ass would be eye-level to him, so maybe she should—?

He solved this somewhat excruciating quandary for her, leaning forward to take her hand and pull her down onto his lap. As if he knew that she was in unfamiliar territory, he directed her.

"Put your legs through there," he said, indicating the space between the armrest and seat. "Now lean back against on me, and I'm going to put my arms around you like this."

With her body sideways against his, she could lay her cheek perfectly on his shoulder.

"You good?" he asked. "Comfortable?"

Tierney couldn't remember the last time she'd felt so good or so comfortable, and she sighed, closing her eyes and inhaling deeply.

"Mm-hm," she murmured.

He cleared his throat, shifting a little. "This might be harder than I thought."

"What?" she asked.

"I've been fantasizing about you for two weeks, Tierney. Suddenly having you on my lap is...well..."

She knew what he was talking about; she could feel a particular part of him swelling and hardening in his jeans beneath her bottom. Her cheeks flamed so she kept her eyes closed and buried her head deeper into his neck, her forehead resting against the warm skin of his throat. She felt him swallow and clear his throat again.

"Tell me what your captain said," she asked him.

"Right. Right. Um...Sean and four of his top guys were arrested. He finally scheduled a meet-up with Ray to find out where I was hiding out. Apparently, he had no idea where I've been. So you've been safe this whole time."

"Of course I have," she said, "because you wouldn't let anything happen to me."

He took a breath, but it was choppy, and she leaned back to look into his eyes. "Are you—are you okay?"

He reached for her cheek, cupping it as he shook his

head back and forth slowly. "No. No, I'm not okay. I'm…I'm dying here, Tierney. I don't want to talk about Sean. I don't want to talk at all. I want—"

"I know," she said, her voice deep and breathless. "Me too."

He pulled her face closer to his, tilting his head as her lips drew closer. "Maybe just…one…kiss."

The first time Burr had kissed her, it was gentle and tender, a mere brushing of lips to tell her thank you, to tell her good-bye. But this kiss was nothing like that one. This one was hot and fierce, hungry and demanding, and Tierney felt it from the tips of her fingers to the nethermost corner of her soul.

His tongue bathed hers in ardent strokes, his fingers threading through her hair. She moaned her pleasure, arching against him, frustrated by the confines of the chair as he tilted his head to reseal his lips over hers, their teeth clashing as they sought closer contact, a more intimate connection.

"*Aisling. Aisling.* Sweet Tierney," he murmured, running his lips over the soft, sensitive skin of her throat, pressing little kisses to her pulse and her jaw and her chin. His fingers tangled in her hair, holding her steady as he brushed his lips against hers. "*Tabhair póg dom.*" *Kiss me.*

She was bolder now, licking the seam of his lips before seeking his tongue, her own sliding slowly against the velvet heat of his. He groaned, his fingers almost painful in her hair as he demanded more from her, but it was a good pain—it meant that he wanted her as much as she wanted him. For a girl like Tierney, who'd never been wanted like this, it was heady and arousing, and she wanted more, so much more…which is why she whimpered softly in protest when he drew back.

"We have to stop," he said breathlessly, breaking off their kiss but resting his forehead against hers. "Oh, God, we should stop."

"No," she mewled. "No. Sean's in jail. I'm safe. We don't—we don't have to stop," she said, reaching for him, trying to pull him closer for more.

He took her hands in his, leaning back a little more so that he was out of reach.

"Lord knows how much I want you, Tierney. It's no secret," he said, shifting beneath her, his erection pressed unmistakably against her. He searched her face as though trying to figure something out. "But…you're so…" He took a deep breath and released. "I need to know…Tierney, when was your last time? How long has it been?"

"Oh. Umm." Her racing heart sank, and she looked away from him, sliding her hands away. "It's been, um…I mean…" She gulped, her voice barely audible when she added, "I mean, I've never actually…"

She couldn't bear to finish the sentence. Pulling her bottom lip between her teeth, she held it for a second, mustering the courage to meet his eyes again. When she finally did, his eyes were wide, his lips parted in surprise. Her cheeks burned, her embarrassment so sharp, it almost *hurt*.

"You'll be my, um…my first," she whispered, wondering if he'd push her away, if sleeping with a twenty-seven-year-old virgin was too ridiculous to fathom.

"Oh, sweet girl," he said softly, reaching up to cup her face. His voice was deep and breathless with emotion, his eyes locked with hers. "Are you sure you want to give that to me?"

Her eyes filled with tears as she nodded at him.

"I'm sure," she said, twisting her head so she could press her lips to the palm of his hand.

"I've already taken so much from you," he said.

"Nothing I haven't freely given," she said.

His tongue slid between his lips to wet them, and he leaned forward, pressing a sweet, soft kiss to her lips. When he leaned back he nodded at her, but his tone was serious. "Take tonight to think about it, okay? Please? So I'll know it was what you wanted and not just…some hasty decision."

"But tomorrow you'll be gone," she said quickly, scanning his eyes.

He looked away for a moment, then nodded. "Then take *two* nights. I'll be back on Wednesday. No matter what you decide, Tierney, I'll be back. I *care* about you."

Gently, he pushed her head against his shoulder and put his arms back around her. Tierney snuggled against him, enjoying the heat from the fire and the warmth from his body, still uncertain about a possible future for them but relieved that he'd be back so soon.

"Tell me what you're going back to."

"Well…Sean's been arrested. The arraignment's on Wednesday. I'm going to say a few words to try to convince the judge not to offer bail. I want him to stay in jail until his court date."

"Will you see your family?" she asked, flattening her palm against his chest, over his heart.

"I don't…I mean, I *want* to, but I don't know if they'll want to see me."

"Burr, they will."

He flinched, then tightened his arms around her. "You don't know them."

"I know Irish people. We're clannish. We love our families."

"We also hold grudges," he said darkly.

She could only imagine how he felt—returning to Boston alone to put away the monster who wanted him dead, then showing up at his sister's house by himself, anticipating hostility. Her heart swelled with compassion, with deep affection, with a longing to soften everything for him, to support him, to let him know that he wasn't alone.

"I could go with you," she whispered impulsively.

He froze. His whole body stilled. In fact, if her hand wasn't resting over his heart, she'd wonder if it had stopped beating.

Had her suggestion upset him? "I mean…I don't have to. I just hate the thought you going back alone and I could—"

"You'd do that?" he asked.

"Of course."

"You'd drop everything and go to Boston with me? You don't even *like* Boston."

She leaned away from him so she could look at his eyes, which were bright and intense in the firelight.

"I like *you*," she said simply, reaching up to caress his cheek with the hand that wasn't on his chest.

"I can't…" He turned his head to kiss her hand as she'd done to him. "*Aisling*, I can't ask you to do that."

"You didn't," she said. "I offered."

His eyes were searing as they looked deeply into hers. "Why? *Why* are you like this? *How* are you like this?"

"This is just who I am," she said, wondering if he was trying to tell her that he didn't want her to go with him. "I just want to be there for you. Unless…Unless you don't want me to—"

Suddenly she was crushed against him, his arms tight around her. "I want you to. I want you there," he said gruffly.

"Then I'll be there," she reassured him.

"Tierney, Tierney," he murmured against her neck, his lips pressing against her skin, his breathing shallow and raspy near her ear. "I want you with me."

Wiggling her hands free, she wrapped them around his neck and cradled him against her chest tenderly, running her fingers through the bristles of his cropped hair.

When was the last time, she wondered, that he'd been held, been supported, been able to trust someone, been free to ask for help, or support, or love? He rested his forehead against her chest, and she held him like a child, like a lover, like a brother, like a human being who was beloved to her. After a few minutes, she realized that they were breathing in tandem, deep breaths in and out, their arms around each other, their hearts close.

"We should get some sleep," she whispered, still gently caressing his head.

He looked up at her. "Together?"

She grinned at him. "I thought you were giving me tonight to be sure of everything?"

He winced like that was a terrible idea. "I'm an eejit."

She laughed softly.

"Do you *need* tonight?" he asked.

Her thoughts slid to her unshaven legs, to the tattered,

but comfortable, white cotton bra and panties she'd pulled on at nine o'clock this morning; to the fact that she was sweaty after a day in the sun, and exhausted, and overwhelmed in such a good way. Is this how she wanted to remember her first time? Given the chance, maybe she'd like to take a little time to get ready, to be freshly showered and wearing her cutest lingerie. After twenty-seven years, what difference did another twenty-four hours make anyway?

"Are you asking if I *want* you?" She leaned forward and pressed her lips to his, her tongue sliding into his mouth to meet his. They kissed passionately for a moment before she pulled away, looking into his mostly black eyes, fully dilated with only a thin circle of light blue around them. "Yes, I do. I know my mind, and I have no doubts. I know I want you to be my first."

"Then…?"

"Hold yer horses, boyo." She pursed her lips. "It's a milestone, for Lord's sake! Give a girl a day to plan a little, huh?"

"And here I worried you'd be impulsive." He chuckled, nodding at her. "I love it when you're sassy, *aisling*. Yeah, sure, of course. Take as long as you need."

"I'm not waiting past tomorrow," she said, raising her eyebrows and grinning at him. "Is it a nice hotel?"

"It damn well will be now," he said.

She laughed, drawing her hands away from him and pushing off his lap. "Then I guess I'll say good-ni—"

"Wait!" he said, reaching up for her hand and leaning forward in his chair as she stood before him. He looked down at her hand, at her Claddagh ring, heart-out, and slipped it carefully from her finger. Gazing up at her, he turned it around, then placed it back on her finger, heart-in. Dropping his lips to her fingers, he kissed the ring, which made her breath catch with longing.

"Good night, *aisling*," he whispered.

And Tierney, who didn't know her heart could hold this much happiness, whispered "Good night, Burr," hurrying inside before she changed her mind about sleeping with him tonight.

chapter eleven

Burr pulled Tierney's Jeep up to the valet attendant at the InterContinental Boston, encouraged by the beautiful harborside location and hoping that the hotel was every bit as nice as the reviews claimed it to be.

He'd be paying over six hundred dollars for the two nights they'd be staying, an exorbitant amount, well out of his usual price range, but it wasn't like he'd spent a lot of money on himself over the last three years. His bank account could certainly handle it.

More importantly, however, he wanted the next two days to be special for Tierney. She had taken him in when he was at his lowest, his neediest, and she'd shown him a kindness and trust he hadn't earned. His feelings for her, born of something as pure as her actions, were fierce now. She deserved the best of everything he could possibly offer her, starting with a luxury hotel for their impromptu getaway.

Aside from the fact that their relationship was about to jump a major hurdle while they stayed here, he wanted to spoil her a little. He'd planned a little surprise as a way to say thank you for all she'd done for him but also to let her know how much he cared about her.

The way she'd offered to come with him to Boston had shocked the hell out of him last night but, God, how much it had meant to him. Everything, he'd quickly learned over the last couple of weeks, felt better with Tierney beside him. She couldn't stand Boston, which made her selflessness, once again, staggering. She was *only* here for him. The least he could do was make the visit as perfect as possible for her.

One valet attendant opened her door and helped her from the car, while another took their bags out of the trunk and pushed them into the hotel on a shiny silver cart.

"Burr!" she exclaimed. "This is…oh, my God, this is *gorgeous*!"

"You deserve it," he said, pressing a quick kiss to her cheek.

He grinned at her, taking her hand and pulling her through the gleaming glass doors, into the spacious lobby, and over to the reception desk.

"Good afternoon, sir, and welcome to the InterContinental."

"Thanks," he said, dropping Tierney's hand to take his wallet out of his hip pocket. "O'Leary. Checking in for two nights."

"Welcome, Mr. and Mrs. O'Leary," said the desk clerk, offering them each a serene smile.

Beside him, Tierney gasped, which drew his attention. He was about to correct the young woman, but when he looked at Tierney, her eyes sparkled with humor and happiness, so he didn't.

Mrs. O'Leary. *Tierney O'Leary*. It was beautiful. It was fucking musical.

"Thank you," said Burr, winking at Tierney.

"Checking in for…two nights?" asked the clerk.

"That's right."

"I have you booked in a water-view guest room, Mr. O'Leary."

"Yep."

Burr nodded as Tierney's elbow dug into his hip. When he slid his eyes to her, she mouthed, *Wow!* And man, but just to see her like this? So happy and excited? Made it worth every cent he was about to spend.

"Very good," said the clerk. "And just to confirm...I have spa services booked for, uh, is it Tierney?" She looked up and nodded at a dumb struck Tierney before continuing. "A Honey Butter Body Treatment at one o'clock and a Signature Honey Butter Mani-Pedi at three?"

"Yes," said Burr. "That's correct."

Tierney turned to him, her green eyes wide with surprise. "Burr!"

He leaned down, kissing her quickly before turning back to the clerk. "Perfect."

"What did you do?" she asked, her voice thready with emotion.

"I had to prove to you that I know how to say thank you, *aisling.*"

"I don't know what to say."

"You don't have to say anything, love."

She stared up at him for an extra second, her eyes brightening, then took his arm, scooting next to him and resting her head on his shoulder.

"Your room is ready," said the desk clerk. "May I have your luggage brought up?"

"That's great," said Burr. "Thanks."

"Eighteenth floor. Elevators are to your left. Enjoy your stay, Mr. and Mrs. O'Leary," said the woman, sliding their keycards across the marble counter with a warm smile.

"Thank you," said Tierney softly, braiding her fingers through Burr's as he pulled her toward the elevator.

As they waited for the polished brass doors to open, he could feel it coming off of her in waves: a mix of excitement, anticipation, and jitters, and while he loved the excitement and anticipation, he hated the jitters. No matter what happened—or didn't happen—between them, he *always* wanted her to feel comfortable with him.

They stepped into the elevator and Burr pressed "18," pulling her into his arms as the elevator started its ascent.

"Hey," he said. "Look at me."

She looked up, her eyes wide, her expression giving away little.

"Nothing's going to happen between us unless you want it to. You know that, right?"

She flinched, just briefly, then nodded.

A wince? No. No winces.

"Tierney, you look terrified. Please tell me you understand. I'd never force you. I—I have no expectations. Whatever happens, happens. It doesn't affect how I feel about you. We could sit on the bed and talk all night and I'd be happy, *aisling*...just to be with you."

Finally, her lips twitched up a little. She took a deep breath and sighed, nodding at him. "Okay."

But her answer was enigmatic. It didn't tell him a thing about what she was feeling, what she wanted, or what she expected.

"I mean it, Tierney."

"I know," she said, squeezing his hand before looking away.

Was it too much? The hotel and the spa treatments? Oh, Lord and all that "Mrs. O'Leary" business? Fucking hell, he wasn't good at this. Sure, Burr had dated in high school and college, but his courtship skills were rusty after three years, and he couldn't get a bead on her.

"Tierney—"

"Burr!" she said, her eyes flashing at him with a hint of impatience. "Stop. I'm just…I'm taking it in. This beautiful place. The spa. You. I've never—I mean, no one's *ever* done *anything* like this for me. I'm not scared. I'm not nervous. I'm just…*overwhelmed* a little. It's all like a dream."

"Oh. Okay," he said, finally exhaling a breath he didn't realize he'd been holding. She stepped out of the elevator, and he pulled her left toward their room.

His free hand—the one she wasn't holding—twitched at his side as they walked side by side down the corridor. He licked his dry lips, pursing them together, reaching for the keycard in his pocket with a sweaty hand, and gulping as they stopped in front of the door, which made him realize—

Oh, fuck. It's not her who's nervous…it's me.

He slipped the card into the reader and pulled it out, pushing down on the lever and letting her enter first.

She gasped, turning around to grin at him before racing to the floor-to-ceiling windows which boasted a spectacular view of the Fort Point Channel and Seaport Boulevard bridge. The door closed behind them, and Burr felt warmth flush his whole body as he watched her stand at the windows.

He wanted to memorize this moment forever.

She was wearing cutoff denim shorts with a polo shirt and pink-checked flip-flops. Her long black hair, pulled into a low ponytail at the base of her neck, was in stark contrast to the powder pink of her shirt. His breath caught just staring at her. He wanted her. He needed her. He lov—

Wait. What? No. Fuck no. Not that. Too soon, Burr. Too fucking soon.

She turned around and sprinted across the room, throwing herself into his arms and dashing any other thoughts from his mind. He lifted her easily, and she wrapped her legs around his waist, pressing her lips against his neck with a sigh.

"I love it here."

"I love…" He inhaled sharply. *Shut up. Shut up. Shut up.* "…it here too."

He held her tightly as she leaned back to look at his face. "You're so good to me."

"I…Tierney, that's because I…I…"

DO. NOT. SAY. IT.

"You what?"

He loosened his arms and she slid down his body, her tits dragging down his chest, which made his dick twitch.

"I have to go see Donnelley," he blurted out, reaching for her arms and untangling them. "I, uh, I need to touch base with him before tomorrow."

"Oh, of course," she said, pushing her glasses up and putting her hands on her hips. "Okay. So I guess I'll…"

"Order room service! If you want," he suggested. "And then…spa!"

"Yeah. Yay," she said, cocking her head to the side. "Um. Are you okay?"

"Me? Yeah! I'm good. I'm great. I'm so glad you like the room, and I'm going to go see Donnelley and I—" *I think I'm falling in love with you.* "—and—and—and—I'll be back in a few hours, okay? We'll go see Suzy, and then, uh, come back here. Okay?"

"You're acting a little weird," she said.

"Just, um, you know, probably just feeling strange about being back. In Boston. Seeing the captain. Suzy. Dad. Lots, um, going on in my head."

"Okay," she said, nodding at him like he had a screw loose, but not willing to press the issue. "I'll see you later?"

He leaned forward and pressed his lips to hers, needing to say something, to let a little air out of the balloon that held his feelings. "I'm crazy about you, Tierney."

He didn't know where the words came from, but her sweet smile made saying them worthwhile.

"You're smiling for me, love," he said, grinning back at her.

"I suppose I am."

"You're not going to tell me to go fuck myself?"

"Nope," she said, seizing his eyes and holding them with her sparkling emeralds. "I'd prefer it if you fucked me instead."

He blinked at her. He blinked at her again, but she held his eyes fast. *Oh, fuck. Sexy Tierney.* He felt her words all over, and his dick hardened like she'd demanded it.

"Fuuuuuuuck," he murmured, his voice like gravel.

"That's the plan," she said softly. "Now go to your meeting. I'll see you later."

She crossed the room and slipped into the bathroom, leaving him with a stone-hard cock, a heart full of love, and words stuck in his head, yet better left unsaid.

***

Love.

When they were standing together at reception, he'd called her "love."

That was the moment she knew.

Not that she was in love with him yet, but that was the moment she knew it was *possible*.

At first, she'd been thrown by being called "Mrs. O'Leary," but there was a certain charm in the desk clerk's assumption, and Tierney hadn't felt like correcting her. But it was the endearment, dropped from Burr's lips, that had made her heart stutter and her breath catch. *Love.* So simple. So much.

And all the way up to the eighteenth floor in the elevator, she'd tried to look ahead to the future, tried to see a clear path to happily ever after, but she still couldn't picture it, and it scared her. But then she'd been so wowed by the view, and the beautiful room, and his thoughtfulness in booking spa treatments for her; she didn't want to spoil the time they had. So she'd decided to put her fears aside and plunge into whatever lay ahead without misgivings.

It had emboldened her to be truly forward with Burr and make it clear what she wanted tonight.

I'd prefer it if you fucked me instead.

She gasped in shock at the memory, pressing her hands to her cheeks in the bathroom mirror as she remembered his reaction. Inked, muscular Burr had looked like a fish out of water, gasping and blinking at her.

"Poor thing," she said, giggling softly at her reflection.

She'd never said anything half as dirty to any man in her entire life. No wonder he'd looked shocked. But unless her eyes deceived her, part of him—a part below the waist but above the knees—had liked it too.

Exiting the bathroom to find him gone, she opened her suitcase on the large, king-sized bed and took out the dress she planned to wear tonight to meet his family.

It was a princess-cut sundress with spaghetti straps, a sweetheart bodice, tapered waist, and full skirt, the fabric a starched cream-colored cotton covered with a light-blue toile. Traditional and sweet, but just a little sexy, she'd been saving this dress for a special occasion, and tonight was it. For underneath the dress, she'd packed pretty underwear she'd never worn: a light-blue satin bra, trimmed with lace, and matching light-blue panties. And to round out the outfit, she'd brought metallic rose-gold flip-flops that she'd purchased at the North Conway Target during the summer clearance last September.

Smiling at the outfit, she hung up everything, then decided to go downstairs, stopping by the lobby café for a croissant en route to the spa. She luxuriated in the body moisturizing treatment Burr had arranged, which made her skin soft as satin. And she had her fingers and toes painted a metallic rose to match her shoes.

Checking the time and realizing she only had an hour until Burr returned to pick her up, she ran back upstairs to shower and shave her legs, change into her outfit, and do her hair and makeup, finishing up just as she heard a knock at the door. And when she opened it, there he was, his face registering surprise, then pleasure, as he stared at her, dropping his eyes to her toes, traveling slowly up her legs to her dress, to the swell of her breasts, to the simple string of pearls she wore around her neck, and finally to her hair in a light-blue hairband. The coup de grace? She'd taken off her glasses, replacing them with seldom-used contacts.

Looking up at him, she held her breath, hoping...hoping...

"Jaysus," he murmured on an exhaled breath. "Tierney. You look...you look..."

She beamed at him, stepping back a little so that he could enter the room.

"*Ta tu go h-aileann*," he finally whispered, his voice reverent and deep. *You look beautiful.*

"*Is maith an scathan suil charad*," she said. *Your eyes are a good mirror.* "Thank you." She reached for the badge hanging around his neck that hadn't been there when he left. She tugged on it, pulling him closer. "What's this, now?"

"I'm official again," he said distractedly, letting her lead him, still caressing her face with his eyes, his breath ragged and shallow. "You smell like heaven."

"Does heaven smell like honey butter?" she asked softly.

"I'm pretty sure it does," he murmured, his gaze lingering on her lips. "If I kiss you, will I wreck your lipstick?"

She shook her head just slightly. "No. It's waterproof."

His arms were around her instantly, his lips ravenous as they fell across hers. He groaned into her mouth, backing her up against the wall. She wrapped her arms around his neck, arching against him, the tips of her breasts instantly hard, her sex throbbing and hot.

Panting by her ear, he moved his hands from her hips to the wall, flattening them on either side of her head, his breath choppy, falling in rough puffs near her cheek. He rested his forehead against hers.

"We have…to go…to Suzy's," he said, grinding out the words like they hurt.

She loosened her hands, skimming them down his arms until they hung by her sides. "The sooner we go, the sooner we'll be back."

His eyes were intense when he leaned back to look at her. "I've never wanted a woman as much as I want you, Tierney. I'm sorry if that frightens you, but it's the truth. I'll try to go slow tonight, but I haven't been with anyone in a long, long time. I'll try to be—"

"Tonight isn't just about me," she said, reaching for his face. She held it tenderly, standing on her tiptoes to kiss him gently. "I want you to—to enjoy yourself too."

"*Aisling*," he said, clasping her wrists and lowering her hands to the fly of his jeans, "there's no chance I won't 'enjoy' myself."

She pressed against his erection experimentally, and his hips bucked forward, filling her hands. *How on earth am I meant to take all of him?* she wondered, her breath catching, her breasts heaving with her panted breath.

"It might hurt a little," he murmured as though reading her mind, "but I swear I'll make it good for you, love. I promise."

Her heart fluttered at the endearment, and she drew back her hands, flattening them over his heart. "I know you will. I trust you."

"Arrrr!" he grunted, pushing away from the wall and surging past her. "Give me a minute, yeah?"

She listened as the bathroom door closed. She knew exactly what he was doing in there, and part of her was so intensely turned-on imagining him touching himself, she almost followed. But if they started making out again, they'd never leave the room. And the only way to get what she *really* wanted was to get out of here so they could return.

She heard the toilet flush and the sink run. A moment later, Burr exited the bathroom, his eyes still dark, though his jaw wasn't quite as taut as before. "That'll only hold me for a little while, Tierney."

"Then let's bloody well get going," she said, beelining for the door with Burr at her heels.

***

Damnú, but she looked a fucking picture when she opened the hotel room door.

And after that sexy-dirty talk she'd laid on him earlier? *I'd prefer it if you fucked me instead.* Christ. He didn't know how the fuck he was going to last through a conversation with his family, but the promise of Tierney's sweet body naked next to his was surely the carrot leading him forward right now.

Throughout his meeting with Donnelley, his thoughts had kept returning to her—to his *feelings* for her, which seemed almost impossible but wouldn't be denied. *In love with her?* Hell, he didn't know for sure. He'd never been in love with anyone before. But he'd never felt like *this* before either. Never felt anything *close* to it.

"Tell me about your meeting with Captain Donnelley," she said, crossing her legs toward him as Burr negotiated the thick traffic from central Boston to Dorchester. Although Suzanne only lived six miles away from the hotel, it would take over twenty minutes to get to her so close to rush hour.

"Hmm. Well, I got my badge back."

"That's good, right?"

"I wanted it back so I could show it to my dad," he

confessed without looking at her, feeling a little sheepish about the admission.

"It's going to be okay, Burr. I just know it."

He was grateful beyond measure to have her sitting beside him. It was like he could draw from her strength, and damn, but he needed it now. He adjusted his grip on the steering wheel. His sister didn't know he was coming. His parents didn't know he was coming. Connor might well punch his lights out before letting Burr in his house. And he'd take it. Like Jesus on the way to Golgotha, he'd take it all.

"Did you see Ray?" she asked.

He shook his head. "Nah. He's under house arrest right now, wearing an ankle monitor and waiting to testify at the arraignment."

"Will he be arrested? For what he did to you?"

And there was that Irish steel in Tierney's voice that he fucking loved.

"Why do I get the feeling you want to kick his ass?" he asked her.

"Is it that obvious?" she asked, giving him side-eye.

He had a brief flashback to Tierney with a spatula and chuckled. "I'll need to keep you away from spatulas."

"When?"

"When...I don't know. When we barbecue, I guess," he said, though he had no house at the moment at which to BBQ.

All he had was a storage unit, which he'd visited today so he could grab some clean underwear and a few clothes before racing back to Tierney. It's not like it was a home. He didn't *have* a home, although the word made him think of the cozy cottage at Moonstone Manor, with beautiful walking trails, a BBQ grill, a fire pit, and a queen-sized bed that smelled like Tierney.

"What else?" she prompted.

"Donnelley said Ray cried like a baby when he confessed. When Sean couldn't get answers out of Ray, he went to Suzy and shot her. When Suzy turned out to be a dead end, Sean went back to Ray and threatened his wife and kids. If he'd shoot Suzy, Ray knew he'd shoot them too. So Ray gave me up. Until then, he swore he was only doctoring reports and giving Sean a heads-up now and then about busts."

"It's still not okay," said Tierney, her tone ice cold.

Burr reached for her hand. "No, it's not. None of it. If Ray hadn't been doctoring reports and informing for Sean, he never would have felt entitled to lean on Ray. You can't be a 'little bit' of a bad cop. Either you're good or you're bad. Corrupt or honest. Ray learned that the hard way."

"I don't feel bad for him."

The strange thing was, Burr did. Just a little. He didn't want to *see* Ray or go *hug* him or offer any conciliatory bullshit like that. But at least he had a reason for why Ray did what he did, and it softened the blow for Burr just a little.

"To answer your question, love, I don't know if he'll be arrested. But I know he'll never be a cop again. He'll never be able to hold up his head in Boston. He's disgraced himself, and there's no way back."

"Unlike you," she said firmly. "*You* have a way back."

He turned down Suzy's street, his chest filling with creepy-crawlies, unwelcome harbingers of anticipation. "Almost there."

She squeezed his hand. "Burr, listen to me. No matter what happens, I'm on your side. I know who you are, and I think you're amazing. And if it all goes tits-up? Well, we'll leave. But we'll leave together."

I love you.

The words rushed through his brain, ratified instantly by his heart without exception, without doubts, without retraction or warning.

I love you. I don't know how, but I do. I love you, Tierney Haven. Absolutely. Completely. For all time.

He pulled into Suzanne's driveway and parked, turning to Tierney. "You're the best thing that's ever happened to me."

She leaned across the bolster, met his eyes, then kissed him, quick and hard.

"Likewise. Now, let's get this over with."

chapter twelve

Burr opened her door, and Tierney climbed into the passenger seat, sitting down with a huff and buckling her seat belt with an angry click.

That did not *go well*, she thought. But she wouldn't apologize for what she'd said. She'd *never* apologize.

She watched as Burr walked back up the driveway to the stoop, speaking to his mother for a few minutes. His mother reached out and hugged him hard before he turned around and headed back to the car.

As he turned, Sheila O'Leary looked for Tierney, searching for her eyes through the windshield and waving to her. Tierney mustered a polite smile and waved back. It wasn't *her* fault. Burr's father, Frank O'Leary, was the horse's ass.

Burr opened the driver's-side door and sat down, resting his hands on the steering wheel for a moment before turning to her.

"Wow, Tierney. Just…wow."

"I'm sorry," she said quickly, taking his surprise for censure. "I should have stayed quiet, but I couldn't—"

Burr reached for her face, his hand landing on her jaw as he pulled her close and kissed her with a wellspring of deep and intense emotion. His tongue tangled with hers, his lips demanding and giving at once, his breath tasting faintly of Killian's beer.

When he drew back, his chest heaved, and his eyes were almost black. "You were…God, you were *amazing!*"

"I couldn't let your Dad talk to you like that," she whispered.

"For the record," he said, leaning away to turn the key and back out of his sister's driveway, "my mother said I should marry you."

Tierney grinned at him, the outlandish suggestion making her smile for the first time in the past thirty minutes.

When they'd arrived, Burr had knocked on the door, and when his mother, Sheila, had answered, she'd enveloped Burr into a massive hug, clutching at her son, crying and laughing at the same time, and saying Burr's name over and over again.

He'd dropped Tierney's hand to hug his mother back, and watching at his side, Tierney had been on the verge of tears, deeply moved by the mother-son reunion and encouraged that the rest of Burr's family would be just as happy to see him.

Well…that's where she'd been *wrong.*

Though his sister, Suzanne, still convalescing on the couch in the living room, had burst into tears, reaching for Burr and hugging him with the devotion Tierney felt he was due, Frank O'Leary and Connor Riley had looked on, stoic and uncompromising, from the corner of the room.

"So you're back," spat Burr's father, tossing a rude look at Tierney. "And who's this piece?"

"Be civil," warned Burr.

His father had nodded curtly at Tierney.

"This is Tierney Haven," said Burr. "Tierney, this is my

father, Frank O'Leary."

"Hello," said Tierney.

"And my brother-in-law, Connor."

"Hi Connor," she'd said.

Neither offered a hand to shake, and both looked at her with some measure of disdain.

"What're you doing with him?" asked Connor, crossing his arms over his chest. "You should call an Uber and get away from here before you get shot or worse."

"Con, come on," said Suzanne from the couch.

Mrs. O'Leary had returned from the kitchen with a tray of open beers and a bowl of peanuts. "We weren't expecting company, but why don't you sit down, Tierney? Tierney. That's Irish."

"Yes, ma'am," she said, taking the beer offered and sitting in the chair Mrs. O'Leary had indicated, with Burr standing beside her. "My mother's from Killarney."

"Ah. Is she, now? Frank and I are both from Limerick."

"That's what Burr said," Tierney answered, taking a small sip of the cold beer.

"So you've come back," said Frank, staring at Burr with disgust. "Got a pound of flesh from your sister. What else can we do for you?"

"Pop, I was hoping that I could explain—"

"Oh!" said Frank, turning to his son-in-law, his cheeks red with anger. "He has an explanation, Connor. You see, there? He has a reason his sister was shot in her front doorway by that pig, Sean Shanahan."

Sheila sighed. "Frank, let's listen to what Burr has to—"

"I don't give a shite what he has to say. He was arrested for dealing, Sheila. I know it breaks yer bloody heart, but the boy's garbage."

"Pop, listen. I was undercover with the New Kil—"

"Ha! Liar!" yelled Frank. "If you was undercover, boyo, my friend, Liam Donnelley, would've bloody well let me know."

"It was Captain Donnelley swore me to secrecy," said Burr, his voice even and low, though his fingers were fisting at his sides.

"*Ná bí ag iarraidh cluain an chacamais a chur orm!*" Frank bellowed. *Don't bullshit me!* His eyes slid to Tierney as he pointed at Burr with one stubby finger. "Yer man, here, is right puir trash." He turned back to Burr. "*Ní mórán thú.*" *You're worthless.*

Burr inhaled sharply beside Tierney, looking down at her. "We should go."

"No, son," said Sheila, wringing her hands. "Your father's just…just…"

Suzanne spoke up. "Pop, please! Can we just listen to what he has to—"

"To say?" demanded Connor. "You got shot by Sean Shanahan in front of our daughter, Suze. And the only reason Sean was here is because he was looking for your fucking brother. Now here he comes, three years after disappearing, talking about being undercover? You're not buying this shite, are you?"

"Sean Shanahan was *arrested* two days ago," said Suzanne, her blue eyes furious. "Did you know that, Con?"

"Everyone in Dorchester knows it," he muttered.

"So you don't think it's a little bit of a coincidence that we don't see Burr for three years, and now Sean's been arrested and he's back? Just listen to him! What'll it hurt you?"

"Me? Nothing. But you, darlin'? You're my wife, and God knows why after what he's done, but you still love him. And if I let him in here to feed you pretty lies, it'll—"

"They're *not* lies," growled Burr. "I was undercover with the New Killeens for three years. The original drug bust was arranged to discredit me."

"Everyone and their brother knows you been runnin' with the Shanahans for years!" said Frank. "Seen you strong-armin' good men down on their luck, and God only knows what other foul deeds. *Go mbeire an diabhal leis thú!* There's no room in this family for you!"

"*Bí 'do thost!*" Tierney yelled, jumping to her feet as she told Frank O'Leary to shut up. "Burr is a *good* man! He *was* undercover. He gave up three years of his life to put those bastards away, and he's only back here in bloody, godforsaken Boston to testify at the arraignment tomorrow and make sure they don't get bail. If you don't believe me, show up tomorrow at the courthouse and you'll see. And if not…if not…then *go hifreann leat*, you old *bastard!*"

And that was the moment Burr had stepped between Tierney and his father, putting his arm around her shoulders and escorting out of the house and back to the car.

Perhaps telling Frank O'Leary to go to hell was a bit harsh, but she couldn't bear the way he'd spoken to Burr, calling his own son garbage, and trash, and worthless.

"He was calling you names," she said softly.

"He doesn't know the full story yet. He's confused."

"*No one* has a right to call you names."

"Tierney," he said, reaching for her hand, "my avenging angel."

"At least your mom and sister seemed glad to see you."

He nodded. "It did me good to see them too."

"I'm sorry I called your father a bastard. I'm sure he's...not. In better circumstances."

He chuckled softly, squeezing her hand before releasing it. "Jaysus, Mary, and Joseph, his face. He was so shocked."

"By the Irish or what I said?"

"You walked in looking like an angel and left yelling like a banshee."

She took a deep breath and sighed. "I'm sorry if I embarrassed you."

"*Aisling*," he said, braking at a red light and looking over at her. "You were magnificent. The most amazing woman I've ever known. You didn't embarrass me. I couldn't have been more proud of you."

"Truly?"

He nodded. "I promise."

"But your father—"

"Probably respects the hell out of you. Probably likes *you* more than *me*," he said, but the pain of his father's rejection slipped into his tone. After a few minutes of driving in silence, he added, "At least that's over now. There's a relief in that."

"And next time will be better," she said.

"I hope so," he said. "Anyway, thanks for being there, Tierney."

"I'm glad I was there."

The bright lights of Boston illuminated the twilight sky ahead, and suddenly Tierney realized that if one part of the night was over, the other was just about to begin. She glanced over at Burr who seemed to be having the same realization.

"Do you, um…want to get dinner somewhere?" he asked. "We could stop on the way back to the hotel."

No. She didn't. There was only one thing she wanted.

"I'm not hungry," she said.

"Me neither," he said, then added, "not for food."

Unexpected butterflies filled her tummy as her heart started thumping, and she took a deep breath.

He reached across the center bolster, taking her hand and drawing it to her lips. "It's not too late to change your mind."

"I don't want to change my mind," she said. "I want to be with you."

He kissed her hand again, then dropped them both to the bolster, his fingers winding through hers. "You remember earlier today, before I left to see Donnelley, when you said I was acting weird?"

"Mm-hm."

"That was me…being nervous."

"You?" She turned to look at him. "But this isn't your first time, is it?"

"No," he said quickly. "But the entire time I was under with the New Killeens, I didn't…that is, I mean…I didn't sleep with anyone." He paused, letting his words sink in. "I was concerned that if I fell asleep next to someone, I might talk in my sleep. Betray who I really am and what I was really doing there."

"So you haven't…"

"I haven't had sex in over three years," he said, shifting in his seat as they neared the hotel. "And it's been a *long* three years."

"I always understood that for men...I mean, sex is something they *need*."

"I can't speak for how the needs of a woman differ from those of a man, but I can tell you that I"—he laughed bitterly—"certainly *missed* it. I'm ready for tonight, Tierney. Long past ready."

"Me too," she said. "You know, just because I haven't done it yet doesn't mean I haven't wanted to. I just wanted to feel..." She thought about what she wanted to say, but the only words that came to mind were these: "...the way *you* make me feel."

"So you've been waiting for me, then, *aisling*?" he asked, his voice soft and reverent.

"I think so," she said as he pulled into the semicircle in front of the hotel.

"Then it should come as no surprise," he said, "that I've been waiting for you too."

Two valet attendants opened their doors, and they exited the car, joining hands again as they walked through the glass doors opened for them. The stood in silence as Burr pressed the button for the elevator, the connection between them palpable, electrifying, like if anyone stepped too close or—God forbid—between them, they'd be fried by the live current that bound them.

In the elevator, Tierney stared straight ahead at the closed doors, not daring to look at Burr for fear that she'd leap into his arms, and once there, never let go. She glanced up at the security camera in the corner of the small box and grimaced. The door opened, and Burr pulled her onto the eighteenth floor.

Without speaking, they walked quickly down the hall to

their room, Burr only dropping her hand to take the keycard from his back pocket and tap it against the reader. The light turned green, the mechanics whooshed, and Burr pushed down on the lever, opening the door to their dark room, illuminated by the brilliant lights of Boston.

The moment the door closed behind them, his arms reached for her, turning her around and pulling her against his chest. His lips came down on hers, hard and demanding, like a thirsty man in the desert, his tongue slipping between her waiting lips, his groan throaty and deep as he sighed with relief.

She wound her arms around his neck, and he slipped his hands under her bottom, lifting her easily. Tierney held him tightly, wrapping her legs around his waist and arching her breasts into his chest as he walked into the room carrying her.

When he reached the bed, he turned, sitting on the edge with Tierney straddling his lap, her pelvis intimately pressed against his erection, which throbbed against her. Sliding her hands down the back of his T-shirt, she dragged it up, and Burr paused in kissing her for a split second, holding her with one hand as he reached behind his neck to pull it off. With his chest bare, he started kissing her again, but Tierney wanted to feel him.

She reached for his hand. "Unzip my dress."

"We can go slow, love."

"I don't want to go slow," she panted. "Unzip it."

"I don't want to rush things for you," he said, moving his fingers to the top of the zipper, his eyes dark and dilated as he looked into hers.

"I'm twenty-seven years old," she said, laughing softly.

"Nothing's been rushed, Burr."

With a soft chuckle, he pushed her hair aside and pulled down the zipper, the teeth giving way as the little straps drooped down her shoulders. Tierney wiggled out of them, and her dress bunched around her waist, leaving her bare, except for her bra. Burr's fingers landed on the clasp, tentative, waiting for permission.

"Off," she murmured, her chest heaving as he flicked her bra open. Reaching for it, she pulled it from her arms. Naked, chest to chest, they collided, their lips bruising, their tongues demanding, the stiff points of her breasts digging into the muscled wall of his chest as they kissed.

She dug her knees into the comforter, sliding her sex as flush against his as possible, but she was frustrated by the clothing between them. She wanted more. She wanted him.

Pushing against his shoulders, Tierney's feet dropped to the floor, her dress falling from her waist to pool around her bare feet and leaving her standing before him in her light blue underwear. She licked her lips, staring at his throat, wanting to look him in the eye but suddenly shy.

"Tierney, *aisling, a ghra mo chroi*," he whispered, *woman of my heart*, "look at me."

She raised her gaze to his, her naked breasts heaving gently with her shallow breaths.

"You are…the most beautiful thing I've ever seen, in all my life."

He reached for her waist, pulling her back between his legs. Bending his head, his tongue circled the sensitive skin around her nipple, and she gasped, reaching for the back of his head to draw him closer. He took her nipple, hard and throbbing, between his lips and sucked gently, his tongue flicking the stiff bud until she cried softly. He skimmed his lips across her chest to her other breast, one hand reaching up to tease the soaked nipple he'd already loved as he sucked its twin between his lips. As he licked one and rolled the other between his thumb and forefinger, Tierney felt a swirling in her stomach—hot and urgent—the sensations fanning out lower to her groin, where the heat pooled, pulsing and demanding.

"I want you," she panted. "Burr, please. I want…I want…"

Releasing her breasts, he stood before her, clasping her cheeks and sealing his lips over hers. As they kissed, his hands skated down her arms to her hands, gently taking them in his and pulling them to the button and fly of his jeans.

Her fingers worked quickly, opening his pants before sliding into the waistband of his boxers to land on his soft, hot skin. Sliding her down to his hips, forced his jeans and underwear down, and used his feet to pull them the rest of the way to his ankles, kicking them onto the floor.

She took his fingers as he had hers, pulling them to the seam of her panties before winding her arms back around his neck. He shoved once, hard, and the panties slid to the floor. His hands landed on her bottom, and he lifted her again. And Tierney, who'd never been completely naked with another man in her entire life, spread her legs and wrapped them around Burr's waist as he laid her down on the bed and fell on top of her gently.

The glorious weight of his body pressed her against the bed, and he surged against her, his erection sliding into her hot, slick folds and massaging her clit. She panted, holding him tighter, the heat that had built before, while he'd loved her breasts, on fire now.

"Tierney," he panted, "I don't want to hurt you."

"It'll only hurt a bit," she said.

With her legs still locked around his waist, Burr reached for the bedside table and pulled out a foil package he must have placed there earlier. He reached behind, gently seizing her ankle and unlocking it. Then he pushed off the bed and stood naked at the foot of it, moonlight and ambient light showing her the hills and valleys of his muscled body. Her eyes slid lower, to his cock, which stood tall and proud from his body. He followed her eyes, staring down at that throbbing part of himself before demanding her eyes.

"Tierney?"

"Hmm? Yes?" She snapped her eyes up, leaning on her elbow.

"You're sure?" he asked, ripping open the condom with his teeth and rolling the thin latex over his erection. He held the stiff flesh in his hand, staring at her.

She nodded. "I want this. I want you inside me. I need you so badly, Burr."

He knelt back down on the bed, and Tierney spread her legs. Leaning forward he kissed her, slowly, gently, his tongue bathing hers reverently before he reached up to cradle her face, the tip of his sex lining up perfectly with her own.

"Do it," she said. "Do it quick."

He winced, his breathing ragged. "It'll hurt."

"I don't care." She moved her hands to his back, then slid them to his ass. "*Now.*"

Surging forward with one hard thrust, he pushed

through any waiting barrier, making her cry out in pain as he embedded himself deeply within her.

"Tierney?" he panted, holding still. "Are you...are you okay?"

"You were right. It hurts," she whimpered, wiggling a little to find relief.

"Stay still, love," he said, keeping himself completely and utterly motionless inside of her. "Relax. Breathe."

She took a deep breath, feeling the walls of her sex relax, then stretch, for him. She could feel him throbbing inside of her, his pulsing flesh massaging the sensitive walls of her sex. She closed her eyes and felt his heartbeat, deep inside of her. And it was so arousing, the pain slipped away, until all she felt was him.

He kissed her jaw and her throat, murmuring sweet things in Irish as her fingers, which had probably drawn blood, relaxed, sliding up his back to the base of his neck. Drawing back, he looked into her eyes. "Better now?"

"Better," she sighed, moving her hips experimentally and watching his face as his eyes closed tightly as though he was in pain. "What do you need?"

"To move," he grunted, staying still inside of her.

She arched her back again, and he grunted, the sound primordial, her hips moving again in response.

"Then move," she panted.

"Look at me," he said, opening his eyes as he slid slowly from her before surging forward to fill her again. "I...Tierney, I...feel more for you than I have ever felt. For anyone. I want...I want so much...with you. Time. Life. Love. More."

His body pulled back and surged forward again, making

her eyes close with pleasure, her feet sliding up the back of his legs to hold him within her. *Love.*

She felt it too.

"Burr. *A chéadsearc*," she panted.

"*A chéadsearc*," he repeated, his eyes brightening at the seriousness of the word she'd chosen. "First in your heart."

Tierney nodded, confirming her feelings, confirming that he was, literally and figuratively, her first. First to claim her body, and first in her heart.

Cupping her face, he kissed her madly, their bodies moving in tandem, giving and taking, welcoming and warm, in the age-old, always-new dance of bodies loving each other for the first time.

"*Aisling*," he panted near her ear, his hips moving quickly, the elbows on either side of her head shaking, his muscles coiled and taut as he readied for release. "I'm waiting for you. Come with me, love."

In the end, it was the word, more than anything else, that hastened her own climax. She didn't know what the future held for her and Burr, but she felt certain, in that beautiful moment, that they would figure it out. *How many had started with even less of a foundation than us?*

Tierney tightened her legs around him, arching her back as waves of heat broke over her like a blessing, like music, like release. And her Burr joined her, crying out her name as he came, clutching her to his chest like he never, ever wanted to let her go.

cbapter cbirteen

After taking her virginity last night, Burr had bathed her gently in the massive hotel tub, then carried her back to bed and made love to her again. They'd fallen asleep hours later, limbs entwined, heart-to-heart, her sweet lips pressed against the base of his throat and his resting on her hair.

This morning, as much as he hated to leave her, Sean Shanahan's arraignment waited, though he insisted that she didn't need to come with him.

"I want to," she'd murmured, looking completely delectable, still naked and curled up in bed.

"It's anticlimactic, *aisling*. You're not missing anything, I promise. The court always runs late. By the time Sean's case is up, I'll say a few words, the judge will make a decision about bail, and that'll be that." He smiled at her, tenderly caressing her cheek. "Thinking about you waiting here for me will make me happy, will give me something to look forward to."

She grinned back at him. "I *am* tired."

"Take a long hot bath. Get some rest. I'm loving you all over again when I get back."

"Loving me?" she asked softly, her eyes downcast, her finger scratching at the snow white sheets distractedly.

"Loving your body," he clarified, sitting next to her on the edge of the bed.

"Oh," she said, flicking a glance up at him, then looking away.

"You want me to tell you I love you?" he asked softly.

"Not if you don't mean it."

"If I said it, I would mean it. But it feels...too soon, doesn't it?"

"To be in love?" she asked, looking up at him. She nodded. "Yes, but..."

"But you feel it too," he said, staring at her.

She nodded. "I do."

"I care for you, Tierney. So much. More than any other woman I've ever known." He took a deep breath. "But I can't see a future for us yet."

She looked like she wanted to protest his words for a moment, but then she dropped his eyes, looking down, probably because she couldn't see it either.

"You hate Boston," he said, "but I work here. My sister's here. My friends."

"Your life."

He gulped, because his throat suddenly felt tight. "But my heart's with you. Wherever you are, Tierney, it's yours."

She took a deep breath and sighed, looking up at him. Her eyes were soft, holding his with abundant tenderness. "Should we talk about it when you get back?"

"Is that okay?" he asked.

"Mm-hm," she hummed, kissing him back when he dropped his lips to hers.

He left the room, heading downstairs and taking an Uber to the Dorchester District Court. As he exited his ride, he pulled his badge from his back pocket and slipped it around his neck, then climbed up the granite stairs and walked through the glass doors and into the courthouse.

Checking in at the clerk's office, he learned that Sean's arraignment, scheduled for ten o'clock, had already been moved to eleven thirty, so he took a seat on one of many benches, thinking about last night, thinking about Tierney.

He hadn't seen her coming, hadn't planned for her, and he was being honest when he'd told her earlier that their future wasn't clear to him. Their feelings had grown quickly—so quickly that they didn't have an actual, physical place for them yet. He had weeks, if not years, of work ahead in Boston. Today was just the beginning. To put Sean away, he'd need to give depositions and testimony to the DA's office, eventually testifying against the New Killeens in open court.

He wasn't free to move to New Hampshire; besides, he didn't have a job there. Besides, she hadn't invited him to. And why would she? They'd only known each other for a few weeks, no matter how fast their feelings had grown or how deeply they felt for one another.

Added to this were *her* feelings about Boston. What had she called it last night? Oh, right. *Bloody, godforsaken Boston.* Not a ringing endorsement, not to mention how, when they'd talked about the city on one of their many walks, she'd made her feelings clear. And it wasn't like Burr felt especially warm and fuzzy toward his hometown right now, but this job wasn't finished. He couldn't just get up and leave.

Maybe they could date long-distance for a while as the case moved through the courts. And maybe, by the time Sean was tried and convicted and Burr had fulfilled his commitment, he could consider relocating…if she'd wait for him.

With so many conflicting thoughts clouding his head, he almost didn't hear his father call his name.

"Burr! Son!"

His head snapped up, and he looked into his father's bright-blue eyes.

"Pop," he said, feeling wary after last night. "What're you doing here?"

"Seat free?" his father asked, gesturing to the empty bench beside Burr.

"Sure."

"See you got your badge back."

"Yeah," he said.

"Came to, ah, hear your testimony at the arraignment."

"You did?"

His father nodded. "Talked to Liam Donnelley this mornin'. Should've let you say yer peace last night."

"I get why you were mad."

"Yer sister could've died."

"I know, Pop."

"But it wasn't yer fault, son."

"If I hadn't been undercove—"

"Liam praised your work, said your partner sold you out, said you took a bullet of your own in the shoulder."

"It's okay now," said Burr, reaching up to rub the scar. "Went through clean."

"You killed Declan Shanahan."

"I did."

"Better days." His father sighed. "Yer girlfriend's a right corker."

Burr chuckled softly. "Yeah, she's something all right."

"Now, I'm not one for speeches, son, but, well, we're proud of the work you done. I'm proud my son brought down the New Killeens."

And while Burr took a mighty dose of pleasure in his father's words, he also marked the conversation as the moment it started: his name bound with the New Killeens. And it lay heavy on his heart.

Sitting on that bench for the next two hours, Burr told his father what he could about his life undercover with the New Killeens, and his father caught him up on family news.

"You've got to meet Bridey. She's somethin'!"

"I've seen her from a distance," Burr confessed. "Can't wait to be an uncle."

"It's time you think of settling down and havin' yer own."

Burr's mind slipped quickly to Tierney. "Someday. Hopefully. When this business with the New Killeens has been put to bed."

"Are ya gonna go back under, then?"

"No," said Burr. "But testifying, assisting the DA's office, the trial. Feels like it'll take forever."

"Hmm. But the undercover part's over now."

"Yeah, but—"

"Mr. O'Leary? They're ready for you now."

Burr looked up at the clerk, who gestured to the courtroom down the hall where Sean and his associates were being arraigned.

"You coming, Pop?"

"Wouldn't miss it, son," said his father, clapping him on the back and following him into the courtroom.

Thirty minutes later, Sean and the rest of the New

Killeens had been denied bail and were sent back to prison to await their trial. Burr breathed a small sigh of relief.

"Proud o' you, Burr," said his father on the steps of the courthouse.

"Thanks, Pop."

"Now you go celebrate with yer girl, huh? And then come by Suzy's later so we can meet her proper?"

"Will do," said Burr.

Impulsively, his father reached for him, enveloping him in a rare hug. Burr couldn't remember the last time his father had hugged him, and he blinked his eyes rapidly against the wave of emotions that threatened to embarrass him.

"Good to have you back, son," said his father, clapping him on the back.

"Good to be back, Pop."

His father cleared his throat. "Now, go. We'll talk later, eh?"

Burr nodded, catching a taxi back to the hotel.

He was relieved that bail had been denied, and now maybe he could start thinking about his life post-undercover. How it looked. How he *wanted* it to look. Glancing at his watch, he realized it was already after one o'clock. As he passed a kiosk selling roses, he considered asking the taxi driver to stop so he could pick up some for his sweetheart, but he was too eager to get back to her. *Another time.*

Back at the hotel, he paid the driver, beelining to the elevators and pressing the number "18" several times before the doors closed. His entire body hummed with longing to see her again, to have her, to hold her, to watch her face as he drove into her, and again as she climaxed with him.

The doors opened, and he stepped onto the plush

carpet but stopped almost immediately.

"Open up the fucking door! I know you're in there!"

Leaning down on impulse, Burr pulled his gun from his ankle holster, then approached the hallway slowly. Peeking around the corner, his breath caught when he realized that the banging and yelling was coming from his door. A man in jeans and a dark hoodie stood outside the door of the room where Burr had left his woman alone.

"I'm going to shoot the fucking lock if you don't open the fucking door!"

His heart beating double time, Burr leaned away, holding up his gun, breathing out three times fast, then turning back into the hallway.

"Boston Police! Put down your weapon!"

The man at the door turned to face Burr, holding a firearm. "Burr O'Leary!"

It was Patrick Griffin, Fat Billy's kid, whom Burr had seen up in New Hampshire loading the body of a blameless handyman into the trunk of his father's car.

"Pat," he said, his gun trained on the kid. "Put the gun away."

"You sold out my dad!"

"Your father's a criminal."

"And you're a feckin' narc!" yelled Patrick.

A hotel guest cracked open a door. "Call 911 and lock your door!" snapped Burr.

"Ima kill you!" Patrick exclaimed, raising the gun and shooting.

The bullet whizzed past Burr, down the hallway behind him. He didn't think. He acted, exactly like he'd been trained to. Aiming small, he squeezed the trigger, watching as Patrick

Griffin screamed out in pain before falling back onto the hotel carpet. Burr raced down the hallway, kicking Patrick's gun out of reach and keeping his own trained on the kid as hotel security came bounding down the hallway.

"Hands up, sir!"

Burr raised his hands over his head and threw his gun behind his back.

"I'm Boston PD," he said. "I'm going to turn around slowly. I'm wearing my badge."

The two armed security guards standing at the mouth of the hallway lowered their weapons, holstering them as they looked at Burr's badge.

"Can you tell us what happened?"

"Cuff him," he said, pointing to Patrick. "His name is Patrick Griffin. I got him once in the shoulder. His weapon is right over there."

"What happened here?"

"Give me a minute, huh? My girlfriend's in our room."

Stepping over Patrick, Burr flashed his card over the reader, racing into the hotel room to find Tierney on the bed clutching a pillow, her face wet with tears.

"Burr!" she screamed, jumping off the bed.

He sat down on the bed, pulling her onto his lap, holding her close and stroking her hair. "It's okay. It's okay. It's okay, *aisling*."

Her body was shaking. "He—He was b-banging."

"I know."

"He was b-banging on the—the d-door. He was—He had a g-gun."

"I know, love. I'm sorry. I know. It's over. It's over now. I'm here, Tierney."

She rested her head on his shoulder, coming down from her adrenaline high, sobbing and sniffling in his arms. And Burr's heart broke for her. Already uncomfortable in big cities like Boston, this would cook her goose. She'd never want to return again. And frankly, he didn't want her to. He didn't want her to be anywhere where her life could potentially be in danger.

Burr winced with the unfairness of it. He'd done his job. He'd just done his goddamned job. How many people he loved would be hurt before he realized that he'd never be free of the New Killeens?

"I w-was so s-scared," she said, her voice catching.

Be calm. Be calm. "I know. I'm so sorry I wasn't here, love. You're safe. You're safe now."

But she wasn't safe. Not at all. Every moment she stayed in Boston was perilous for her. Who knows who'd come after him next? After him and those he loved.

What if he'd stopped for roses? What if he'd gotten here five minutes later? Would she be dead? If that had happened, he'd just as soon turn the gun on himself. Life wouldn't be worth living if the woman he loved had been killed because of him.

Never again. He would *never* put her in danger again.

"Officer...?" called one of the security guards from the doorway.

"O'Leary," he said, quickly pulling a blanket around Tierney's naked body.

"Police are here, sir. We need to understand what happened."

Burr looked down at Tierney. "Can you get dressed? We need to give our statements."

She sniffled, her body still shuddering in his arms. "Y-Yeah. And then…c-can you t-take me home?"

"Of course," he said. "As soon as we talk to the police."

"Th-Thank you," she said, pulling the blanket around her body as she walked to the bathroom and closed the door behind her.

It'll never be over, a voice whispered in Burr's head as he pushed off the bed and went out to the hallway to explain what had happened.

The drive back up to Tierney's cottage was silent and strained. Although nothing could erase the beautiful night they'd spent together, Burr saw how shaken up Tierney was by what had happened at the hotel.

She'd been clear in her statement: One minute she'd been in bed, waiting for Burr, watching TV. The next, some madman had been banging on her hotel door. She'd crept to the door and looked out the peephole to see a young man in a hoodie. At first, she thought he must be in the wrong place, but when he said, "Get out here, O'Leary, you fucking rat!," she knew he wasn't.

She'd run back to the bed, clasping a pillow to her naked body, shaking, too scared to organize her thoughts, to pick up the phone and call the police or dial 0. She'd literally *frozen* with fear until Burr had gotten there.

And that's what killed him more than anything. Tierney was one of the bravest woman—no, bravest people—he'd ever met. The fact that she'd been frozen with terror chilled him to the bone.

"I'm sorry," said Burr softly, breaking an hour of silence. "I'm so goddamned sorry, Tierney."

"It's not your fault," she said.

"It is," he said. "People I love—people I care about are getting hurt because of me."

"It's not…your fault," she said again.

He glanced over at her to find her eyes puffy and cheeks red. She'd been crying off and on since the incident, though she'd been relatively calm for the last hour in the car. He'd hoped that she was recovering a little.

"I'd die for you," he said, his voice breathless and strained.

"But I don't *want* you to die for me," she said, her voice breaking through more tears. "I want you to live. I want you *alive* for me."

He reached for her hand, and she clasped his, raising it to her lips and kissing his warm skin, then rubbing the back of his hand against her cheek.

"Can you stay with me tonight?" she asked.

"Donnelley needs me back by seven o'clock tomorrow morning to give a statement on what happened with Patrick."

She made a tiny whimpering noise that made his heart clench.

"I'll stay until four," he said. It was the best he could do.

She was quiet for several minutes before sniffling. "You *arrived* at four. That first night. It feels so long ago."

"Are you sorry?" he asked. "Are you sorry I ever arrived at your doorstep?"

She shook her head as tears slipped down her cheeks. "Never. I'll *never* be sorry."

"Do you—" *Oh, God, was it even fair to ask her this?* "Do

you still have hope for us?"

"I'll *always* have hope for us," she said.

For the rest of the drive to her cottage, she held his hand in hers, but he felt something terrible brewing between them—a stalemate, the beginning of a long good-bye—and he hated it so much, he didn't know how to contain his rage.

What was the answer? To hunt down every single member of the New Killeens and dispatch them one by one? He wasn't a murderer. But how was he ever going to have a normal life?

When they reached her cottage, Burr carried their bags inside, placing them on the floor just inside the front door as Tierney walked wearily upstairs.

Standing alone in her parlor as the late-afternoon crickets chirped outside, he remembered the first time he left her, brushing a kiss to her sweet lips and telling her, *Maybe this isn't the end of you and me, aisling.* But now? Now he felt like maybe it was.

Not that she'd want to, but even if she suggested it, he'd forbid her to come to Boston. As much as he loved her, he didn't want her there. In part because she wasn't comfortable. But more because she wasn't safe. He'd rather walk away and never see her again, rather than risk her well-being.

And so this might be all they'd ever have. Today. Tonight. Until four o'clock in the morning.

He walked up the stairs slowly, turning left at the top of them as he had that first night. She was curled up on her bed, quietly weeping, and without thinking, he kicked off his shoes and lay down behind her, drawing her into his arms, against his chest.

"I'm so sad," she murmured through tears.

"I am too," he said.

She placed her hands over his. "Do you think we could just sleep like this? For a little while? I'm so tired, Burr."

Of course she was. He'd kept her awake for most of last night, and she'd been scared out of her mind earlier today.

"You sleep, love. I'm here."

It took a little while, but after a time, she slept, her body relaxing against him, the weight of her head on his arm welcome, her breathing deep and easy.

"I'll go back to Boston and leave you be, *aisling*," he whispered. "I promise I'll never put you in danger again."

She murmured in her sleep, turning in his arms, and Burr rolled onto his back, taking her with him, her sleeping head resting over his heart as he also succumbed to sleep.

Hours later, he woke up, still fully dressed, to find her standing beside the bed, looking out the window.

"What time is it?" he asked.

"Almost three," she said, coming back to the bed and sitting down beside him. "We slept hard."

"What are you wearing?" he asked, realizing that she wasn't in jeans, but little shorts and a tank top.

"Pajamas. I changed when I woke up."

"How long have you been up?"

"Half an hour."

Her voice was steadier than it had been at the hotel or in the car. Rest had done her good.

"I have to go soon," he said.

"I know."

"Tierney, I never meant to bring danger into your life,

and yet…that's what keeps happening. First the phone call to Mass General…then, Patrick Griffin at the hotel." He scooted over, and she lay down next to him, facing him, the moonlight through the window making her eyes shine. "I can't…I won't do anything that puts you in further danger."

"I know," she said.

"So you know what that means?"

"That you won't be back for a while," she said, leaning forward to press her lips to his, and despite the fact that her voice was steady and even, he tasted the salt of her tears and knew she was crying.

"Don't cry," he said, reaching up to cup her face. "Please don't cry, *aisling*."

She kissed him again, and his hands slipped under her top, sliding along the silky softness of her back. Rolling away from him, she stood up beside the bed and pulled off her top, then pushed her shorts down, standing naked before him, lit only by the moon and the stars.

He pulled off his own shirt, unbuckled his belt, unbuttoned his jeans, and pushed them down, kicking them to the foot of the bed. As naked as she, he reached for her and she climbed on top of him, straddling his abdomen as she leaned forward for another kiss.

When she drew back, she reached for something on her bedside table, and he realized she held a condom packet in her fingers. She ripped it open, holding it out to him. "I don't know how."

She slid from his chest, kneeling beside him as he reached down and sheathed his erection. Once he was finished, she climbed back on top of him, taking his cock in her hand and lowering her body over him.

Tight and hot, she was heaven around him, fisting him like muscled silk and sucking him forward with every thrust. Her tits bounced with each plunge of his hips, and he reached for them, teasing her nipples into tight points and feeling her innermost muscles tighten around him.

He held her hips, driving up and into her again and again, and wishing that they had more time, every day, every night, to explore each other and love each other and learn every nuance and every sound and every beautiful fucking thing about each other. When he came, he bellowed her name, calling her his love and the woman of his heart, and it was all true, but fucking hell, he was leaving her in half an hour and his fucking soul was in shreds.

He held her hips as she leaned back, running a hand through her dark hair, her eyes glistening with tears.

"I love you," she said, her voice breathless with exertion and emotion, his semihard cock spent but still within her. "I don't know anything else, except that I love you, Burr. That's how I feel, and I don't know when I'll see you again, so this is my chance to tell you. I love you...and I want you to know it."

He stared up at her—his heart bursting with the purity and rightness of her words—miserable to the very core of his being.

"I have to go back, Tierney, and I can't ask you to come with me."

"I know," she said brokenly, lifting the back of her hand to her face to swipe the tears away.

She rolled from his body onto her back beside him, and he got up, disposing of the condom in the bathroom before returning to her. She was still naked, on her side now, with her back to him. He lay down beside her, pulling her warm body against his and trying to memorize how it felt to hold her, wondering if he'd ever have a chance to hold her again.

"You are my *aisling*," he said, softly. "The sweetest dream. Everything I could ever want."

"*A chéadsearc*. First in my heart.," she murmured. "When you're ready, come back to me, my love. I'll be waiting."

chapter fourteen

Three Weeks Later

When you're ready, come back to me, my love. I'll be waiting.

The words haunted him mercilessly, but Burr's reality was this:

He couldn't have her if he couldn't keep her safe.

And honest to God, he didn't know how to do that yet. And until he figured it out, he wouldn't reach out to her, because it would only be giving both of them false hope.

For now, he was staying with Suzanne and Connor, and while he welcomed the chance to reconnect with his sister and get to know his niece, he couldn't deny it ached to be around them too. He wanted what they had. He wanted it with Tierney.

Tierney.

Fuck, but thinking about her hurt.

Sitting on Suzanne's patio, watching Bridey playing on her swing set, he reached for his chest, rubbing the place over his heart and remembering the sweet weight of her head resting there. Had it only been three weeks ago? Because it felt like three hours ago. He could still remember every look, every word, every touch and smell and feeling in such intricate, perfect detail.

Patrick Griffin had been arrested for disturbing the

peace and the attempted murder of a policeman, but how many other New Killeens were waiting in the wings, gathering their strength to come after Burr, and those he loved, again? It was a question that tormented him endlessly.

For most of the past three weeks, Burr had buried himself in work, recounting his dealings with the New Killeens in intricate detail for the Boston DA's office. But yesterday morning he was told that while he would be needed as a star witness closer to the court date, his usefulness in this part of the process was at an end.

Reporting to Captain Donnelley yesterday afternoon, he was advised to take "a couple of weeks" off for R&R, before being reinstated and reassigned at District C-6.

And that's when the *real* torture had begun.

He was only on day two of said R&R, and he felt neither relaxed nor rested.

He felt frustrated. He felt tired. He felt lost. He felt…empty.

He longed for Tierney with an ache that bordered on anguish, dreaming of her every night and reaching for her every morning in the moment between sleeping and waking. And when he finally woke up? The crushing disappointment of being alone was almost too much to bear.

All he wanted was her, and not having her made life feel worthless and pointless.

But what was the alternative?

His dark mood lifted just a touch when Bridey waved to him, asking him to watch her go down the slide. But the slight boost he felt was quickly swept away when he considered that the only woman in the world with whom he'd want to have children was three hours away.

A chéadsearc…come back.

His eyes burned suddenly and unexpectedly, and he blinked them furiously.

She loved him.

She *loved* him, and he loved her so fucking much it was killing him to be apart from her.

"Burr!" said Suzy, appearing at the back door with two beers. "Help me down the stairs, huh?"

He climbed up the steps, carefully pulling his sister into his arms and carrying her to one of the comfortable chairs in her patio sitting area. She could get around the house with a cane for now, but stairs were still off-limits.

"Nice out here today," she said, offering him a beer.

"Yeah," he muttered.

"Oh, Christ. We need to talk."

"What about?"

"Tierney." Suzanne's ice-blue eyes bored into his. "And how miserable you are without her."

Exhaling a long-suffering sigh, he clamped his lips around the top of the beer bottle and tipped it back, taking a long sip. It sluiced down his throat, the bubbles sharp and burning.

"I liked her," said Suzanne. "She has a backbone."

You're the bravest woman I've ever met.

"Yeah, she does," he said, leaning his head back on the chair cushion and closing his eyes.

"Told Dad to go to hell in Irish."

"That's her," Burr mumbled.

"And the way she looked at you," continued Suzanne, "like God broke t'bloody mold after he used it for you." She sighed. "She's in love with you."

"Jaysus, Suze!" he exclaimed, opening his eyes and leaning forward, his body coiled with anger. "Are you trying to fucking *kill* me?"

"No, Burr," she said evenly. "I'm trying to fucking understand."

"Understand *what*?"

"Why you aren't together."

"Take a look at the scar on your hip and ask me again," he growled. "You think I'd ask her to come stay here with me in this shithole of a city? After what happened to you? After Patrick Griffin tracked us down at that hotel? Where her life would always be in danger? What kind of man would that make me? Not to mention, she bloody well *hates* it here, not that I blame her."

"Got it." Suzanne nodded. "So why not go see her?"

"What's the point? I'm here. She's there. My *life* is here. Her *life* is there. What're we going to do? Torture ourselves by drawing out the inevitable?"

"Which is…?"

"Stop, Suzy. Please," he said, feeling beyond weary. "Please, just stop."

He leaned his head back again, hoping that Suzy would shut up and leave him be. It did no good talking about it. They lived two different lives in two different worlds. He was a Boston cop. She lived hours away in the country. End of story.

"I'm going to talk," she said. "And you can listen or you can block me out, but I need to know that I said this, Burr. I'm your sister and I love you and I can't stand to see you like this. Not to mention, I got shot. You owe me." She paused, waiting for him to argue, he supposed, but he was too tired. *Say what you want*, he thought. *It won't help.* "For the last three years, your life was dangerous, and you were isolated from your friends and family, very much alone. I'm sure you saw and did some things you wish you hadn't seen or done, and I know you'll hold those things in your heart, and when you think of them, they'll hurt you. But I also hope you'll remember that the New Killeens are finished because of you. That's a good thing you did, Burr. It was a hard job, and you were betrayed by someone you trusted along the way. But you did your job to the bitter end, even testifying at the arraignment and spending the better part of the last three weeks giving testimony to the DA. And sure, you'll need to be there in court for the trial, but who knows when that'll happen? Could be years from now."

"Exactly," he bit out. "So there's no point in talking about it."

"There are two more things I want to say," said Suzanne, "and when I'm done, you can tell me to shut my feckin' gob, deal?"

He huffed with annoyance. "Fine. Christ."

"The first thing I want to say is that your time with the New Killeens is over."

"Yeah, I know."

"No, you *don't*," she said slowly and carefully.

"What?" He stared at her. "What does *that* mean?"

"Look around, Burr. Declan's dead. Sean, Billy, Gordon, Frank, and Paul are all in jail now. Patrick's in jail. They're *not* a danger to you and yours anymore." She paused to let her words sink in before continuing. "A stupid kid did a stupid, reckless thing showing up at your hotel room, because his father was arrested, and he was sad and terrified, and he blamed you for it. But it's not foreshadowing the future. It was a onetime thing. It's over now, Burr. It's *over*. I'm safe. You're safe. I mean, as safe as a cop in a big city with various enemies can ever expect to be."

Boston, *safe*? *No*, he thought. *Absolutely not*. Boston would *never* be safe, never *feel* safe. Too many terrible things had happened here for Boston to ever feel like home again.

"You're wrong," he said. "Boston isn't safe."

She cleared her throat. "So why are you staying here?"

His lips dropped open, and he stared at her, trying to understand what she was saying. "Staying…?"

Suzy nodded. "She doesn't belong here in Boston, right? Tierney? She doesn't belong here."

"Right."

"Well, the second thing I want to say to you is this, Burr: neither do you," she said, her voice gentle but firm.

"What do you—Suzy, this is my…"

"Home? No, it's not. Not anymore." She took a deep breath and sighed. "We've been here in Dorchester— O'Learys—since the 1850s, right? Sure. Six generations in this neighborhood, and Mam and Pop never let us forget it. Our people are here. Our work. Our homes. Our churches and schools. Our lives. Boston proud, right? Except…" She leaned forward, reaching out to place her hand on Burr's knee. "Except this *isn't* your home anymore, Burr.

"I think you went undercover to make a change, and based on the results, you did grand. But…you didn't escape that life unscathed. More changed for you than just bringing down the New Killeens." Her eyes were sympathetic as she squeezed her fingers. "I know that you're *from* Boston, and I've no doubt that some part of you will always *love* Boston.

But I don't think you *like* it very much anymore."

It was like blasphemy to hear her articulate these words, especially because she was right. He was one of Boston's finest, born and bred, a fourth-generation police officer. Boston proud. Boston *go bragh*. And yet...

Would he ever feel comfortable here again? Or would he be looking over his shoulder for the rest of his life, waiting for some disgruntled New Killeen like Patrick Griffin to take a shot at him or someone he loved?

He knew the answer. He'd known it for weeks now.

"I wanted to do good," he murmured. "I just...wanted to do good."

"And you did," said Suzanne. "You did something great for Boston. That's the gift you leave behind. But this isn't your home anymore, Burr. It hasn't been your home for a long time." Her fingers squeezed his knee before she withdrew her hand and sat back. "Unless I'm mistaken, and we both know I'm not, your home is with a certain black-haired Irish girl up north." She took a swig of her beer and gave him a look. "Boston isn't the only city with a police department, you know. I have it on good authority they have them all over, even in little towns in New Hampshire."

"There's still work to do here. Testimony to give."

"Nah. It's done for now. And if there's more to do, come down and do it, and then go back. Back *home*."

"I told Donnelley I'd report to work the week after next."

"Oh, then," she said, her voice dripping with sarcasm, "by all means, take a new assignment, and stay here where you're puir miserable."

He stared at her.

"Or...stop being a damn eejit!" she cried. "Get out of here. Go be with your woman! Find a new home! A new job! A new life! Go now! Scat!"

Go maire sibh bhur saol nua. May you enjoy your new life.

"Just like that?" he asked.

"No," she deadpanned. "Make it tougher on yourself. You're good at doing that."

"But what about you?" he said. "I almost lost you. I just got you back."

"And I'll *always* be here. This is my home and I'm happy here, and since you put Sean Shanahan away, *I* feel safe again," she said. "But Burr...you're *unhappy* here. Now, you can be unhappy for a week or two before you make a change, or you can stay here and be unhappy for the rest of your life." She took his beer from the coffee table and finished it. "What you want—*what you need*—is a fresh start with your girl."

He stared at his sister, her words and his thoughts a maelstrom in his head, swirling into reason, into change, into a plan.

Enjoy your new life.

New life.

Fresh start.

Your home is wherever your Tierney is.

I'll always have hope for us.

A chéadsearc.

And suddenly, something inside of Burr that was wound very, very tight sprang free. Looking up at Suzanne, he felt his smile start small, growing, growing, growing until he was chuckling softly.

"And...now you're just being crazy, laughing at

nothing," she said, pursing her lips before joining her brother with a small giggle.

She was right…about everything.

He was sick of his grim, gritty life in Boston. He didn't want to be a part of it anymore. He didn't want to be known as the cop who'd gone undercover with the New Killeens, no matter how much good it did. It would follow him for the rest of his life; something by which he would be identified, for better or worse, for the rest of his life, and he'd never be able to leave it behind.

And fuck, but he didn't want that.

What he wanted—more than anything else—was a fresh start with Tierney.

He wanted to live in a little stone cottage on the edge of a great estate and play hockey with her brother in a local league. He wanted to eat burgers and drink beer and watch his woman lean over a pool table without worrying someone was coming for him. He wanted to give her brothers shit and tell her he loved her in Irish and take long walks with her at twilight and worship her body all night long until he didn't know where her pleasure ended and his began. He didn't want the life that lay before him in Boston. He didn't want any part of it. He wanted a new one altogether.

He wanted a new life with Tierney Haven.

"You want another beer?" asked Suzanne.

He shook his head. "Nope. It's Wednesday. If I leave now, I can drop off my badge with Donnelley and make it to her place in time for family dinner."

"Speaking of family dinner…how about coming back for one?" she asked with a sly smile. "Say…in a month or two?"

"Yeah," he said, standing up, eager to get back to his apartment and start packing. If he hurried, he might make it to Moonstone Manor in time for Wednesday night dinner. "Or how would you, Connor and Bridey feel about coming up to New Hampshire for a weekend?"

"There we go." Suzanne smiled up at her brother and nodded. "Now *that* sounds like a plan."

***

Tierney could tell the second Brittany and Rory walked in the door that they had some news to share. Brittany was bouncier than usual, and Rory, who was already a sap when it came to his girlfriend, looked at her with such sheer and utter devotion, it almost hurt to see them together. It made her unending longing for Burr all the sharper.

"So what's up with you two?" asked Tierney, taking their raincoats and hanging them on the pegs by the front door.

"Eeeeep! I can't wait!" cried Brittany, holding out her left hand where a diamond ring sat perched on her fourth finger. "We're engaged!"

Tierney had known that this was coming, of course, and she was deeply, genuinely happy for her brother and Brittany, though she couldn't deny that her heart cracked and bled a little as she witnessed their happiness. It had been three weeks since Burr had returned to Boston, and she hadn't heard from him since.

"Oh!" she gasped, tears filling her eyes. "Oh, my!"

Brittany threw her arms around Tierney, and she hugged her future sister-in-law, closing her eyes against the sharp, salty burn.

When Brittany stepped away, Tierney looked up into

her brother's eyes.

"*Comhghairdeas, Rory. Go maire tú an lá!*" she said, congratulating him in Irish before letting him pull her into a tight embrace.

"I see you, Tier," he whispered near her ear.

She closed her eyes tightly, but tears slipped free, sliding down her cheeks.

Both Rory and Ian had expressed worry about her, gently and in their own ways, since Burr had left. She'd explained everything in detail, and they understood why he'd left. And while they liked him, her safety and happiness came first. Though they would have supported her if it was what she really wanted, being the wife of a Boston cop wasn't the life either brother would choose for her.

Tierney had seen, firsthand, how much Burr's family meant to him and how good he was at his job. She loved Burr desperately, but Boston frightened her. The noise. The pace. The people living on top of each other with barely a patch of green. People showing up at hotels and waving guns around. If she relocated to Boston, she'd be alone a lot while Burr worked, and she wasn't good at making friends. Would she be able to make a happy life for herself, or would her *un*happiness eventually chip away at everything that had made her relationship with Burr so special? To leave her home and job and family only to end up destroying any potential happiness with Burr would be the biggest mistake of all. So she was stuck. Here. Without him.

Her heart clenched as Rory squeezed her before leaning back. She opened her eyes, swallowing over the lump in her throat.

"I'm so happy for you, Rory," she said. "Truly."

Brittany trained her gleaming smile on Ian. "I'll expect *you* to behave. Hallie's coming up for the wedding."

"H-Hallie Gilbert?"

"Who else?" Brittany nodded. "She's agreed to be one of my bridesmaids…and I hope Tierney will agree to be the other!"

"Of course!" said Tierney, engulfed in another overenthusiastic Brittany bear hug.

"Yay! It's going to be so fun! You're going to love Hallie, and her little girl, Jenny, is going to be a flower girl!"

When Brittany finally released her, Tierney asked, "So when's the happy day?"

"Well," said Brittany, shooting a quick look at Rory, who winked at her. "We have a little more news." She placed her hands over her stomach then looked up at Tierney. "We're expecting."

Tierney's neck whipped to the side, her eyes connecting with Rory's. "You're having a baby?"

"We are."

"Oh, my God! That's—that's amazing! Oh, Rory—wait. Does Mom know?"

Rory chuckled, shaking his head. "Are you mad? I'm attached to my balls."

"When are you telling them?"

"*After* the wedding," he said.

"And when's this wedding happening?" asked Ian, his voice stilted and eyes troubled, like he was still processing the idea of seeing Hallie again.

"Thanksgiving weekend at Summerhaven," said Brittany. "We'll have friends and family come up on Wednesday and stay until Sunday! Thanksgiving dinner on

Thursday. Rehearsal dinner on Friday. Wedding on Saturday! I'm counting on you to help me, Tierney. I only have six weeks to plan everything!"

Still chattering about wedding plans, Brittany followed Tierney to the kitchen to get dinner ready, and once seated, Tierney and Ian toasted the happy couple with sparkling cider, digging into a baked ham and mashed potatoes.

Brittany and Rory left soon after dinner, but Ian lingered, standing beside Tierney as she washed the dinner dishes and he dried.

"First of us to get married," he said.

"Weird, right?"

Ian nodded. "Yeah."

"You looked pretty surprised about Hallie," said Tierney.

His chest swelled as he took a deep breath. "Haven't seen her in a long time."

"What happened between you two? How come you never said anything to me and Rory about her?"

"Leave it, Tier," he said softly, taking a dripping plate from her hands and drying it distractedly.

"Are you going to be okay?"

Ian opened the cabinet beside the fridge and put the plate away and then turned to his sister. "Are you asking about my heart or my sobriety?"

"Both," she said, then added, "but I guess I'm more *worried* about your sobriety."

"I'll be okay," he said. "If anything…" His voice drifted off for a moment before he finished his thought. "I'm *not* backsliding." He looked up at her, his eyes searing. "What about you? Are *you* going to be okay?"

"What do you mean?" she asked, focusing all of her attention on scrubbing out the baking pan she'd used for the honey ham.

"I mean you've been a zombie for the last three weeks." He paused, then added, "I mean you miss Burr."

She blinked, the suds in the sink suddenly blurring. "I really…" She gulped before continuing. "God, I miss him so much, which is crazy because I barely knew him, right? We only…I mean, we only spent a couple of weeks together. It wasn't enough time to—"

"Yeah," said Ian. "It was."

"I don't know what to do."

"Have you thought about going to Boston?"

Only every minute of every day! She used the sleeve of her cardigan to swipe at her tears, scrubbing the pan with renewed vigor. "I can't go live in Boston, Ian. It would eat me up and spit me out. I'd be miserable."

"Even with him?"

"Especially with him! He's an inner-city cop. I'd always be scared for him. I'd stay up every night waiting for him to come home, half-crazy that someone had hurt him. I can't love him like I do and bear that life. I…I can't."

Ian raised an eyebrow. "Maybe you should give it a try before you make that decision."

She turned on him. "Do you think it's *easy* for me to let him go? It's not! It's torture. It's fucking misery every day since he left. I don't *know* what to do. I don't *know* how to forget him. I don't *know* how to stop loving him. I hate where I am. I hate where he is. I don't know how…I don't…I don't…"

Her tears were falling so fast, she couldn't speak

anymore, and she rested her sudsy hands on the side of the sink, her head bowed, her shoulders shaking with sobs.

Suddenly Ian's arms were around her. "I'm sorry, Tier. I know how much you care about him. I have no right to judge you."

She relaxed in his arms, bawling against his solid chest as he rubbed her back. Finally, little by little, her tears subsided and she hiccupped, looking up at her brother's face. "It s-sucks. I don't—I d-don't know what to do. And b-besides, he hasn't *invited* me to come to B-Boston."

"Would you go to him if he did?"

"I d-don't know. Maybe I'd t-try. Even B-Boston's got to be b-better than this." She shrugged halfheartedly. "Sorry for crying all over you."

"Nah. It's fine. I love having your snot on my shirt."

She chuckled softly, grabbing a paper towel and wiping her cheeks. "Tears are useless."

"I wish I knew what to tell you. I wish I could help."

"You can't," she said, taking a shaky breath. "Just be patient while I try to figure it out."

"Well," said Ian, rinsing the pan before drying it, "if you don't cheer up soon, I'm going to have to resort to drastic measures."

She shook her head, giving him a warning look. "No drastic measures. I'll be okay. I promise."

"Okay," said Ian, pulling the drain from the sink and hanging his damp drying cloth on the oven handle. "I have to get going. Meeting at eight."

"I'm proud of you."

"I know," said Ian, leaning down to kiss her forehead. "Be good, huh?"

She nodded, telling him she loved him in Irish before closing the back door behind him.

Alone in the quiet of her cottage, she turned off the kitchen lights and stepped into the living room, remembering the dark and stormy night so many weeks ago when Burr had arrived on her doorstep.

She'd had no idea then how much her life would change: the rush of falling for someone, the delight of learning that they longed, in turn, for you. The way it felt to touch him, hold him, kiss him, and give herself to him. The way it felt to love him. The lump in her throat doubled, and she sat down on the couch despondently.

Have you thought about going to Boston?

She thought about it, but she'd seen Suzanne's house in that close-knit Dorchester neighborhood. People living on top of each other. For happily reclusive Tierney, the idea made her skin itch. Not to mention, it was Burr who'd insisted that he return to Boston alone—that his life was there and hers was in New Hampshire. More than anything else, that's what was keeping her from him. She knew that he cared for her—or he *had*—but maybe not enough to change his life for her, which made her hesitant to consider changing hers for him.

And it left them both in a terrible, awful place.

A stalemate.

Which might be okay if her feelings would just go away. But they wouldn't. Her heart was fixed on him. Her body longed for his touch. Her ears coveted the low hum of his voice. It was hell, and there was nothing she could do to stop the yearning.

A knock at her front door made her sit up. Ian. Sighing,

she slid off the couch.

"Ian!" she exclaimed, stepping over to the door and turning the knob, "I *said* that there was no need for drastic…"

Her voice trailed off, the breath knocked from her lungs as she looked up into the clear blue eyes of Burr O'Leary. She pressed her palm to her chest, trying to take a deep breath, but unable, her eyes shuttering, blinking back tears, and wondering if he was real.

"Tierney."

His voice.

Oh, God, his beautiful, familiar voice.

She tried to get control of herself, but she couldn't. Her face crumpled, and her shoulders shook as a sob she tried to swallow escaped from her lips.

"*Aisling*," he said, reaching for her. "Can I come in?"

Unable to speak, she nodded, grabbing at his forearms and pulling him inside.

He pushed the door closed with his foot and stared down at her, his eyes searching her for a second before he pulled her against his chest urgently, his lips against her hair, his voice gritty and soft with emotion.

"I missed you. Fuck, I missed you, Tierney. I missed you. I missed you so much."

The words were a soft litany as he kissed her head, reaching up to cup her cheeks, his lips landing on her forehead, her cheeks and finally, flush on hers, where she wanted them, where they belonged. He kissed her desperately, like it had been far longer than three weeks since they'd last been in each other's arms, and Tierney closed her eyes, tears running down her cheeks as she remembered the taste of him, the perfect feeling of being in his arms.

"Are you here?" she sobbed, looking up at him. "*How* are you here?"

"I drove," he said simply, grinning down at her.

"A visit will only make things harder," she lamented, then shook her head, holding him tighter. "No. I don't care. I needed this so badly. I missed you so much."

"It won't make things harder. I promise," he said. "Come sit with me."

He took her hand and led her to the sofa, pulling her down on his lap and clasping his arms around her. He kissed her again, slower this time, like he had time. Gently exploring the crevices of her mouth, he slid his tongue alongside hers, groaning softly before leaning away.

"I love you, Tierney," he said, looking deeply into her eyes. "I love you so much, it was hell to be away from you."

"For me too," she murmured, caressing his cheek. "I missed you so much. I love you too, Burr. I tried to let you go, but…I couldn't. I waited."

"I left Boston," he said. "I don't—it doesn't—it's not my *home* anymore."

"But your job, Suzanne—"

"I quit my job," he said.

"What?" she gasped. "But you *love* your job!"

"No, Tierney. I love you," he clarified, pressing a quick kiss to her lips. "And yeah, I loved being a Boston cop, but the New Killeens took that love away from me. I don't want to be there anymore. I don't feel like I can do good there."

"But you're a *great* cop!" she insisted.

"And I still *can* be," he said slowly and carefully. "Somewhere else."

"Somewhere...else?"

He nodded. "Uh-huh. Somewhere like Wolfeboro...or Meredith...or Gilford...or—"

Her heart started thumping and her breath caught with a mixture of hope and caution. "Those are towns in New Hampshire!"

He chuckled, his eyes glistening as he nodded at her. "And all of them will have my resume by tomorrow."

A sob broke free from her lips and she buried her face in his neck. "You're moving here? You're staying!"

"I'm staying," he confirmed, his voice breaking.

"I'm not a crier," she insisted, her voice muffled as tears streamed down her cheeks. "I'm not. I promise."

"I don't mind," he said, rubbing her back as she wept. "You cry all you want, *aisling*. I'm here now, and I'm not leaving you ever again."

"Promise?" she asked, drawing back to look in his eyes.

"I'll stay as long as you'll have me."

"What about Suzanne and Bridey? You just got them back in your life. I don't want to be the reason you—"

"Oh, yeah! I almost forgot. Suzanne, Connor, and Bridey want to come up for a weekend in October. Think Rory could reserve a cottage for them?"

"Yes!" she cried, throwing her arms around his neck as more tears spilled from her eyes. "Yes, yes, yes! Rory could reserve *anything* for them!"

"Know what else?" he continued, whispering near her ear. "I'm going to need a place to stay."

"No, you're not," she said, leaning back and cupping his cheeks. "You have a place. With me. This is your home too, Burr."

He grinned at her, his eyes sliding to her lips and lingering there for a hot minute before he seized her eyes again. "You're sure? Our story began on a dark and stormy, night, *aisling*. Those tales don't always end well."

"This one does, *a chéadsearc*," she said. She smiled at him with all the love in her heart. "This one has a *very* happy ending."

"I believe it does," he said, lowering his lips to hers. "In fact, I'm sure of it."

epilogue

A Thanksgiving Wedding

"I now pronounce you husband and wife," intoned Pastor Clarke of the Center Sandwich Congregational Church. "You may kiss the bride."

As Rory leaned down to kiss Brittany, Tierney looked over the heads of the happy couple to catch Burr staring back at her, an intense expression in his light-blue eyes.

I love you, he mouthed.

Her lips wobbled a little, trying not to cry for her brother's happiness *or* her own.

I love you, too, she answered.

Since Burr's return, they hadn't spent a night apart, which added up to a lot of perfect nights in his arms, their bodies slick with sweat and their hearts beating as one.

When Rory asked Burr to join Ian as his other groomsmen a few weeks ago, it hadn't surprised Tierney too much. Burr had secured a job at the Center Harbor Police Department within two weeks of his return, impressing Rory and Ian with his commitment to Tierney by putting down roots. Besides, his slap shot was already leading the Gilford Griffins to victory. At this point, he was pretty much considered a member of the family.

Speaking of family, Burr's sister and her family had come up for a weekend in early November and stayed at

Summerhaven. Rory and Brittany were in one cabin, Tierney and Burr in another, Ian in his own, and Suzanne, Connor, and Bridey in another. Surrounded by the Technicolor glory of autumnal New Hampshire, they'd fished and hiked—and toasted marshmallows around a bonfire, much to Bridey's delight.

Well, actually…Bridey and *Jenny's* delight.

As Rory and Brittany finished their kiss, Tierney slid her eyes to Ian, who looked like a thundercloud, staring at the woman standing next to Tierney, wearing an identical black bridesmaids' dress: Halcyon Gilbert Silveira.

Hallie, and her daughter, Jenny, had moved back up to their Squam Lake summer cottage just before Halloween, and since then, Ian had been just about impossible. Tierney wasn't talking about his sobriety, which seemed intact, but his moods. Dear Lord, he'd been a grumpy bastard since Hallie had appeared, grunting and growling at everyone, with barely a smile for anyone.

Well, actually…anyone except Jenny.

For little Jenny? Ian's frown was neutralized. And Jenny *adored* Ian. With her dark-brown braids trailing down her back, Jenny followed Tierney's gruff brother all over the camp like a wee duckling, talking his ear off.

Rory and Brittany took hands and stepped down the stairs of the church altar, followed by Ian and Hallie, who, Tierney noted, were careful not to touch as they walked side by side in stoic discomfort. Finally, Tierney turned to face her escort, and as her eyes smashed into Burr's, she felt it again—as she always did—*BAM.*

His hair had grown out a little bit, as jet-black as hers, and less edgy than his gangland buzz cut. As handsome as the devil in a tuxedo, today was the first time she'd ever seen him dressed formally, and good Lord, it had taken her breath away.

She grinned at him, clasping the hand he offered.

"Look at you, now, Smilin' Irish," he said in a light brogue, winking at her. "I mentioned you look a picture in that dress, right?"

"You did," she said, her cheeks flushing from his compliment.

"An' do ya' know where that dress will look even better?" he asked.

She knew what was coming but shook her head back and forth, looking up at him with pursed lips. "Where?"

"On the floor of our bedroom," he said, chuckling as she rolled her eyes at him.

"You're insatiable."

"That's because you're delicious."

"Burr, stop it. We're in a church."

"Not a Catholic one. Doesn't count."

Giggling quietly, she squeezed his hand as they swept up the aisle, her happiness filling her heart to overflowing.

***

Tierney stood in the receiving line in front of the church, shaking hands with the departing guests, while Burr stood off to the side with Hallie Silveira and her little girl, Jenny. When Suzanne, Connor, and Bridey had visited Summerhaven in October, Bridey and Jenny had become "besties," spending the whole weekend together.

He squatted down in front of the little girl. "Hey, Jenny. I was talking to Bridey yesterday, and she said to say hello."

"I miss her," said Jenny. "When's she coming back?"

"She misses you, too," said Burr, "but I think she'll be back for Christmas."

Jenny's whole face brightened. "Bridey's coming for Christmas? Oh, my gosh!" She looked up at her mother. "Mommy! Bridey's coming for Christmas!"

Burr stood up, looking into Hallie's blue eyes. "Think you'll still be here?"

"We have nowhere else to go," she said softly, sliding her eyes to her daughter and adding in an animated voice, "I heard, baby! What great news!"

"I'ma tell Mr. Haven!" Jenny exclaimed, running over to the receiving line and tugging on the hem of Ian's tuxedo jacket.

Burr watched Hallie's eyes follow her daughter, her lips tightening into a thin line when she stopped in front of Ian. As he squatted down to talk to Jenny, celebrating her news with a huge hug, Hallie's face softened, her head cocking to the side as she watched them.

"She likes him," said Burr softly. "Ian."

"She's crazy about him," said Hallie, her face still troubled as she watched Ian lean away from Jenny, still grinning at her from behind his trimmed-back beard.

"They say that kids are good judges of character."

She looked up at him, her lips unsmiling, her eyes flat. "Kids are naïve."

He nodded. There was no sense arguing with her, especially since Jenny was already running back to them, her smile wide and eyes sparkling with excitement. "Mr. Haven said he'd take me and Bridey sledding if there's snow over Christmas!"

"I can take you, too, baby." Hallie forced a smile,

pushing a lock of her daughter's dark hair behind her ear. "Remember what we talked about? We don't always have to bother Mr. Haven, right?"

"Okay, Mama," said Jenny, her smile dimming.

Hallie turned to Burr. "I think we'll go freshen up before the reception. See you there?"

Burr nodded at the young mother and daughter as they took hands. "See you there. Save me a dance, Jenny, okay?"

"Okay, Mr. O'Leary," said Jenny with a gap-toothed grin.

He watched them walk to their car, no doubt headed for their little cottage before proceeding to Summerhaven for the reception. He felt bad for Hallie. He didn't know her very well, but from what he gathered, her ex-husband had been a regular fucker, running up enormous debts before leaving Hallie and their daughter for a woman barely out of high school. Aside from the humiliation of his betrayal, Hallie had been left flat broke, with nowhere to go except a dilapidated summer cottage, adjacent to Summerhaven, that her parents had left her.

It was clear that something simmered between her and Ian, though Tierney and Rory swore they had no idea what had happened between them, and Brittany refused to spill the beans. Burr sighed, turning back to watch Tierney say hello and thank you to the last of the guests still filing out of the church. He hoped the best for Hallie and Jenny, but today he had other things on his mind...important things that wouldn't wait anymore.

He'd only known Tierney Haven for three months, but he'd known himself for over twenty-eight years, and she was it for him. He'd felt it in his bones the moment he'd woken up on her bed, those emerald eyes staring back at him and the honeyed words *I'm not scared of you* falling from her sweet lips.

A montage of Tierney played in his head like a movie: the first time he kissed her in her living room, the second time he kissed her in front of the fire pit in her backyard, the way she leaned over a pool table pocketing balls like a boss, the abysmal way she'd first lied for him to Dr. Weasel, and the way she looked all decked out for her date. The way she'd stood up at his sister's house and told off his father, and the way his heart exploded every time he slid inside of her.

He loved her.

He loved her so hard and so well, it didn't matter that there were still plenty of mysteries about her for him to unravel. It didn't matter that he'd never spent a winter or spring with her. It didn't matter that he didn't know the answer to every question he had about her. None of it mattered, because he would do whatever it took—bend, mold, learn, change, flex, and adapt—to make her happy.

Because there was only one absolute in the heart and soul of Burr Brian O'Leary, and it was this:

Life could *only* be spectacular if he was living it with Tierney.

"All done," said Tierney, suddenly appearing in front of him. "Ready t—wow. You're deep in thought. Everything okay?"

"Yeah," he said, putting his arms around her and pulling her against him. "Everything's perfect, *aisling*."

She leaned back to look up at his face, tilting her chin to offer her lips to him. He took them with his, kissing her soundly in front of the church where her brother had just gotten married.

When he drew away, her eyes were still closed, but they opened slowly to look up at him. "Whoa."

"I love you," he said, the words guttural and gritty with emotion.

"I love you too." She smiled at him. "Weddings, right? Everyone gets a little—"

He shook his head. "Not weddings. *You.*"

"Me?" she asked, tilting her head to the side. "Are you sure you're okay?"

"Yep. I'm good. Thanks to you." He took a deep breath. "*Life* is good because of you, Tierney. You're my fresh start, my new life."

"And you're mine," she said, cupping his cheek tenderly.

"See you guys there?" called Brittany, holding hands with Rory, who pulled her toward a waiting limousine.

Tierney waved at them, then turned back to Burr with a wide grin. "Ready?"

"Yeah," he said. "I am."

Reaching into his back pocket, he withdrew a small black velvet pouch and loosened the draw string before kneeling down on a carpet of autumn leaves in the old churchyard before her.

She gasped, covering her mouth and nose with both hands.

"What are you doing?" she squeaked through her fingers.

Tipping the bag over, a ring dropped into his palm: a gold band with a small, perfect diamond flanked by platinum

Celtic trinity knots. He held it up to her.

"I don't know what the protocol is about proposing to your woman at her brother's wedding, but I don't—I don't want to wait anymore, Tierney. You're it for me. Yesterday. Today. Tomorrow. Forever." He reached up for her right wrist and pulled her hand away from her face, holding it tightly. "And I'll do whatever it takes—I mean that, *aisling*, so I'm going to say it again—I will do *whatever it takes* to make us last forever. I promise you that, and I will never, ever break that promise. You are my priority. You and no other until the end of my days." He paused, taking a deep breath as he looked deeply into her eyes. "*Bean mo chroí. Ah ghra mo chroí. An bposfaidh tu me, aisling?*"

Woman of my heart. Love of my heart. Will you marry me?

With tears rolling down her cheeks, she started nodding, slowly at first, then faster and faster, happy laughter escaping from her lips as she dropped her left hand from her face and held it out to him.

As he slipped the ring on her fourth finger, she cupped his cheek and whispered, between tears, "*A chéadsearc. M'Burr. M'fhíorghrá.*"

First in my heart. My Burr. My true love.

Looking up at his fiancée, Burr thanked the Lord above for His many blessings but couldn't resist asking her one last question:

"Smile for me, *aisling*?"

And his Irish girl—perfect for him in every way—traded in her old response for a new one before letting him swoop her up in his arms:

"*Go deo.*"

Forever.

LOVING IRISH, *The Summerhaven Trio #3,*
will be available in June 2018.

For announcements about upcoming Haven family books,
be sure to sign up for Katy's newsletter at!
http://eepurl.com/disKID

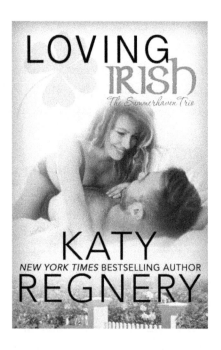

THE SUMMERHAVEN TRIO

Fighting Irish
Smiling Irish

Loving Irish
Coming June 2018

THE BLUEBERRY LANE SERIES

THE ENGLISH BROTHERS
(Blueberry Lane Books #1–7)

Breaking Up with Barrett
Falling for Fitz
Anyone but Alex
Seduced by Stratton
Wild about Weston
Kiss Me Kate
Marrying Mr. English

THE WINSLOW BROTHERS
(Blueberry Lane Books #8–11)

Bidding on Brooks
Proposing to Preston
Crazy about Cameron
Campaigning for Christopher

THE ROUSSEAUS
(Blueberry Lane Books #12–14)

Jonquils for Jax
Marry Me Mad
J.C. and the Bijoux Jolis

THE STORY SISTERS
(Blueberry Lane Books #15–17)

The Bohemian and the Businessman
The Director and Don Juan
Countdown to Midnight

<u>*a m o d e r n f a i r y t a l e*</u>
(A collection)

The Vixen and the Vet
Never Let You Go
Ginger's Heart
Dark Sexy Knight
Don't Speak
Shear Heaven

At First Sight
Coming 2018

Fragments of Ash
Coming 2018

Swan Song
Coming 2019

STAND-ALONE BOOKS

After We Break
(a stand-alone second-chance romance)

Frosted
(a romance novella for mature readers)

Unloved, a love story
(a stand-alone suspenseful romance)

About the Author

New York Times and *USA Today* bestselling author **Katy Regnery** started her writing career by enrolling in a short story class in January 2012. One year later, she signed her first contract, and Katy's first novel was published in September 2013.

Thirty-five books later, Katy claims authorship of the multititled *New York Times* and *USA Today* bestselling Blueberry Lane Series, which follows the English, Winslow, Rousseau, Story, and Ambler families of Philadelphia; the six-book, bestselling ~a modern fairytale~ series; and several other stand-alone novels and novellas, including the critically acclaimed, *USA Today* bestselling contemporary romance *Unloved, a love story*.

Katy's first modern fairytale romance, *The Vixen and the Vet*, was nominated for a RITA® in 2015 and won the 2015 Kindle Book Award for romance. Katy's boxed set, *The English Brothers Boxed Set*, Books #1–4, hit the *USA Today* bestseller list in 2015, and her Christmas story, *Marrying Mr. English*, appeared on the list a week later. In May 2016, Katy's Blueberry Lane collection, *The Winslow Brothers Boxed Set*, Books #1–4, became a *New York Times* e-book bestseller.

Katy's books are available in English, French, German, Italian, Portuguese, and Turkish.

Katy lives in the relative wilds of northern Fairfield County, Connecticut, where her writing room looks out at the woods, and her husband, two young children, two dogs, and one Blue Tonkinese kitten create just enough cheerful chaos to remind her that the very best love stories begin at home.

Sign up for Katy's newsletter today: www.katyregnery.com!

Upcoming (2018) Projects

Loving Irish, The Summerhaven Trio #3
At First Sight, a modern fairytale novella
Fragments of Ash, a modern fairytale

Connect with Katy

Katy LOVES connecting with her readers and answers every e-mail, message, tweet, and post personally! Connect with Katy!